"You are aware that we have to make slippers for four hooves?" Vince asked.

"I did actually notice that horses have four legs, thank you. Shall we get started with Tom?"

After an hour, even Tom had about reached his limit. He had begun to fidget and stamp as they fastened the last sneaker around Tom's right front hoof.

Anne sat back on her heels. "There. But I'm not certain I can get off the floor without help. I'm so tired."

"Here." Vince took her hand, waited while she got her feet under her, then pulled her up.

Vince caught her around the waist with his free arm. "I've got you," he said.

Their eyes met and held a moment too long.

He bent to her and brushed her lips with his. When she didn't back away, he pulled her closer. She could have stayed within the circle of his arms forever...

Just then, Tom nickered and shoved his small body between them.

Dear Reader,

When Dr. Vince Peterson is landed with the veterinary care of eight untrained, completely wild miniature horses, he finds himself on a collision course with Anne MacDonald.

Anne has been hired to train the little guys as helper horses, but first she has to prove to her employer and to Vince that she can do the job. Vince doesn't believe she can teach the minis even the basics of horse etiquette, much less how to act as guides for the blind and helpers for the elderly.

Anne feels Vince treats her like an incompetent underling, undercutting and second-guessing her training at every step. But they are forced to work together for the good of the program. They move from grudging respect to a fondness neither one wants. Boy, does that cause problems.

Vince comes from a family where divorce is nearly a seasonal activity. His father is on his fourth wife and not happy with her. His brothers are either divorced or considering divorce. Vince does not intend to marry—he's certain he'll mess it up.

Anne was raised by loving parents and knows what a good marriage is. She wants lifelong love. And for her, that means Vince.

At a family reunion with Vince's dysfunctional family, Vince and Anne have to choose to take their chance at love. With the help of their favorite mini, Tom Thumb, will they make the right choice?

I hope you enjoy this third installment in the Williamston Wildlife Rescue miniseries!

Carolyn

HEARTWARMING

Tennessee Reunion

———

Carolyn McSparren

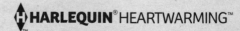

Recycling programs
for this product may
not exist in your area.

ISBN-13: 978-1-335-51060-0

Tennessee Reunion

Copyright © 2019 by Carolyn McSparren

Printed in U.S.A.

RITA® Award nominee and Maggie Award winner
Carolyn McSparren has lived in Germany, France,
Italy and "too many cities in the US to count."
She's sailed boats, raised horses, rides dressage
and drives a carriage with her Shire-cross mare.
She teaches writing seminars to romance and
mystery writers, and writes mystery and women's
fiction as well as romance books. Carolyn lives
in the country outside of Memphis, Tennessee,
in an old house with three cats, three horses and
one husband.

Books by Carolyn McSparren

Harlequin Superromance

The Wrong Wife
Safe at Home
The Money Man
The Payback Man
House of Strangers
Listen to the Child
Over His Head
His Only Defense
Bachelor Cop

Harlequin Heartwarming

Williamston Wildlife Rescue

Tennessee Rescue
Tennessee Vet

Visit the Author Profile page
at Harlequin.com for more titles.

This book is dedicated to Fran Kamp, who breeds and trains miniature horses known as VSE's (very small equines) as helper horses.

Her minis won my heart and made me a firm believer in the job they and the people who train them do to open the world for people with disabilities.

CHAPTER ONE

SOMETHING'S ALIVE INSIDE that van, and it wants out now.

It squealed.

Thwock!

Veterinarian Vince Peterson recognized the sound of hooves kicking the inside wall.

Then came a whinny. The vehicle's windows were tinted, so Vince couldn't see inside, but from that soprano neigh, he could guess what was causing the fuss.

Sounded as though someone who should have known better had shut one of the miniature horses this farm raised inside that van.

Minis *could* be transported in a van or the bed of a pickup truck, but leaving them unattended for long was a recipe for disaster. Most horses settled down once they were on the road, but they tended to get fractious when they were left parked for long, and as small as those hooves were, they could do major damage. These confined creatures were notifying whoever was in charge that they had been abandoned, and they didn't like it. Besides, the inside of that van probably smelled too much of human and not enough of horse to be comfortable for them.

Another squeal erupted, followed by a couple of stomps and a kick that reverberated outside like a rifle shot.

From under the trees at the far side of the nearby paddock came an answering neigh. A buddy? A son? A stallion talking to one of his mares? Vince glanced across the paddock to identify the source.

Suddenly the windshield of the van exploded into glass pellets that rained down on the hood and on Vince. He jumped back and brushed at his face.

"Hey!" he shouted as a fuzzy brown-and-white streak shot through the empty space where the windshield had been, scrabbled across the hood and hit the ground.

"Whoa!" Vince yelled. In the moment the little horse took to get over its surprise at sudden freedom, Vince grabbed the lead line attached to the halter. Then they were off.

The horse had the forward momentum of a tank and the belly circumference of a miniature hippo. Vince found himself skiing through the mud on the heels of his boots.

From his vantage point he could see he had hold of a mare. Possibly a wounded mare from all that glass. She raced toward the five-bar paddock gate that was taller than she was.

Was she going to try to jump it? If she chose to try, either he followed and crashed, or he dropped the line. He'd run hurdles in college, but no way he could clear this gate even at a dead run.

Surely the mare would never attempt a jump that high. She'd veer off along the fence line. He'd be able to catch her again.

He let go of the lead line.

Veer? No way! If she'd been a regular-sized horse, she could have jumped over Mars. She cleared the gate and skidded to a halt beside the other little horse, the one that had neighed at her and caused this breakout in the first place.

They whinnied at one another, while the little mare nibbled the other horse's neck. Vince checked for the sheen of blood on her coat. Nothing obvious, but against her chestnut hair, blood might not show up until he ran his hands over her and felt the moisture. He had to catch her again before he could do it.

She was probably the other horse's mother.

Possibly the colt wasn't fully weaned, although it was an inch taller than its mother and wouldn't fit under her to nurse.

Vince slipped through the sally port beside the gate and took several careful steps toward the pair. They were more interested in their reunion than in him, but he didn't attempt to get close enough to pick up the mare's lead line again in case that started them running.

Vince was not used to a horse of any size getting away from him. Certainly not one no larger than a full-grown ram. At least she didn't have horns to poke him in the gut. He'd never enjoyed that sensation, and rams *would* do it if their ewes were threatened. Assuming they didn't prefer to belt you one behind the knees and knock you flat. That was fun too.

"Hey!" a female voice called from inside the stable at the far end of the paddock. A moment later a woman ran toward him. She wore a broad-brimmed hat that kept her face in shadow, and she sounded annoyed. "What the heck happened?" She pointed to the pellets of broken windshield on the hood of the van.

"She wanted her colt. I assume he's hers. He is a male, isn't he? From this angle I can't tell."

Mother and son noticed the woman coming toward them and trotted over to greet her, but not close enough to catch. Vince followed.

"Yeah, he's a colt all right, and becoming tougher and tougher to handle safely. His mother thinks he's weaned. He doesn't necessarily agree. If he tries to nurse, she's likely to hand him his head on a platter." She glanced up at him. "Or he'll kick and bite somebody like you. You're a bigger target."

She reached down, grasped the little mare's lead line and flipped her hand at the colt. "Scat." The stud colt shook his mane and ambled off. Not far. He hovered, ready to insinuate himself back into contact with the mare.

"What possessed you to pull an idiotic stunt like leaving that mare alone in the back of that van?" Vince snapped. "She could have been cut to ribbons on the windshield."

She brushed her own mane of shining auburn hair out of her eyes, squared her shoulders and took a deep breath. "I did not put her in the van in the first place. I just got here, *Doctor*. Mrs. Martin must have thought she'd be okay alone and went off for a few minutes. If I'd known she was inside the van, I'd have unloaded her before she broke out. I am not in the habit of shirking my responsibilities."

Uh-oh. She made "Doctor" sound like a swear word.

"You are Dr. Peterson, right? You were supposed to be here an hour ago. If you'd been on time…"

"Had an emergency at the clinic," he said. "I got here as quick as I could. And you are? Are you in charge?"

From behind them came a soprano shriek and a thud.

Vince spun around in time to see the mare wheel, buck and land a solid kick on her colt's chest. So much for mother love. The colt backed out of range.

"I'd say he hasn't been weaned long enough to have forgotten she was the one who nursed him," Vince said. "If he keeps trying, he's going to get his teeth handed to him. Come on, we need to get her out of this paddock before she decides today is the day to remind him about his manners."

"Have fun with that." She turned away from him. "In case you can't see from that high up, he has a whopping umbilical hernia. It's your most immediate job. And for your information, I am Anne MacDonald, and I am not by any stretch in charge here. Not yet. You have glass pellets in your hair."

"Good thing windshields don't break into shards any longer. Where can I safely brush off this stuff?"

"In the back of the van she came out of. It's going to have to be detailed anyway before we can drive it." She put her hands on her hips and sighed. "How am I supposed to explain this to the insurance company?"

"Most insurance companies replace broken windshields," Vince said.

"When they're broken by a miniature horse jumping through them from inside?"

"So lie."

At least the mare didn't run from them this time. She was content to stand near her colt so long as he didn't try to nurse. Vince reached for the line attached to her halter, but this Anne kept hold of it. Her hat fell back as she looked up at him. He got his first good look at her.

He was used to horse women whose sun-baked skin looked like an iguana's. Hers was fair and as smooth as a two-year-old's.

She must have left her sunglasses in the barn.

Her eyes weren't green and they weren't blue. Sort of blue with green flecks. Whatever color they were, he'd remember them. They reminded him of the cold mountain tarns in

Wyoming that looked warm and inviting after a hot morning working cows. The only time he'd jumped into one, he'd darned near had a heart attack from the chill. He'd like to see those eyes warm up when they looked at him. Not happening.

"I'll put the mare in a stall," she said and turned away from him to check the son. "He'll come with her. I can probably get him into a separate stall, but don't count on it. Where do you want to sedate him so you can examine him and do his hernia surgery? You are planning on taking care of that, right?"

"And whatever else needs done. We'll put him out in the grass over there. Cleaner, better light if I actually have to open his belly to get at the hernia. Let me go get my stuff out of my truck. When was the last time he had his shots?"

"I have no idea. Probably never." She walked off, leading the mare. The youngster tracked her step by step. "He's one of the six Victoria adopted when they were abandoned. They're totally wild."

"Did Mrs. Martin put that mare in the van to take her somewhere else? Give her to someone else to foster?"

"Again, I don't know. I wouldn't think so. She only picked them up a few days ago."

"So you have six minis total?" he asked. Since this place is called Martin's Minis, I figured you'd have more than that."

"Actually, Victoria has been concentrating on serving the clients who board big horses here. When she stopped breeding and showing her minis in horse shows several years ago, she sold off all of them except her mini stallion. He's over there in his paddock. Now all of a sudden she has this additional bunch that are wild as March hares."

Vince had been expecting to meet the owner, Victoria Martin, who must be considerably older than this woman. This was his first time at Martin's Minis. He'd barely had time to get his assignment this morning from his boss, Barbara Carew, at her clinic. This woman could be a trainer or even a groom. Whoever she was, she sure was touchy.

Most likely, she was a client who boarded her normal-sized horse at this stable. He didn't yet know precisely how many equines were stabled here.

He checked out her skin-tight riding britches and her tall riding boots. Yeah, she had to be a client all right. Those boots cost nearly as much as his first semester at vet school. Stable hands generally spent their days in jeans and paddock boots.

She obviously held limited authority when Victoria Martin was off the property.

He prided himself on his ability to charm both animals and women. Most animals liked him and eventually came to trust him. This particular human seemed immune. Not his fault the owner had left the mare unattended in the back of a passenger van. Not his fault he'd assumed *she* did it. He hadn't seen anybody else since he got here. Not his fault he'd parked his van beside the one the farm owned. That probably didn't trigger the mare's bid for freedom. She was bored and annoyed at being confined. Lucky she didn't get hurt in her great breakout.

Barbara Carew, the senior vet at the clinic, had barely hinted that this assignment might not be precisely the piece of cake he'd expected. He'd barely had time to get the directions to Martin's Minis before he headed out after an emergency C-section on an English Bulldog this morning.

Working on miniature horses. How hard could it be?

Six newly arrived miniature horses, alias

VSEs, very small equines, to be vet-checked, wormed and brought up to date on vaccinations. He needed to examine their teeth and file off any sharp points. Draw blood for more tests. Check their hooves for abscesses—the usual stuff on a first exam. A lot of work, but not that challenging.

Hernia repairs were generally uncomplicated. A small incision, tucking any stray guts safely back in place, a couple of stitches and done. He'd learned his first year in vet school always to lay the horse down before he jabbed a needle into its belly after he'd narrowly avoided getting kicked in the head by a gelding he was certain was zonked out.

He had expected a straightforward morning's work. Except that apparently these little guys had not had either handling or training.

He scratched at his shoulder and dislodged a few more bits of glass. The glass didn't itch, but something did. He looked down at the hairs on his forearm.

Fleas! Either mare or colt had fleas. Horses almost never harbored them. Ticks—yes. But fleas? He *hated* fleas. Suddenly he felt itchy all over. He'd have to go home, shower and change before he went back to the clinic for the afternoon.

If he finished here before the clinic closed. If he finished before dawn, more like.

If the other minis were as wild as these two, he might never get home. Or not in one piece.

The mare and colt were filthy, probably had worms and ear mites, and their hooves were so long that they turned up at the ends like elf shoes. It could take months of expert trims to get those hooves back into shape. He prayed the rest of the herd was in better shape, but he doubted they were. It was his first visit to Martin's, and he wanted to make a good impression. That meant he had to keep his temper, but he tended to lose said temper when dealing with animal owners that didn't care for their charges properly.

He'd put himself through his last two years at Mississippi State vet school working for a farrier, shoeing horses. But if, as he suspected, the Martin horses had never had their feet picked up by a human hand, trimming their hooves would be like trying to trim full-grown musk oxen on speed. He couldn't afford to be laid up with broken bones or a fractured skull. The minis were so low to the ground that just holding their hooves up was going to give him the mother of all backaches before he'd finished.

His boss, Barbara, had told him that the animals he was here to see were rescues, but he assumed they had been given up by someone who could no longer afford to feed them and basically kept them as pets. They weren't like the wild mustangs he'd broken and trained in Wyoming or even the Chincoteague ponies in the outer banks of North Carolina that were left on their own most of the time and only rounded up once a year. These little guys had been on a regular farm with fences and pastures.

It might as well have been Antarctica. They seemed to be as feral as wolves. Fortunately, it shouldn't be nearly as hard to gentle them.

No one could say they were starving. They were past fat—obese, even.

Mrs. Martin, who had taken them in to her farm, was obviously trying to remedy the neglect they had suffered. Barbara said the lady who owned this operation was a longtime animal rehabilitator and colleague of hers. And man, these little horses certainly needed rescuing. In the meantime, he suspected they were about to make his life miserable for the foreseeable future.

What on earth could you do with a mini once you got it tamed and trained and fit enough to act like a horse? They usually stood between twenty-eight and thirty-four inches tall at the withers. Smaller than a Shetland pony. By the time a child was ready to ride, these guys would already be too small.

Not his problem. All he had to do was to get them healthy. Until Victoria Martin showed up, that touchy woman was the closest to an authority figure he could see, so it was up to her to figure out what to do with them. Even if she was just a boarder, she must be aware of what was going on. He watched her walk away beside the mare. Pity she was mean as a snake, because he liked the looks of her in her skin-tight riding britches. He liked long legs, and hers ended somewhere around her collarbone. In the sun, her hair shone bright mahogany and lay as sleek as an otter's pelt.

He had to persuade her to "volunteer" to be his de facto assistant until somebody else showed up. He had no intention of being fired from a job this big before he'd gotten well started. Barbara trusted him to make friends with the clients and give their animals the best care possible. He'd simply have to work a little harder to enlist her services. Seemed he was losing his touch.

If Barbara intended to assign him as lead

vet for a crazy herd of equine munchkins, he'd better win the woman over. He sure couldn't handle that herd of hellions by himself.

He'd have to walk a very fine line between charming her and keeping his professional distance. The last thing he needed in his life was an attractive female human. The female animals he worked with kept him plenty busy. Besides, the men in his family tended to change partners with the seasons.

In vet school he'd hated statistics, but he'd sign up for five years' worth of courses if he could avoid a single freshman class in what his friends called "relationships." He had no frame of reference. He'd flunk.

His cell phone vibrated. He usually kept it muted when he was working. Having an alarm go off when he was pregnancy-checking a thousand-pound Brangus could get him kicked. He checked the caller ID and sighed. Cody. He had to answer. "Hey, brother. What's wrong?"

"Sorry to bother you, Vince, when you're working. It's Daddy."

Vince felt a stab of adrenaline.

"Why do you figure there's something wrong?" Cody asked.

"It's got to be something wrong. That's the only time you call me."

"Calm down," his brother said. "Daddy's fine physically, but he's driving Mary Alice crazier than usual. He just threw a coffee cup at her."

"Full?"

"Empty, thankfully. He missed, but she's hysterical and threatening to walk out. He's egging her on. He told her he had wife number five hiding in the bushes until she drove out the driveway."

Vince ran his hand down his face. "Lovely, but I'm not sure what I can do about it from here. I'm a hundred and fifty miles away and getting ready to cut open a horse."

"She's in their bedroom with the door locked, crying her eyes out. Probably packing. Can you try to talk some sense into her?"

"Somebody needs to talk some sense into *Daddy*. Call the sheriff."

"Mary Alice refuses to do that. She made me promise not to."

"He knows he went too far. So far as I remember, he's never raised a hand to any of the wives or any of us boys, either. He really loves Mary Alice."

"How would she know?"

Vince sank onto the grass with his back against an oak tree. "Give the phone to Daddy and tell him if he hangs up, you'll go upside his head with an anvil. In the meantime, call the doctor and get him in today for a checkup to rule out any new physical problems."

His brother snickered. "Heck, I can't even pick up an anvil. And the only physical problem Daddy has is a bad temper. Okay. Daddy? Vince is on the line. He wants to talk to you."

Vince heard inchoate grumbling in the background, then his father's voice. "Boy? When you gonna quit that job working for that woman and come on home to look after our animals, where you belong?"

"And walk into this?" Vince said. "You go tell Mary Alice you did a stupid thing and you're sorry. Maybe she'll forgive you. I doubt I would."

"Tarnation, no."

"Daddy, do it or I swear I will call the cops down there and tell them to arrest you for spousal abuse, whatever Mary Alice wants."

"Heck, I didn't *hit* her. I wasn't even aiming for her. I was just mad she put the milk jug where I couldn't reach it from my wheelchair at breakfast."

"And that's reason enough to throw a temper tantrum? Go apologize right now. Ask Mary Alice to call me after you've finished."

"I'll send her some roses."

"This is way beyond roses."

"I never meant to do it, son. Sometimes I get frustrated being stuck in this blasted wheelchair. Mary Alice understands. I need you to come home. I'll build you a clinic right here on the property. You'll be working for yourself, not some woman."

"I'd be working for *you*. No thanks."

Not in this lifetime. He wanted a quiet life where he could build his career among people who respected the work he did. At home he'd always be at his father's beck and call. The more he accepted from Daddy, the deeper in thrall he'd wind up.

He could tell from his father's voice that this time he'd won. His father would go apologize to wife number four, who loved him in spite of everything. The thing was, his father loved her back, but like all the Peterson men, he didn't know how to express love. A good reason never to go home and never to get married.

VICTORIA MARTIN WOULD have a fit about the broken windshield, although it was definitely not Anne's fault. She had no doubt the arrival of that arrogant vet—late, of course, they invariably were—had triggered the great escape.

The mare could have hurt herself jumping that gate. He'd snapped at Anne without bothering to find out if she was responsible for leaving the mare inside the van alone. Serve him right if the horse had yanked his arm out of the socket.

Anne had never worked with miniature horses before, and definitely not with six of them, as well as a stallion that thought he was a Clydesdale and spent half his life walking around on his hind legs, screaming for attention from his ladies. Spoiled rotten. Reminded her of some of her ex-boyfriends, except that he was better-looking. And had better manners.

She'd not even had time to put her bags into the guest cottage where she'd be living for the next six months—permanently, if she and Victoria got along. Anne would see that they did. She had to make this job work. She liked Victoria and agreed with her goals. It wasn't precisely the job she'd been aiming for, but it came at the perfect time.

She hadn't expected to have to prove herself to the new vet working for her stepmother, Barbara.

Why had Barbara sent Dr. Peterson on this call instead of coming herself? She and Victoria had worked together for years rehabilitating wild animals and rescuing starving and abandoned livestock. They were comfortable with each other. Maybe this guy didn't intend to be overbearing, but it made her feel as though he found her less than capable. The heck with him.

Barbara was a very competent vet and had recommended her for this job. Anne would prefer to work with Barbara, but it made sense that she wanted her clients to get used to having Dr. Peterson answer their calls.

Anne led the mare into the barn and the first stall. The colt shoved her against the door in his rush to get back to his mother. "Hey! Stop that!"

He turned liquid brown eyes up at her and rubbed his cheek against her shirt.

"Oh, so you love on me and all is forgiven?" She scratched between his eyes. He sighed in ecstasy until his mother pushed him aside to get her face scratched as well. "I don't even know your names yet, little guys." She unclipped the line from the mare's halter and shut the stall door on her. If she left them together, the colt could get in trouble again.

She managed to get the colt into the stall beside the mare's, unclipped his line and shut him in. "Can't leave this dragging. You could strangle yourself."

She'd better go back to find Dr. Peterson. She'd probably need help getting the colt away from his mother long enough to sedate him and keep him under. The little guy was lucky Victoria had realized how big the hernia was before it strangulated.

Anne started toward the wide-open barn doors.

Her phone rang twice before she could slide it from her tight britches pocket and answer it.

"Anne? It's Victoria. Did the vet show up yet? Have you had any problems?

"Yes, ma'am. To both."

"Is Molly hurt? Is he?"

"No, ma'am. Did you intend to leave Molly in the back of the SUV?"

"Just for a few minutes. I meant to be there when Vince arrived, but Bunny Metcalf emailed me that she needed a place for two more VSEs and asked me to come get them right then because she had to go to work. I was sure I'd be back before Vince showed up. I shut Molly in the back of the SUV so I could put her out in the mares' paddock myself to intervene in case she had a problem with her colt. I couldn't catch him, but I could catch her. The big horse van was already hooked up, so I just drove away with it. I know I should have left you a note, but I was in a hurry, and I figured I could leave Molly in the back of the SUV for a few minutes while I made the trip. What happened?"

"Whoa. Slow down. I'll tell you when you get here. Don't worry, nobody's bleeding," Anne said.

"We had a horrible time loading the horses I was picking up. Bunny got her ankle stomped on, so I had to wrap it. I'm five minutes away from you. Is everything okay now?"

"Uh—not quite. Should we wait until you get here before Dr. Peterson operates?"

"Not quite?" Victoria sounded panicky.

Anne interrupted. Once Victoria started talking, she tended not to know when to stop. "No broken bones, no blood, horse or human. But we could definitely use your help."

"I'm not sure Grumpy has ever been in a stall more than half a dozen times at the place he's from. He was born in that pasture and stayed there on his own. Otherwise surely somebody would have called the vet over that hernia. Tell Vince I'm sorry to be late. Make nice with him. We certainly don't want him to walk out."

Anne now had two horse names. The mare was Molly and her colt was Grumpy. Two names down, and four—no, six, counting the two in the trailer behind Victoria—to learn.

Working with minis was definitely not her dream job, but at the moment it was a blessing. And the position did come with a guest cottage to live in. Thanks to Barbara, she wouldn't have to stay in her attic apartment in the family home in Memphis. She simply could not go home to live again. She had reached her limit of snide remarks from her older sister, Elaine, about getting a real job. She intended to make Victoria glad she'd hired her. She'd handle that vet.

Handling the untrained VSEs looked like being above and beyond the call of any sane person's duty. They were wilder than mustangs running loose on the Great Plains. They might look cuddly, but they could bite and kick and paw as well as any regular-size horse, and do it faster.

Victoria was bringing back two more minis? Anne hadn't a clue what to do with the six Victoria had already acquired. Could they all be put in paddocks together?

Obviously, the stallion had to stay in the stallion paddock alone. Stallions did not believe in sharing their ladies or their space. As the only stallion on the property, he would automatically consider himself the leader of his herd of mares and would fight any other male, gelding or not, that tried to join him in his paddock.

Anne had not yet worked out which of the minis considered herself boss mare, but there would be one.

Horses were generally comfortable with their pecking order once it was established. The boss mare's job was to lead and keep the herd disciplined. Her word was law. The stallion's job was to protect, even at the risk of his own life. He might think he was the leader, but the mares knew different.

In any herd, keeping the balance between boss mare and stallion invariably led to squabbles over dominance, but that didn't prevent a blossoming romance between the two when the time was right.

The stallion paddock had extra-high fences that should keep the horse inside, but the way that Molly mare had jumped the five-bar gate to get to her colt…even high fences might not be enough. He was not used to having females that close.

The colt could join the rest once he'd given

up bugging his mother. His mother would teach him manners, but he might not survive the experience in good shape.

Anne had a couple of ex-boyfriends, including Robert, who might have benefited from being kicked and bitten to teach them how to behave.

Peterson could fix the colt's hernia by himself, but she'd have to help halter and control the other minis while he checked them over. Didn't *that* sound like fun? At least he was a big guy with a lot of brawn. He was probably capable of wrestling them to the ground.

She met him at the wide doors of the stable. He was carrying two large medical satchels.

"Here, give me one of those," Anne said. "Show me where you want to set up for the procedure."

She figured he'd refuse to hand her part of his load. But he swung the smaller bag at her, turned his back and walked out onto the grass in front of the stable.

"This looks like as good a place as any." He glanced over his shoulder and smiled at her.

His smile transformed his face. Gone in an instant were the glower, the set jaw and tight lips. He'd only needed to relax. She considered telling him he ought to concentrate on smiling, but she decided he'd be annoyed. He was almost handsome.

And he wasn't wearing a wedding ring.

Not that she cared. Since she had moved away from Memphis and kicked two-timing Robert to the curb, she was definitely off men for the foreseeable future, and maybe forever.

CHAPTER TWO

"Is MOLLY ALL RIGHT?" Victoria Martin climbed from her truck and rushed over to the van to check out its missing windshield. "Oh, my word, would you look at that?"

Not, Vince noted, an inquiry as to whether he and Anne were all right. But then, horse people invariably checked out their animals first. Sometimes they ignored the humans completely.

"What happened?" Victoria asked.

"When I pulled *in*, she decided she'd go *out*," Vince said. "Right through the windshield and over the hood. She may be little, but she jumps like a gazelle."

"Cleared the gate to get to Grumpy," Anne said.

"I should never have left her alone like that," Victoria said. "But she was so calm when I loaded her, and I only planned to be away for a few minutes." She ran her hand through her mop of short curls. "I gave her a handful of treats to keep her busy.

"Not enough treats." Anne grinned. "Once the ones you gave her were gone, she decided to go hunt for some more."

"I cannot believe she cleared the gate," Victoria said in awe. "Amazing."

"Then she kicked the stew out of her colt when he came over to reintroduce himself," Vince said.

"Why did you put her in the van in the first place?" Anne asked.

Victoria flapped her hand. "I was in a big hurry, and it was closer than a stall in the barn. I didn't want to take the time to watch how she and Grumpy got along. I should have known better. If minis can find trouble, they will."

"Why is the little male with the hernia called Grumpy?" Anne asked.

"Because he is," Victoria said. "Oh, dear, I need to get the two minis I brought back with me into the mare's paddock."

"Together?"

"They're not fond of one another now, but they should get along after a little jockeying for position in the herd."

"With Grumpy?"

"Depending on the size of that hernia repair," Vince chimed in. "He ought to be less grumpy immediately. He needs handling badly. I doubt he's ever worn a halter before."

"Probably not," Victoria said. "Between us, Bunny Metcalf and I and the resident groom managed to get halters on the two I brought back with me and manhandled them into the trailer. One mare, one gelding. They don't get along too well as yet either, although I'm sure they will. I didn't tie them up on the trip, so that they could get away from one another. I decided they'd be marginally safer that way. I didn't want to make the trip twice with only one horse each trip."

Victoria knew miniature horses much better than Anne did. The problem was that they didn't need any more minis, period. This job looked less and less like a gift from heaven and more like a curse from another direction. She'd have to work harder to countermand its effects. She intended to make Victoria glad that she'd hired her.

"Come on, people, let's do this," Vince said.

Anne tossed him a couple of lead lines from the front seat of Victoria's van.

"We need to open the tailgate of the horse trailer only enough for Anne and one of the minis to come out at a time," Victoria said.

Anne gave her a *why me?* look. Victoria refused to meet her eyes.

"I'll go in the front escape door," Anne said. "Keep the tailgate shut until I tell you to open it."

Oh, well, this was why she was getting the big bucks. As if. She took the lines from Vince, opened the access door in the front of the trailer and slipped in. She started crooning to the two lumps that peered at her from the shadowy rear of the trailer. One was a small gray ghost that stood stock still and studied her as though trying to figure out what she was and how she should be dealt with.

Anne thought that the other horse was lying down. He wasn't. He was the smallest horse she had ever seen. He stared at Anne a little longer, then ambled over to her with a massive sigh. He was drenched with sweat. Either the mare had been bullying him, or he'd been frightened by the ride. He apparently saw Anne as a refuge. He walked around to hide behind her, leaned against her leg and closed his eyes.

Anne reached back and scratched between his ears. Another huge sigh. "Okay, little guy, let's get you out of this dark old trailer." She clipped one of the lead lines to his halter and walked forward. He refused to budge. "Little shy, are we? Let's see if Big Mama will lead the way."

She reached across the intervening space and clipped the other lead line into the mare's halter so quickly that it didn't register with her. She remained staring at Anne, stiff-legged, ears wiggling, head lowered so that she could swing into fight-or-flight mode in an instant.

"Don't know where you'd run to, Mama." Anne picked up her rope, slipped by her and called through the rear door, "Victoria, guard the door. Big Mama and I are coming out." She turned to her other little companion, who still leaned against her leg. He stared up at her in perfect trust. "Whither thou goest, huh?"

As the doors were pulled apart, a shaft of sunlight hit the mare. She reared straight up, shoved Anne out of the way like a bulldozer, jumped down the ramp and was off to the races.

Anne kept her balance down the ramp, but as she reached the ground she caught the toe of her boot, stumbled forward and landed face-first in the mud.

She grabbed the end of the rope with both hands for a better grip. The mare was desperately trying to race away to freedom—any freedom.

"No, you don't! Whoa, right there!" she sputtered. She tasted mud. Her eyes were blurry with it.

A large hand reached down in front of her and grabbed the line from Anne. "Whoa!" Vince shouted.

Anne rubbed her eyes with the sleeve of her shirt so she could see.

Vince braced himself as the mare galloped away. When she reached the end and the line went taut, she reared straight up in the air and somersaulted backward into the mud. She started to roll to her feet, but Vince slammed his boot down on the line close to her halter.

"Don't you move, missy. You are well and truly got, so stay got." He dropped to his knees and laid his free hand on her neck. "It's all right, baby girl, nobody's going to hurt you."

Anne thought she'd never heard a more reassuring voice. The little mare seemed to agree. She lay there unmoving while he petted her. Anne could see her muscles relax, her breathing slow, her eyes blink and her ears point forward as she listened to him.

Anne pulled herself to a sitting position.

What the heck, she was baptized in mud. Hardly mattered if her rear end got as wet as her front.

She hadn't given the tiny gelding behind her a single thought. He was loose somewhere with a lead line dragging behind him. She started to get up and felt something tickle her ear.

"*Hmhumhumhum*," came a soft whuffle. A moment later the little horse laid his head on her shoulder.

She reached up and petted him. "Well, hello, little guy. You're my little guy, aren't you? Let the rest of these nuts misbehave. You're mama's angel, aren't you?" He sighed and closed his eyes.

"Are you all right?" Victoria asked.

"I need a shower and some clean clothes is all."

"Hey," came Vince's voice. "Might as well stay dirty until we've finished with Grumpy's hernia repair." He reached a hand down to her. A clean hand.

"Don't touch me. I'm filthy."

"I noticed. Who's your friend?" He leaned down to scratch behind the little horse's ears.

"His name is Tom Thumb," Victoria said. "He's actually a dwarf VSE."

"He's a saint is what he is," Anne said, and wrapped her arms around him. "And after today, he's *my* saint."

CHAPTER THREE

IN THE END, Molly came along with her son, Grumpy. He refused to move without her. Once Vince shot him with a tranquilizer, however, he lay down in the clean grass and went peacefully to sleep. Molly allowed herself to be led to the far side of the paddock fence, apparently convinced he was simply taking a nap.

Gloved and gowned, Vince did his regular exam, took blood, knelt beside the horse and probed his belly gently. "What were the people that owned him doing? This hernia is as big as a baseball. Amazing it hasn't strangulated, cut off the blood supply and killed him."

"You're going to have to open him up?" Anne asked.

"Ya think? Right now if not before."

The hernia repair looked much more difficult than it was. Repositioning the gut and stitching the belly took Vince less than twenty minutes. He finished by giving Grumpy a shot of antibiotics.

"I'll leave trimming his hooves and the rest of his exam until tomorrow," Vince said. "Right now he needs to rest and recuperate."

Grumpy struggled to his feet and staggered off toward the manger full of hay under the trees in the big paddock.

"He's eating," Vince said. "Good. One problem solved. Next."

"You want to go from worst to best or best to worst?" Anne asked.

"Molly's here. Let's start with her while Grumpy's out of the way. The last thing he needs is another kick."

While Anne held Molly, Vince did his preliminary check.

Then he looked at her hooves and shook his head. "I don't know how they are managing to walk with those overgrown hooves, much less gallop and sail over fences. People in the middle ages used to make the toes of their shoes so long they had to button them to their knees to keep from breaking their necks. These guys could use knee buttons on all four hooves. How did they get this long?"

Victoria Martin leaned over the fence. "Didn't Barbara tell you anything about their history?"

"Ma'am, back at the clinic we haven't had

time to breathe since yesterday when you called, and then we went different directions. I had an emergency waiting for me when I walked in this morning. All I have is a note that gives me your name, your address, and says you have rescued minis. No time to talk."

"Huh. If I know Barbara, she didn't want to scare you off. So what do you do first?"

"You mean while we're still ambulatory and not in the ambulance yet?"

From the look in her eye, Vince suspected Molly was planning how quickly she could make that happen. "I can feel her muscles bunching up, ready to explode. First off, I'm going to hit her with a little tranquilizer," he said. "Not enough to knock her down like Grumpy, but maybe enough to mellow her out a tad."

As he popped the needle into the ridge of muscle beside her tail, she cow-kicked straight out to the side and missed Vince's shin by centimeters. The syringe flew from his hand and landed in the dirt.

"Shoot!" he snapped. "I think I got enough tranquilizer in her, but we'll see. Give her a couple of seconds, then I can draw some blood." He readied another syringe, then bent over her. "Come on, pretty baby, let Daddy have some of your nice red blood. You weren't serious that they've never been wormed, were you?" he asked Anne. "I'll have to start out with a low dose of wormer, otherwise they could be so stressed out they might colic. It'll take time to get their guts back in working order. We'll figure out the proper diet later."

He managed to feel Molly's teeth without getting his fingers bitten off and found that hers, at least, didn't need any points filed smooth.

"Yes, indeed, she has ear mites. They must itch like crazy." He dosed them. She flicked her head in irritation.

He picked four fat ticks out of her mane. "She needs a flea bath and fly spray and her mane trimmed, not to mention trimming those hooves."

"One doesn't trim a Very Small Equine's mane," Victoria said with a sniff. "They are supposed to flow—long and luxuriant."

"Uh-huh. Well, they've developed dreadlocks. I'd actually roach them—trim them completely off—then let them regrow. Just so long as I don't have to try to comb them."

"Oh, very well," Victoria said, obviously unhappy. "It's not as though we'll be showing them anytime soon."

He gaped at her. "No way you are showing until they're healthy. I'll start hoof trimming today, but they're all going to require extensive farriery over the next few months. You have a patient blacksmith?"

"Nobody's that patient," Anne said under her breath.

Vince grinned at her. "I am definitely not."

"I have a farrier, but I'd feel better if you did the first couple of trims," Victoria said.

Without warning, Molly shook her head and humped her back.

"She's starting to come out of it," Victoria said. She had stayed comfortably on the far side of the paddock fence where she was out of Molly's line of fire.

"We've about reached her limit today. I'll start cutting on her hooves this afternoon." He turned to Anne. "In the meantime, maybe you could attempt to teach her to walk on a lead line?" He made it into a question, but from the way Anne's shoulders tightened, he suspected she'd taken it as another complaint.

"Why don't I just train her for third-level dressage and skip the small stuff," Anne said.

"I didn't mean to imply…"

"Right. If you intend to work on her this afternoon, shouldn't we get her back in a stall?"

"Yeah. Tom Thumb, too. Grumpy will not be happy, but he needs to learn to live without her. It's almost as though he's never been weaned."

"So, you want him back in a stall as well?" Anne rolled her eyes. "What fun." She brought Tom over from the small area in front of the stable where he'd been waiting his turn without fussing. She didn't bother to use a lead line. He ambled along behind her like a hound at heel. She caught Vince's flash of annoyance.

"Do you always walk strange horses without a lead line?" he asked.

Another shot. Did he intend to question everything she did? "I wouldn't try this with any of the others. Besides, if he wanders away I can always get him back. It's not as though he can outrun me. You saw the way he reacted in the trailer. I do know what I'm doing, Doctor."

CHAPTER FOUR

ONCE THEY WERE in the barn and getting ready to work on Tom Thumb, Anne did attach a lead line to his halter. Vince did not comment.

Working over the little gelding was a piece of cake. Anne stood in front of him and scratched his face.

He really was sweet and trusting. He responded to the pressure on his halter. He obediently opened his mouth to get his teeth checked for sharp points, and barely flicked his ears when Vince probed for mites. They were abundant. He didn't wriggle while Vince cleaned his ears out and treated them.

"Darn," Vince said as he ran his fingers through Tom's tangled mane. "You got some clippers?" he asked Anne. "Whatever you choose to do about the others, I absolutely have to shave Tom's mane. I'm feeling scabs. Maybe bites from the other horses. Could be they've been picking on him."

Anne raced to the tack room and came back

with the large electric clippers and some heavy shears to cut the mane first so that the clippers could cut it off.

"He may freak at the whir," Vince said. "Don't get kicked."

"Let me," Anne said. "He won't kick." She didn't know why she knew that, but she did. She turned on the clippers. Tom moved uneasily, but didn't buck, not even when she shaved the hair completely off.

"Work around the bad places," Vince said.

"Yes, Doctor." Anybody with half a brain knew not to tear off the scabs.

"Can you bring me a bucket of warm water?" he asked. "I'm going to scrub his mane with antiseptic and hold off on antibiotics."

This would be fun, Anne thought. Antiseptic on Tom's raw skin would cause a meltdown.

It didn't. Tom snorted and wriggled, but he seemed to understand that these creatures were trying to help him. That in itself was unusual. Animals almost never appreciated help offered by a human being. They had a point.

After Tom, Anne was impressed at how carefully and quietly Vince worked over Grumpy and Molly. Tom had been easy. Vince seemed to have a Jekyll-and-Hyde personality—gentle with the horses, snappish with the humans.

Anne wanted Victoria to recognize that she, too, knew her job. She'd worked with a couple of trainers who treated their staff and students like idiots. This new job would be no fun if she had to put up with a less than congenial work environment.

"Okay," he said. "That's Tom, Molly and Grumpy at least partially done."

"Do we have to put Tom in a stall?" Anne asked.

"He's been with other minis," Victoria said. "Even if they pick on him a bit, he'd be miserable by himself."

Vince nodded. "Just keep an eye on him in case they start to bully him."

The minis stood under the shade at the far side of the pasture. They didn't exactly welcome Tom, but they made no attempt to run him off either.

"Good," Victoria said. "Hey, people, it's already past noon. I'm hungry even if nobody else is. I'll throw a pizza in the oven. We can go back to work after we eat."

"I can't walk into your house until I've had a shower and put on clean clothes," Anne said. "I put my stuff into the guest house when I got here, but I haven't unpacked yet."

"Then, Vince, you mind helping with lunch?"

"Sure."

The guest house Anne would be using had been built down the hill from the swimming pool beside the patio. Both the cottage's main and second bedroom had en suite baths. It wasn't palatial, but it had heat and air-conditioning, a kitchen and a big stone fireplace with an even bigger TV screen above it.

It was definitely a step up from her cramped apartment in the attic of her old home in Memphis.

Victoria had hired Anne for a trial period of six months. Anne didn't doubt her ability to manage a stable and train riders and horses. She'd started and run the program for special-needs riders at her previous job. It had been highly successful until they lost their grant because of budget constraints.

When Victoria offered her a job, free board for her horse, Trust Fund, and a chance to train the minis, she'd jumped at it.

That was before she heard the history of the crazy minis and found out what Victoria wanted to do with them. Anne knew how to train big horses, but had no hands-on experience training miniature horses to be helper animals for the disabled. That was what Victoria planned to do with them.

She'd read everything she could find and talked to several people who were getting minis ready to be helpers, but that wasn't the same as actually doing it from scratch.

Jobs with horses—any sort—that paid a living wage weren't that thick on the ground. She was lucky to find this position after the stable she worked for in Memphis closed down. Doubly lucky that her stepmother, Barbara, knew Victoria and recommended her.

She had to make this work. She'd given up her part-time bartending job in Memphis and her apartment to come up here.

She realized she had a great deal to learn about miniature horses. The point was that they were *horses*.

The friends she'd graduated from college with had gone to law school or med school or married men who had. They all thought she was crazy to believe she could make a career with horses.

She fell in love with horses the first time she saw a pony ride at the zoo. There was something about equines that called out to certain girls. Oddly, boys were seldom affected the same way. *The infected girls*, as her father referred to them, progressed from spending their allowances on horse models to pony rides at the zoo to riding lessons, and eventually, if they were lucky, to a horse of their own. Most of them moved on when they went off to college, started careers, married or when daddy stopped footing the bills. Some of them came back to riding when their own children fell under the equine spell, when they began to long once again for the feel of a foot in the stirrup and a rump in the saddle.

A few never considered any life but a life with horses satisfying.

Anne was one of them. She'd endured her sister Elaine's criticisms ever since she climbed on her first pony. To Elaine, Anne's horse craze was silly, expensive, and led nowhere. She should have outgrown it.

Anne intended to prove her wrong. She could make a career with horses. Maybe she'd never be rich, but she'd be happy. Sooner or later she hoped to find a man to share her dream. Someone with whom she would have the kind of love her parents had.

That dream was possible. Her father and mother had proved it, and after her mother died, her father had found another great love with Anne's new stepmother, Barbara.

Anne didn't have to ride or drive a horse to be content. Even shoveling manure out of stalls was preferable to working in an office—any office. Anything to avoid wearing a suit and heels.

Team sports like soccer or gymnastics or swimming had never appealed to her. Her tunnel vision had a horse at the end of it. Her father was right—it was an infection. Equinitis?

Now she was in a new horse environment where she needed to establish a place.

That meant dialing back the antipathy she'd felt when that Vince person treated her like some kind of incompetent. He was the vet after all, not her. She was willing to give him the benefit of the doubt. This was his first visit to Martin's. He probably knew less about VSEs than she did. And he knew nothing of what she and Victoria planned to do with them.

After a long scrub she changed into fresh jeans and a T-shirt and then headed over to Victoria's house. Before she even walked into the mudroom she could smell the pizza. She hadn't realized how hungry she was after her drive up here from Memphis at the crack of dawn. She had left her riding boots at the cottage. They were filthy. She'd polish them tonight. She stashed her rubber boots in the mudroom and put on the pair of clean sneakers she'd brought with her.

"I was just telling Vince the background on the minis," Victoria said. "I was concentrating on big horses. They pay the bills, after all. When I got the call about this abandoned herd, the only mini we still had was our stallion, so I agreed to take a few. We are set up for minis, after all—low stalls, small paddocks, mini-sized tack, even a training cart to teach them to drive."

"A few?" Anne asked. "Six in one load?"

"Hey, you're actually lucky this barn only took six—no, eight now. Our rehabilitation group managed to place most of the herd with other members. I have no idea how many were running free over at the farm they came from and were adopted by our other members. Thank heaven I wasn't in charge of counting them. One of our members said it was like counting ants on an anthill.

"None of us had any idea what we were getting into when we got the call from the sheriff's office that there were a bunch of VSEs that needed to be rescued. Nobody realized they'd been abandoned. If they hadn't had that pond for water and a lush pasture, I don't know what would have happened to them. They would probably not have survived the winter without hay and grain."

"Nobody reported them to the ASPCA?" Vince asked.

"The man who bred them lived on a large farm with lots of woods at the end of a back road," Victoria said. "Toward the end of his life he became a recluse. He was estranged from what little family he had, and as he grew older, he simply didn't have the physical strength to take care of the horses. He had too much pride to admit he'd gotten in over his head. Then he started having dementia issues.

"I don't think he knew the last year how many he had in the pasture. He definitely kept no breeding records. There were foals that should have been weaned, a number of mares…

"No vet care, no blacksmith, no halter breaking—not even the most rudimentary training. If that fancy developer hadn't wanted to buy the property for his mansions, the whole thing would have turned into a tragedy when the old man died. He tracked down the owner's son, and discovered the herd."

"What do you intend to do with them, Mrs. Martin?" Vince asked.

"I do not intend to keep eight additional horses, small or not, as yard art. I can't afford that, even if I had enough land to house them separately from my normal-sized horses and my clients' horses. We've been discussing it among ourselves, and we're going to keep the stallion and a few of the mares to breed. The rest will be Anne's problem. More pizza?"

"No, thank you. What can *you* do with them?" he asked Anne.

"Drive them—they are easily trainable to a cart. They're popular at driving shows. We're also going to experiment with training them to be therapy and helper animals like Seeing Eye dogs."

He choked on his iced tea. "You can't be serious. I can see how little Tom Thumb might wander down the halls at a nursing home and get fed treats by a bunch of elderly ladies, and maybe there's a couple you could calm enough to drive a cart, but how could you ever trust them enough to use them like helper dogs?"

Anne felt her hackles rise. "They're used all over the world as companion animals. Just like dogs. Not as many yet, but they live longer than dogs, and they can carry a lot more weight."

"You can't housebreak them."

"Sure you can. They can do almost anything a dog can do indoors, and a bunch more outdoors. They're stronger than dogs for their size. They can pull wheelchairs, open doors, turn lights on and off, carry saddlebags full of books to and from class…"

"And you've actually done this how many times?"

"This is a new program for this area."

"In other words, you've never trained minis before, and certainly not that bunch of demons who have to either stomp or run from human beings."

"You just watch me, Doctor. It'll take a while, but I will do it. What do *you* think we should do with them? Leave them untrained in the pasture until they founder from too much food and too little work?"

"Not at all. Of course, they need to be brought back to health. It's why I'm here. But I don't think turning them over to people who don't know how to care for them is a good idea. They are likely to actually wind up as yard art or be abandoned all over again. They're not toys."

"And I am not a toy maker. Whatever size they are, I can train them and I will." She pushed away from the table, picked up her boots and left the house.

As she stalked back down to the barn, she

wondered why on earth she had made a promise she might not be able to keep. She was banking on the minis being like other horses, just in smaller sizes. She already adored Tom Thumb. He would be her first test case. The others—a bit later. She'd barely had time to read books on the subject of minis. That included miniature donkeys as well, although Victoria had fostered none of *those*, thank heaven.

She'd spent hours on the telephone and the computer talking to the people who had successful helper horse programs, but she hadn't visited any or helped train any on her own. She and Victoria had discussed sending her off for tutoring after she had some experience on her own. Not yet. When she had a successful track record with the VSEs. She'd know the basics, but trainers who had been doing this job for years would know much more than she would.

At the moment, she wanted more than anything to climb on her own horse—all seventeen hands of him—and go for a nice, quiet trail ride without either Victoria or Dr. Pessimist around.

There were a bunch of people she had to prove herself to with this job, starting with her family. Her ancestors weren't farmers or ranchers. She had no ties to what her sister, Elaine, called "the horsey set." Anne was the first to go foxhunting on a borrowed pony when she was nine and sent her poor mother into hysterics when she'd come home bruised and battered from a fall.

Her sister, Elaine, played tennis. It was a great place to meet boys. Besides, she liked the tennis dresses.

Anne played polo and rode jumpers in local horse shows. Her darling father supported her, but she knew he secretly hoped it was just a phase.

It wasn't. She learned to train horses because she couldn't buy million-dollar already trained "made" horses the way her rich friends did. The day she won her first Grande Prix jumping challenge in Memphis on a horse she'd bought cheap as a two-year-old and trained, even Elaine was proud of her. Or said she was.

Now she also had to prove herself to her family, Victoria and Barbara. She added Vince Peterson to the list of doubters.

AS MUCH AS Anne liked Victoria, she did tend to start a project only to wander off to another before she finished the first. Like leaving Molly in her van and driving off to pick up two more minis.

She shoved her feet back into her boots, then tied the shoestrings of her sneakers together and slung them over her shoulder. She'd drop them at her cottage and go try to halter one of the other mares for Vince.

As she opened the door of her cottage, her cell phone rang. She read the screen. "Barbara?"

"How's your first morning?"

"Don't ask. What's with that fancy doctor you sent over? He thinks I am an idiot."

"I'm sure he doesn't, Anne. He's a sweetie. He adores animals and people both. He's just had a bad morning."

"He's not the only one. He's all over the horses' health issues, but he doesn't seem to see their true value."

"How are he and Victoria getting along?"

"They're getting along, sort of. She took one look at those blue eyes of his and those broad shoulders and melted."

"Didn't he fuss at her about the state of the minis?"

"I assume he gave her points for rescuing them in the first place."

"Obviously you noticed those shoulders, too."

"I'm on this job to charm a bunch of horse imps into behaving themselves, not to simper at Vince Peterson."

"He's a good vet."

"I don't doubt his professionalism. His stall-side manner leaves a bit to be desired. I don't think he has much patience with people."

"He's now the one in charge of Victoria's vet service, so make nice with him. You're going to see a lot of one another."

"Oh, goody." She took a deep breath and changed the subject. "How's my daddy's career in front of the camera progressing? He was worried that he'd lose the feeling of contact with his students."

Barbara chuckled. "Not from the feedback he gets. They can interact when they set it up with some app. I have no idea how it works, but he's happy, so I am."

"And the new house? How soon can you move in?"

"The new house is close enough to completion for me to start planning a housewarming party. Stephen and I have managed better than I thought we would in my old apartment behind my barn at the clinic. Neither of us had shared living accommodations for a long time, and my barn apartment isn't all that big. I was afraid we'd kill each other instead of settling into wedded bliss." She chortled. "Bliss won by a mile."

"I never doubted it. I'm glad Daddy's keeping his hand in."

"Your father is a natural in front of the camera. Now that he's teaching his classes over the net from here rather than commuting to Memphis every other day, he's having a great time with his students online, and doing classes for half a dozen community colleges as well. We're both looking forward to having you living so close. Victoria's guest house is less than twenty miles from my clinic. Get to know Vince. He works so hard he hasn't had time to make many friends up here in Tennessee. Williamston is not exactly a hotbed of social interaction. He's quite a ways from his homeplace down in Mississippi. He swears he's turned himself into a Tennessean since he works for me, but his father still wants him to move back. He says he'd rather eat glass."

"I'll bet he has girlfriends coming out of the woodwork."

"They flirt, all right. There are some cats

and dogs around that are seeing much more of their vet then they're used to. He doesn't seem to be interested. He swears he hasn't left a girl behind in Mississippi. Anyway, you've got VSEs to treat. Why don't you come to dinner Thursday night? My kitchen is still not functioning fully, so Emma's feeding us."

"I can't just invite myself."

"She told me to ask you. I think she wants to show off baby Diana."

"Will Vince be there?"

"No idea. Emergencies take precedence. But he's invited. Come."

Anne nodded. She and Emma were old horse show friends. Anne could use her company and her advice right now. "What shall I bring?"

"Not a thing. Just yourself."

Anne grabbed her bush hat on her way out the door and walked through the barn to the stallion paddock. Whatever Vince planned to do with the stallion, he could do it in his paddock. She had no intention of bringing the little stud through the stalls of horses large and small that lined both sides of the center aisle. He'd be trying to climb into the stalls of every mare he passed, whether VSE or draft horse. One thing about stallions—they always assumed they were the most important creatures in the barn. She giggled. Kind of like Dr. Vince.

CHAPTER FIVE

THIS WAS NOT going to be a satisfactory professional relationship, Vince thought as he added wormer and vaccination ampules to his kit from the supplies in the back of his van. It was mostly his fault. He'd come on too strong with Anne. His clients mostly liked him and appreciated him. Okay, so he had an ego. Most doctors did. But he didn't need Victoria's trainer bad-mouthing him or worse, undercutting his decisions.

He still tended to look for a human to blame when something went wrong with one of his patients. Invariably he wound up snapping at the creature that walked on two feet rather than four. Unfortunately, he'd assumed Anne was the two-legged culprit in this case, but she was blameless. He probably owed her an apology.

He didn't do apologies. In his family an apology chalked up one for him in the loss column. The entire family kept score. His father had still not forgiven him for taking out one of the peach trees with the ATV he was forbidden to drive. He'd been thirteen at the time.

Had to hand it to Anne. When he'd tossed his heavy case to her, she neither backed off nor dropped it despite the weight. Blood didn't bother her. From the expensive boots and britches she wore when he met her, he'd figured she must be one of the Horse Princesses that more often than not made his life difficult.

On the one hand, they drove him frantic demanding he dance attendance on them as well as their animals. He didn't have time to schmooze when an animal was in trouble.

On the other hand, they were the ones with plenty of money to pay their vet bills and order expensive tests when necessary. He just wished he could keep their horses healthy without dealing with some of the owners.

Most of the clients were careful, thoughtful people trying to do the best for the animals in their charge. But when he had to work on horses like these minis, full of ear mites and ticks and worms and who knew what all else, the situation made him want to hit a wall. Or the person responsible.

If he were at home in Mississippi, he'd run a couple of miles along the edges of the soybean fields, or shovel manure out of stalls, or use the gym equipment he and his brothers had installed in the barn when they were all playing football.

Or get into a fight with one of his brothers. More satisfying than a gym. He usually won, although Joshua was older than he was, and both he and baby brother Cody were equally large. He was trying to avoid the physical stuff with both of them, but it was hard to break the dynamics of a lifetime. Over the years his temper had become a survival mechanism. When he lost it, his brothers frequently backed off.

Now, however, it was turning into a liability. He needed to keep it in check so that things would remain comfortable for his clients.

He met Anne coming up the path from the guest cottage and headed for the barn beside her.

"Uh," he said. "Sorry I snapped at you." There. Did that hurt? Well, yeah, a little. All depended on how she responded.

"Fine," she said and walked past him into the barn. "Can you help me get a halter on one of the mares?"

"Sure." Maybe that was as close to an olive branch as he would get, but it was a start.

BY MIDAFTERNOON THE mini stallion had been examined and treated—no ear mites or ticks—

and released into his paddock. He had behaved fairly well for a stallion, but as a resident of the farm he was used to regular vet care.

Tom Thumb had seemed to be looking forward to his flea bath. Now that his mane had been roached—shaved off—his scabs seemed to be drying up. A bath would clean them up further.

The hose on the wash rack boasted a state-of-the-art sprayer attachment and warm water. When Anne turned it on his legs to see how he'd react, Tom decided this was a new game and began to dance.

Anne moved up his shoulders and ran the hose down the now hairless strip where his tangled mane had been cut away.

He tossed his wet head and gave Vince a solid smack with his skull just below his belt buckle.

Vince jumped back and fell over the saddle rack behind him. Only grabbing the chain of the cross tie kept him from falling on his rear end.

Anne laughed. "Close one, Tom."

"Give me a hand, blast it," Vince said.

Anne reached across to pull him up at the moment Tom decided to attack the hose with his teeth. A blast of water hit her full in the face. She squealed and dropped the hose, which morphed into a writhing snake under Tom's feet.

Tom began a tap dance worthy of Fred Astaire while Anne tried to grab the hose and drag it out from between the horse's front legs before all three of them wound up in a tangle.

Vince's jeans were wet from the waist down, Anne's shirt from the waist up. Tom was barely damp.

Vince shoved Anne out of the way.

"Hey!" she said as he reached down, snatched up the sprayer and narrowly avoided catching a small hoof on the back of his head. "Get out of the way. I'll do it. I'm not the one that got smacked in the crotch." She grabbed the hose out of his hand.

He looked down at his jeans as she began to snicker. Then laugh.

He could have throttled her. Instead, he grabbed it back from her. It seemed appropriate to pay her back in kind, so he turned it on her. She threw up her hands, shrieked and hurled a currycomb at him. Since her eyes were closed, she missed, but the comb hit the wall with a satisfying *thunk*.

Tom skittered sideways.

"Are you two trying to drown one another?" Victoria said from the barn door.

"She dropped the hose…"

"He sprayed me on purpose."

"Thereby drenching both of you. Tom, on the other hand, is practically dry."

"It was an accident," Anne said and pointed at Vince. "The hose slipped and Tom smacked him in the groin…"

"He did nothing of the sort. She upset him…"

"Does he look upset?" Anne asked.

"He doesn't even look *wet*," Victoria said. "Do you plan to bathe him before or after you put on dry clothes? I assume you have a change in your van, Doctor?"

He glanced away from Anne, suddenly aware how long her legs looked in her damp jeans. He turned to Victoria. "It's warm in here. I'll dry off fast."

"Me, too," Anne said. "Let's keep going. We've got more horses to bathe. I doubt they'll be quite so easygoing. We'll probably get wet all over again."

"Make sure it's because of the horses, you two, and not each other." Victoria turned on her heel and stalked out the barn door. Her shoulders were shaking with laughter.

"Give me the hose," Anne said. "I do too know how to bathe a horse. I'll soap, you rinse. Faster that way."

"Be my guest." He stepped back out of range.

She flashed him a frown, took in their bedraggled appearance and began to laugh. "Looks like we could both use some lessons. The point is, Doctor, to get more water on the horse and less on us."

"What a concept!"

Tom Thumb bumped him with his forehead, and Vince started laughing as well.

"He thinks we're crazy," Anne said.

"He has a point. Let's get this done before we drown him."

Instantly, the laughter died, and they became sober and businesslike again.

That was fine with Vince. He felt they'd achieved a tiny moment of agreement. And he hadn't behaved like such a bear this time. Now, if he could just keep it up. Anne's impression of him was important because of her influence on Victoria. He picked up the soap sponge, squeezed it nearly dry and washed Tom's face.

Some horses relished being around humans and being petted. Tom Thumb ranked ten on the scale of one to ten. He seemed to have a preference for Anne. Not surprising. She was closer to his size and hadn't dosed him with nasty stuff or stuck him with a needle.

Anne and Vince managed to stay out of each other's way, and once Tom was clean, he seemed perfectly content to stand under the hose as long as they'd let him. Eventually, Anne took him out in the paddock where there was plenty of hay and shade.

Vince watched her, but did not offer to help. Maybe that was the key. If he and Anne could figure out a way to work together without communicating in words…

Vince had expected Victoria to supervise what he and Anne were doing with her minis, but she'd disappeared. He and Anne barely said two words to one another the rest of the afternoon. Fine with him. He didn't snap more than four or five times when he saw the state the minis were in. She raised her eyebrows at his tone, but didn't comment.

He knew she was not personally responsible for the condition the horses were in, but his stepmother, Mary Alice, reminded him frequently that he was what she called "an equal opportunity snarler." He took out his annoyance on the nearest person. He needed to cut that out, but in his family, he'd learned to snarl first before someone snarled at him.

Late afternoon, his cell rang. The caller was the clinic answering service. He released the hind hoof of the mare he was trying to trim to answer it, and she promptly stepped on his foot. Hard. Vince yelped with pain. Her hooves had edges as sharp as knives, and he was grateful for the steel toes on his work boots.

"Dr. Vince? This is the office. We just got a call for a case of choke down the road a piece from where you are, and Dr. Barbara's off the other side of Williamston County. You through over at Mrs. Martin's?"

"I'll be through sometime next century." He took a breath. "How bad?"

"Bad enough. Can you go?"

He glanced at the three untrimmed elf toes on the mare beside him. "Have to. Where?" He held the phone under his chin and gestured to Anne. "Write this down."

"Sorry, my third hand is occupied at the moment." The mini tossed her head and bopped Anne on the side of her face.

"Then remember it." He repeated the information, hung up, pulled a sticky note from his shirt pocket, wrote the info and shoved the note back into his pocket. "Don't you carry a pad to take instructions?"

"Not generally, no. I remember the ones that matter. As you can see, my hands are otherwise occupied."

"Get one. Tomorrow be prepared to take notes accurately."

"Uh… I'm not your clerk."

"You are when there's nobody else here. Consider it under the heading of 'other duties as assigned.' I'll clear it with Victoria, if it's important to you. Right now I have to go. Do you know how I get to Bar-Q Farms?"

"Stop that!" Anne gave a fast tug on the line attached to the mare's halter. "I've been there. Out our gate, turn left, three miles to Marcy Road, turn right. Their gate is a couple of miles farther."

"Thanks."

"Hey!" She trotted along behind him and hauled the mare with her. "We've still got horses to do. You coming back?"

"Tomorrow morning."

"What about Harriet here?"

"She'll be fine." He left Anne standing beside the mare, who was now in full fidget mode.

ANNE TURNED TO the horse. "Quit it, you. One jerk is enough for one afternoon. 'Get a notebook. Other duties as assigned. Take notes. I was starting to think I was wrong about his status as a world-class jerk. He must put on a whole different personality with Barbara. Or maybe it's just me."

Anne walked the mare back out to her pasture, pulled off her halter and turned her loose. She checked that the little horse wasn't lame from having one trimmed and one untrimmed hind hoof. Apparently not. Her striking surface was flat. Okay, that was one for Dr. Charming.

What was his problem?

She walked through the patio door into Victoria's office. Her boss sat hunkered in front of a big desktop computer with her glasses halfway down her nose. "He's gone."

Victoria looked up. "Finished already?"

"Still three and a half more. He had to head off to an emergency. A choked horse down the road. He said he'll be back tomorrow morning, goody, goody."

"Whoa. What about him rubs you the wrong way?"

"He is impatient, opinionated and bad-tempered."

"With the horses?" Victoria leaned back and listened.

Anne waved her away. "He's peaches and

cream with the horses, but he treats me as though I was doing everything possible to delay him or get in his way. He must have been fun to work with in vet school. Oh, I forgot. In vet school he had a lot of techie minions prepping and cleaning up. And taking notes. I'm supposed to carry a notebook with me at all times to take his instructions." She dropped into the chair.

"Surely you've worked with prima donna trainers and owners before."

"He makes me feel as though I am a lesser being, and that I am his employee, not yours. I just got out of a relationship with a man who was a rage-aholic. I never knew what would set him off, so I walked around on eggshells all the time. Then I got smart and dumped him. I hate feeling I have to justify myself. I've spent too much of my life justifying my need for horses with non-horse people. Either they're afraid of the size of them…"

"Not in this case, obviously."

"…or they talk about the dirt or the expense. I tell people that horses got me through all the bad parts of adolescence. When my sister Elaine's friends were going to sorority balls and coming home drunk, I was fast asleep because I had to feed my horse at six-thirty in the morning."

Victoria leaned back in her chair. "I'll talk to Vince. If he needs notes, he can take them himself."

"I know you need him. He's good, and he's conscientious. Just set me my boundaries and I'll deal with him. I don't want to lose this job because the working atmosphere is a tad tense."

"No danger of that." Victoria finished the soda she'd been drinking and tossed the can in the trash. "I need you both. Barbara adores Vince. She says his surgical skills are the best she's seen in twenty years. I'm sorry you got off on the wrong foot, but even you admit he seems to be good at his job. Since it's still early, how about we take a trail ride, so I can show you the property? Get you on a normal-sized horse for a change? That should smooth out your emotional wrinkles."

"You're on. Right now, I definitely need to hug a horse."

Victoria tacked up her bay Morgan gelding while Anne got her big hunter, Trust Fund, ready. Trusty was still getting used to his new pasture and his new herd out back of the barn. She hadn't been paying enough attention to him. He showed his displeasure by spooking at nothing as they walked down the road shoulder to shoulder. He settled, however, when she was in the saddle and walking beside Victoria's mount.

"There're lots of deer trails down past the woods," Victoria said, "but we'll stick to the gravel roads. It's easy to get lost back here."

"We're riding west, yes? I had no idea you had this much land."

Victoria nodded. "We don't need it at the moment, but that could change. My husband, Edward, is thinking of renting it next year to someone who wants to cut it for hay, then we could share the crop for our winter forage instead of charging actual money. Now we keep the horses safely in their pastures closer to the barn. Just so you'll know, there's a creek at the end of this road that can flash flood in a storm. The area around it is swampy and can turn treacherous. Stay out of it."

"Snaky?"

"Very. We don't see them in winter when hey den up and seldom in the summer, like w, when they run away fast. In the spring d fall when they're chilly, they can't react ckly, and if they're sleeping or sunning, one he horses could step on them."

"I don't do snakes," Anne said.

"The ones around the barn are speckled king snakes. They keep the bad snakes away and the mice down." They had reached the end of the road that led to the creek and the bog. "It looks harmless now. The horses could ford it easily. In a big rainstorm it's deadly."

"Listen," Anne said. "Frogs."

"More than one kind. Hear that? It's a big bullfrog."

Anne leaned down, wrapped her arms around Trust Fund's neck and laid her cheek against his pelt. "Out here everything smooths out. Our horses don't judge us. Together we become one unit. We're free. I love this big guy, and I think he cares about me, not simply because I feed him. Out here all that stuff with Vince seems overblown and silly. Don't worry. I'll make it work. Now, is there any place around here where we can have a nice relaxed canter? That would really mellow me out."

"You bet." Victoria led them through the woods beside the road to where the trees opened into a field. The hay had recently been baled and left in the field to be picked up later.

"Lovely," Anne whispered. She laid her legs

against Trusty's sides and took a good hold of her reins. They were off.

Twenty minutes later they walked the horses to cool them down as they started back up the trail toward the fenced paddocks.

After they detacked their horses, rinsed them off and put them in their stalls to eat, Anne said, "Thank you. Nothing can get on my nerves now. There's something about a leisurely ride that reaches in and reminds me why I often prefer horses to people. They don't have hidden agendas."

"And people certainly do," Victoria said. "Come on. Time for a swim. Don't worry so much about Dr. Vince. It'll work out."

CHAPTER SIX

VINCE COULD TELL at once the choked horse was suffering. Head hanging, the horse stood on the wash rack of the Bar-Q quarter horse barn, dripping sweat and coughing so hard to try to dislodge the food caught in his throat that his back humped up with every attempt. Jack Quarles, the "Q" of Bar-Q, stood at the horse's shoulder and ran cold water over his back. Despite a big fan aimed at the horse, the afternoon heat inside the stable was intense.

After he introduced himself, Vince asked, "What happened?"

"Lil Joe here gulps his feed. We keep rocks in his trough to force him to eat slower. This afternoon one of my grandsons came out after school to help feed, and he put Lil Joe here in the wrong stall."

"No rocks, huh?"

"By the time I caught what had happened, the feed was gone, the horse was heaving and coughing, and my grandson was having a fit for fear he'd killed him. He loves Lil Joe, but he's an eight-year-old kid. He didn't know."

Looking at Mr. Quarles, Vince realized he wasn't far off from having a fit himself. The kid must be in agony.

"Let's see what we can do." He took care of the preliminaries quickly, then began the laborious process of easing the thick rubber tube down Lil Joe's esophagus while avoiding the trachea. "I'm going to try to clear as much as I can frontways, and then we'll see if we can move the rest down into his stomach. Where's your grandson?"

"I sent him in the house with his mother, my daughter. Didn't want him seeing this in case it went bad."

"Probably a good idea. Once we're sure he's okay, you ought to bring him out."

"Can you fix it?"

"Let's hope." The kid had done a stupid thing and put the horse in jeopardy. If it had been an adult who should know better, he'd have torn a strip off the offender while he tried to save the animal. This kid was eight. He'd been trying to help, to do something he could be proud of with an animal he loved. He was suffering more than from any pain Vince might cause him.

CAROLYN McSPARREN 83

It was a case of "been there, done that." Vince still shivered at the memory of walking in the barn when he was ten and discovering he'd left the door to the feed room open after the evening feed the night before.

His brother Joshua had warned him that horses would devour tasty sweet feed so long as it was available to them, even if they overate so badly they killed themselves with bloat.

The three horses clustered around the spilled feed knew they were in trouble when he came in, realized what they'd done and spooked away from him.

Those were the worst two days of his life up to that point and among the top ten overall. He worked with the vet to dose the horses to calm their guts. He walked them in turns until his ten-year-old legs cramped from dehydration, and he thanked God for every pile of manure that landed in the aisle.

It was a close thing. By rights his daddy's Tennessee Walking Horse mare should have died. Miraculously, she survived, as did the other two, but the vet told him that they might all be susceptible to gastric problems for the rest of their lives.

That was his first lesson in how much damage being thoughtless or careless could do to an animal. He still experienced flashes of guilt over that open feed room door.

He'd expected his father to take his belt to him, although for all his faults, Thor Peterson, his father, was never a hitter. In the end, Vince would have preferred the belt. A beating would cause finite pain that would subside and eventually go away. Instead, his father dumped a load of guilt on him he still carried. The wound never healed because his father never let him forget what he'd done. He could still feel his skin tighten when he thought of that near-disaster.

Over the years whenever his father's mare showed the faintest sign of distress, Daddy accused him all over again of trying to kill her. The old man had perfected the art of inducing guilt in the whole family. He never forgave or forgot. Daddy had total recall. Vince had found his only escape was to stay beyond his dad's influence. That translated to staying away from home.

That open feed room door was probably the reason he became a vet. It was his job to protect animals from the human beings who too often didn't protect them. He hated watching an animal suffer and figured he needed as many skills as he could accumulate to make them better.

Sweat dripped off Vince's face and ran down his back between his shoulder blades. He worked with the tube and syringes of water, watching as the undigested gunk that was blocking the horse's gullet gushed out onto the concrete floor. The horse coughed and shook. He was miserable, but he could still get enough air down to breathe, if shallowly. Vince worked to keep him on his feet.

"I explained to Jack Jr. that horses can't up-chuck," Mr. Quarles said. "He already knows Lil Joe here is a gobble-gobble eater. We've tried everything from feeding him in a foal-size manger to putting a wire grid across his feed bin so he has to suck little bits at a time. So far the only thing that's worked is the rocks."

"They ought to keep working after this, Mr. Quarles."

"Shoot, until he finds a way around them too. I had me an old Thoroughbred mare learned to pick up them rocks—big dudes, size of bricks—in her teeth and drop 'em on the floor of her stall." He laughed. "Horses—worse'n women. Well, maybe not. How come you're not pouring mineral oil down him the way you do with colic?"

"Too easy to get droplets into the lungs. Nope. Only water. Okay, let's see what we got."

Vince leaned over and gently worked the long rubber tube farther down. Then he blew into it. A moment later, he lifted his head and smiled. "I'm in the stomach. His throat is clear. Need to start him on a course of antibiotics. Otherwise, he might develop aspiration pneumonia three days from now."

"Thank the Lord. Let me get my grandson to show him."

Vince held up a hand. "You might want to wait a minute until I get this tube out." He gently withdrew the tube, moving slowly and carefully. "Yeah, thought so." As he removed the final inches of the tube from the horse's nostril, a gush of blood followed and cascaded down to the cement floor.

"Shoot!" Quarles shouted and skipped back.

"It's almost inevitable we'd get a nose bleed. Don't worry. A horse can lose twenty percent of his body weight in blood with no ill effects."

"Looks like he'll reach that in five minutes. My heaven, would you look at it?"

Vince put a hand on his arm. "Promise you,

he's fine. See, it's already slowing. You want your grandson to see this?"

"Indeed I do." The older man called his grandson on his cell phone. "Jackson, boy, how 'bout you run on down here to the barn." He listened for a moment, raised his eyebrows at Vince and received a nod in return. "Yeah, Dr. Vince says Lil Joe is gonna be fine, but he could use some loving on." He hung up, slipped his cell phone back into the pocket of his overalls, and shook his head at the blood still dripping, but only dripping, from the horse's nose. "My grandson could use some loving, too. That's a better object lesson than anything I could tell him. I don't expect ever to mention it. Won't have to. He'll never make that mistake again."

"No, he won't. I went through a similar situation when I was about his age. I never forgot it."

Half an hour later, Vince unfolded the plastic tarp he kept in his truck onto the front seat, and climbed in on top of it. He hated blood on his fancy leather seat cushions. He probably shouldn't have splurged on them, but they were his graduation gift to himself. He did love them, even in the summer when sliding in unprotected could result in third-degree burns.

He drove away with a view through his side mirror of a joyful eight-year-old carefully sponging the blood off Lil Joe's face and chest, while his grandfather stood by, ready to help if needed, but letting his grandson savor the glory as he had suffered the pain.

Now, that was the way to *discipline* a child, Vince thought. How wonderful it would be if all object lessons could wind up happily, and not, as so many did, in tragedy.

He used to believe his daddy kept an actual list of all Vince's offenses that he pulled out whenever the occasion arose. Now that list probably resided on his father's laptop. Not on the farm PC, which was the size and complexity of something designed by NASA.

That computer was probably where his brothers kept *their* lists.

Was he treating Anne the way his father treated him? Commands, demands, bad temper? Guilt? Nobody deserved that. His deepest fear was that he'd turn into his father. Thor seemed to enjoy hurting people. It was as though the only way he could feel big was by making everyone around him feel small. Vince had watched his father tear down one wife after another. His father had managed to drive them all away, except for his current wife, Mary Alice. She was sticking it out. So far.

That could change. She might reach her limit and walk out as Vince's mother had walked out, as Cody's mother had left.

CHAPTER SEVEN

AS SHE WAITED for Vince the next morning—
he was late again—Anne felt as though she
had already done a full day's work. She'd fed,
hayed and watered all the stock, large and
small, checked for any wounds or signs of
distress, and made herself a rough list of the
minis she'd be training. She had six months to
make progress in turning the VSEs into helper
horses. Would it be enough? Would Victoria
be willing to extend her contract if Anne made
a hash of it?

She decided to start with Molly.

Dosing Molly with a repeat of the ear mite
treatment required hanging on to one of her
ears while shooting liquid down the other, then
repeating the process on the other side. Although Molly's ears were about the level of
Anne's waist, hanging on to them reminded
Anne of the goat herding contest for kids at
rodeos. Small or not, Molly was stubborn and
could toss her head like a water buffalo.

"Promise you won't bring home any more minis," Anne begged Victoria over bacon and eggs.

"Martin's Minis has done its bit," Victoria said. "Eight is definitely enough."

"Promise?"

Victoria smiled and walked away without answering. Uh-oh. If Victoria brought any more in, there wouldn't be enough hours in the day to train them. Shoot, Anne wouldn't have enough stamina left to do the job properly.

In the barn, Anne closed her eyes and heaved a sigh that topped Molly's. "Little girl, I have no faith that she will not come back with half a dozen more of your kith and kin. So we'd better start training you to go live with somebody else." She hooked the twelve-foot lunge line to Molly's halter. Come on. Let's go try working out."

Anne had trained a number of young horses—big horses, like her seventeen-hand gelding, Trust Fund. How hard could it be to teach this lawn ornament–sized critter?

Obviously, Molly intended to prove that size was no object when it came to acting out.

Anne walked her to the end of the line and led her along the perimeter of the pen to give her the idea that she was supposed to circle by the fence.

The twelve-foot whip Anne carried was purely a pointer to keep the horse out on the circle. She kept it pointed at Molly's shoulder without coming close to her actual body. Molly decided it was a dragon that planned to scarf her up for breakfast—dragon chow instead of cornflakes.

She couldn't make up her mind whether flight or fight was more appropriate, so she tried to do both at the same time. This was not Anne's first rodeo, but Molly was determined to make it her last.

Most horses stayed away from the creature in the center of the circle at first, and bucked and fussed out on the rim.

Molly pawed with her front feet, kicked with her hind, jumped forward two steps and did it again. And again. Repeated as necessary.

Anne stayed in the center.

Apparently deciding that ploy wasn't working, Molly turned and charged into the middle, straight at Anne.

"Hey, cut that out!" Anne shouted and threw her arms up. It was supposed to work against charging grizzlies. Anne hoped it worked against twenty-eight-inch equine hellions.

Molly swung away, wrapped herself in the line and fell flat on her back with all four hooves flailing the air.

From behind her Anne heard slow, rhythmic clapping.

She spared a glance over her shoulder. Vince Peterson leaned on the fence with a broad grin on his face.

She felt her cheeks flush and thought, *I am going to kill him.* But before she did, she had to get Molly untangled and on her feet without getting kicked or bitten. Anne might suggest to the little mare that she go bite Vince, but she'd probably love on him instead. Just like a female.

"Need some help?" he asked.

"No. The last thing we need is another pair of feet tangled up." At the moment, she wouldn't have accepted help from the leading rider of the Spanish Riding School in Vienna. Not with Vince Peterson looking on and grinning.

The mare was not stupid. She lay still until Anne had her safely unwound, then climbed back to her feet, shook herself and gave Anne a haughty "I meant to do that" look.

She looked so silly Anne laughed. "For our next trick…" she said.

Vince laughed, too. But he was laughing at the situation, not at Anne. A definite step forward.

Maybe she had been supersensitive about his opinion of her. Just maybe. *Anne* hated being laughed at almost as much as she hated to have her skills disrespected. Probably because she'd devoted her life to sports that a lot of people thought were silly. And then there were the falls—so long as she wasn't actually hurt, some people thought falling off horses was funny.

"Turn her loose," Vince said as he climbed over the fence into the ring.

"I beg your pardon."

"I'm not kidding." He reached for Anne's whip.

"Fine. On your head be it." She let go of the whip, but kept her place in the arena beside him. If Molly charged again, he was big enough to hide behind. Let *him* get run over.

"Stay behind me and out of the way," he said. "Come on, mare, get crackin'." He whistled between his teeth. Molly bucked, spun away and started to gallop around the perimeter of the round pen. Every time she slowed, he clicked and whistled her back into a canter, ignoring her frequent bucks and occasional attempts to turn and run over him in the center.

Anne had used the same technique before with unbroken horses, but never one as small as Molly. She hated to admit that after ten frantic minutes, Molly had slowed to a steady canter, and a moment later began to drop her head and chew her lips. An indication of submission.

This time when she slowed to a trot and then to a walk, Vince let her.

She stopped and turned to face him, but stayed on the circle. He moved up to her slowly, reached across and scratched behind her ears. Then he walked back to the center. Molly followed him like a dog at heel.

"Impressive," Anne said. Not that she wanted to compliment him, but she had to give him credit. She'd watched the best horse trainers fail at that technique through impatience or anger. Sometimes it was hard not to credit a horse with malice. They were notorious for getting on your last nerve. Vince hadn't let her best him, or showed the first sign of annoyance. He reserved his snarls for human beings. For Anne in particular, it seemed.

"You did the hard part," he said as he checked Molly's ears for any remaining mites.

"Used to drive the bronco busters in Wyoming nuts when I did that after they'd been tossed in the dirt a dozen times. By the time I got here this morning, Molly was ready to cooperate and not act like a donkey rather than a mini."

Anne ran her hands down Molly's withers—dripping wet from exercise and ambient heat. "I need to rinse her off and put her out to roll in the grass. She likes you, you know."

Deciding that if close was good, closer must be better, Molly butted against Anne's side and shoved her against Vince.

They jumped apart and looked anywhere but into each other's eyes.

Anne caught her breath and a handful of Molly's mane to steady herself. *Molly, you devil.* Horses couldn't snicker, but Molly was trying. It seemed almost as though she knew these two had more in common than they were willing to admit. Molly was simply helping to show them.

Vince followed Anne and Molly into the barn and to the wash rack to give the little mare a cooling shower. Except that Molly had no intention of being trapped with her face to the back of the wash stall—obviously sprouting wall-to-wall trolls ready to devour small horses. Her rear end stuck out in the aisle. She braced all four feet and refused to take a single step onto the concrete pad.

"Here, let me," Vince said.

Again with the Mr. Rescue, Anne thought. But she gave him the line.

He hauled forward. Molly hauled back. He wrapped the line from her halter around her rear under her tail and back up to her nose, so that he was pulling her from the back rather than the front.

Molly sat down on her rear end like a donkey.

Ha ha, Anne thought. "Here, let me." She took the line from him, shooed him out of the way, poked her toe into Molly's shoulder so that she stood up, then backed her rump into the barn aisle. She turned the mare face forward, put a hand against her chest and moved her, tail-first, into the wash rack. Molly did not put a foot wrong, and once there, stood as though she had been doing it all her life.

Anne cut her eyes at Vince. "No problemo." So there.

Anne remembered the debacle with Tom Thumb, the dancing mini. Molly might react the same way, so Anne held the end of her line rather than cross-tying her in case she freaked.

"Here," said Vince, "I'll hold the line for you."

"I'll wet her down, and then we can scrub her. Same as yesterday." Anne ran the warm spray over Molly's feet and ankles so that she could get accustomed to the feel. She seemed much more relaxed than Tom. That was an illusion.

As Vince turned back with the shampoo, Molly swung her rear end toward Anne. Off balance, Anne let the hose slip out of her hand. This time Vince leaned across Molly's back and grabbed it midair. It twisted in his grasp and shot a solid stream of water between her eyes. Momentarily blinded, she reached out and found herself hanging on to Molly's tail. Molly bucked and shoved her against the wall.

"Get out of the way!" Vince snarled. He steadied the flailing hose from under Molly's rear feet.

One of her little hooves landed squarely on his instep.

He yelped and dropped the lead line. Anne dove and caught it as Molly decided that since these people were dangerous to horses, she had better get out.

Limping and biting back a groan, Vince shoved the mare back into position. When he caught the start of a snicker from Anne, he looked down at his jeans. He was soaked again.

Anne knew he did not enjoy being laughed at, certainly not by her. In retaliation he turned the hose on her again.

She squealed, grabbed a currycomb and threw it at him. Again.

"What is this thing you people have with hoses?" Victoria shouted from the barn door. She ran toward them. "Here, you," she said and caught Molly before she'd taken all four feet off the wash rack. "Are you trying to drown Molly or each other?"

"Each other!" they said in one voice.

"Somebody turn off the water right this minute. I can't let go of Molly." The little horse stood calmly gazing up at Victoria with innocent eyes. "Oh, come on, Molly. I'll put her out in her paddock. You can bring her back in later. Do you plan to change to dry clothes? It's plenty warm in here. Might be counterproductive."

"I'm fine, thank you," Anne said. "This is one of those quick-dry shirts."

"My jeans aren't," Vince said. "I've got another pair in the van, but I'll keep these on until we're finished with the hose just in case."

As she led Molly out to her paddock, Victoria said over her shoulder, "I suggest you bathe Big Mary next. She's filthy, has bugs and may not run over you or drown you. Probably." As she kept walking toward the paddocks, she was laughing.

They studiously avoided one another's eyes. Calm and businesslike was the ticket.

"I'll bring in Big Mary," Anne said.

"Shall I come with you?"

"I don't *think* so." Anne heard the sarcasm under her words. "There's a heavy-duty horse hair dryer in the tack room if you want to work on drying your jeans."

"I'm good."

Anne felt his eyes on her as she walked out to the paddock. She pulled an apple-flavored treat from her pants' pocket. Today, Vince had taken the head butts and the majority of the shower, too. He had shot her back on purpose. She'd get him for that.

He was at least trying hard to keep a handle on his temper. Why did he have to act so pompous, and treat her as if she'd never laid a hand on a horse before?

Big Mary met her at the gate to the paddock and greedily scarfed up the treat she offered.

"Okay, girlfriend, one more, but that's all."

She gazed at Anne from under her long lashes as if to say, "Aw, Mama."

"This is going to be fun. You're going to love it." Mary didn't seem convinced, but accepted the little halter easily enough and allowed her to clip on the lead line and head for the stable where Vince stood in the doorway, hands on his hips, glaring. He seemed to glare a lot.

Amazing that a pair of horses could be so different. Big Mary enjoyed the shower, even when Vince sprayed her face and dosed her ear mites again.

"She really doesn't much care what we do as long as somebody is paying attention to her," Vince said. "She seems like the perfect candidate for your helper horse training. She seems to like people." He hesitated. "Not that it's my call."

"It remains to be seen if she's smart enough to handle the commands."

When they let her back into her paddock, she trotted a dozen steps, lay down in the grass and rolled on her back, side to side, while her short legs flailed in the air.

"Dirty again already," Vince said with a grin. "Typical horse behavior."

"Oh, well."

Halfway through bathing the last horse, Vince's phone rang. He checked it, gave the lead line to Anne and walked off into the barn to return the call in private.

"Got to go," he said when he came back.

"Now?"

"Emergency."

"Are you coming back here afterward?"

"I doubt it. I'll call." He trotted to his van, climbed in and drove away.

"Thank *you*, Doctor," Anne said. *Drat the man. He might have told me what the emergency is. I do not intend to wait on his majesty, thank you very much. I can do this.*

She did, too, but by the time she finished, she'd been stepped on twice and run in circles.

Before she went back to her cottage to shower and change to dry clothes, she walked out to the far pasture to give a couple of apple treats to her Trust Fund. "I miss you, big guy," she whispered when he came up to her and whickered softly. "Maybe there'll be time for another trail ride tomorrow." After the minis, it felt strange to lean against his shoulder without being able to see over his back. Tom Thumb could easily walk under his belly. She laughed. Trusty would be horrified.

While she showered, she considered how

best to structure the training for the helper horses. She had already decided Tom Thumb should be her initial candidate. When Vince suggested the same thing, she felt as though Victoria would think he had made the decision.

That was petty. They were both right. Tom was the obvious choice. He was smart, he was kind, and he liked people. She'd work with all the horses, of course, but she'd ask Victoria to let her focus intensively on Tom first. At this point she wasn't even sure what behaviors he should be able to do.

So, first thing was a curriculum. She wanted to speak to someone who needed a helper horse. No one in the area was actually working with one as yet. Should be relatively simple to train Tom Thumb to visit nursing homes, once she'd house-trained him, but that didn't make him a helper horse. He could be trained to carry saddlebags, but could he learn to open cabinet doors? Could he learn to alert his deaf owner that the phone was ringing? Or his blind owner that he was about to step off a curb or into traffic? Could he walk up stairs? Or ride elevators? Or airplanes? Or escalators? Or ignore dogs and cats and motorcycles? Or children running at him? Or adults petting him when he was working?

"I have no idea what I'm doing," Anne said to her reflection. She dragged a comb through her damp hair, pulled on a clean T-shirt and denim shorts, sat down at her desk and called her friend Emma Logan, who lived two miles down the road from Barbara's clinic.

"How's Baby Diana?" she asked.

"Teething. Don't ask. You can hear her in the background. What's up? How's the new job?"

"Other than being saddled with Barbara's vet Vince Peterson, who I would like to slug about half the time? I do not have a clue what I'm supposed to be doing…"

"Uh-oh. You are coming to dinner tomorrow night, aren't you? Maybe I can help."

"That's the thing. I need a guinea pig."

"Oooh-kay. I don't have any handy right this minute."

"A people guinea pig. I need to know what a person requires in a helper horse."

"What about the kids you trained at your old stable?"

"I've talked to them and made notes, but that's not the same thing as having them right here with the horses."

"I haven't been in the horse show world for a long time. Let me think about it. Maybe I can come up with a couple of candidates for guinea pig of the month."

THURSDAY EVENING, ANNE, Victoria and her husband, Edward, drove to Emma's house together for dinner.

Emma was older than Anne, but their love of horses had created an early bond that remained strong even though they no longer lived close to one another. Emma's father, David French, and Anne's father, Stephen MacDonald, had played handball and golf regularly until Stephen married Barbara Carew and moved to Williamston.

When a newly jobless Emma moved into Barbara's old cottage, she found herself the foster mother of three orphaned baby skunks. She managed to con her neighbor, Seth Logan, a fish and game officer, into helping her raise the babies. Along the way she and Seth fell in love, married and now had an eight-month-old daughter named Diana. According to Seth, Diana was the smartest and most beautiful child in the history of mankind.

Anne had found Seth intimidating when she first met him. He arrested poachers, fined people without hunting and fishing licenses, and from time to time had to deal with well-protected marijuana crops and illegal stills.

Now comparing Seth's size to Vince's, Seth didn't look so intimidating after all.

After they were settled, the women with

white wine, the men with beer, Stephen Mac-Donald proposed a toast. "Next time, dinner at our new place. Mine and Barbara's—without horses in the foyer."

Barbara added, "We're near enough finished to sleep there, but we're far from being ready to entertain anyone."

Since they married, Stephen and Barbara had been living in her old apartment attached to the clinic's stalls, while they built their new house in a grove of woods in the pasture.

"Vince, are you managing all right living in The Hovel?" Emma asked. Before the renovations, Emma had christened the Victorian cottage she inherited from her great aunt The Hovel. The joke had stuck. Now everyone including the mayor, Sonny Prather, called it that, though Emma's stepmother, Andrea, a decorator, had turned it into a charming house.

"I shared a student apartment off campus with three other guys in vet school, then I lived in a bunkhouse in Wyoming the summer I spent there breaking mustangs. The Hovel is palatial by comparison. In our apartment, the roaches battled the geckos for floor space."

"Eeew," Emma said. "Hate roaches."

"You love geckos," said Seth.

"Not in the house with the baby. Vince, Barbara says your father raises cattle in Mississippi."

"On a very large chunk of the delta," Edward added and lifted his glass to Vince.

"My family's homeplace has been added onto over the years. If land was for sale, my family bought it. Then they'd add more rooms onto the house. I could never live there again. Look up 'dysfunctional' in the dictionary— you'll find pictures of my family."

"Everybody has a dysfunctional family," Seth said. "One of these days I'll take you out fishing and tell you about mine. Least your family could afford to send you to college. I'm going to be paying off student loans until Diana has grandchildren."

"Gifts from my family don't come with strings. They come with bridge cables. Daddy still wants me to practice at home. Look after all his cattle. He'll build me a clinic…"

"Watch it, buster," Barbara said. "You promised when I hired you that you wouldn't go work for Daddy."

"He'd have to send both my brothers up here to hog-tie me and drag me home. Come to think of it, I can whup both my brothers. I think you're safe."

"How about the girl next door?" Anne

asked. As the words left her mouth, she wondered why on earth she'd asked. She could feel her face blush, took a drink of her wine and nearly choked.

"The girl Daddy picked out for me…" He held his hands up. "True, I promise you. He offered to build her a big house down the road from our homeplace, as well as build me that clinic."

"Hey," Seth said. "Not a bad deal. Want to swap?"

"You're out of luck, buster," Emma said. "Diana and I have you and do not intend to let you go. You are stuck with us in Tennessee. You will not, I repeat not, think about moving to Mississippi. Besides, you don't like cows." She leaned over and kissed him on top of his head.

"Oh, shucks, just my luck."

Everybody laughed, then Barbara said, "Finish telling us about the girl next door. Imagine turning down an offer like that."

"I never asked her, but she would have said no. She lives across the road, not next door. We're friends, but that's all we'll ever be. She's not interested in anything more. Neither am I. Since all I've learned from my father and my brothers is how to get divorced, I plan to avoid divorce by never getting married. Easier in the long run." He raised his glass. "Cheaper, too."

"Hey," Emma said. "No babies?"

"Joshua and Cody, my two brothers, each have a pair of boys. What the Brits call an heir and a spare. I'm off the hook. There are heirs in place after the three of us brothers are gone."

"Have girls," Seth said. "I like them."

"You like Diana." Emma slapped him on the shoulder. "Vince could have holy terrors. Come on, y'all. Let's eat before Diana wakes up and wants to eat, too."

THE NEXT MORNING, Vince joined Anne and Victoria for coffee beside Victoria's pool in what had become a casual daily staff meeting.

Anne said, "As of early this morning, I think I've found a guinea pig for our training program. Emma reminded me about her last night." She leaned back on the chaise longue beside the swimming pool and rested her sore neck and shoulders.

"What are you talking about?" Vince asked.

"We need someone with actual needs to work with me while I train Tom."

Vince sat up. "Whoa, there. Do you have the faintest notion how much trouble you could get into working with a person with disabilities when you don't know what you're doing?"

"As a matter of fact, I do. I have trained blind kids and kids with cerebral palsy. They've learned to ride and to drive. One of my carriage driving kids is showing her horse at shows and winning. She's in a special carriage fitted with a wheelchair. I had a student paralyzed from the waist down. I trained her sixteen-hand Friesian gelding to lie down so she could mount him."

"That's different from relying on a mini horse like Molly to help you while you shop in a big box store."

"Not that much. That is why the person who works with us the first time has to have a limited disability that can benefit from having a helper horse, but won't be in danger if something goes wrong in the initial phases of training." She topped off her coffee, added artificial sweetener and carefully avoided looking at either Vince or Victoria. "I'll be working closely and supervising…"

Vince rolled his eyes. "Do you have any idea how you're going to accomplish this so-called training? Or where you're going to find a…" he held up his first and second fingers in a quotation mark gesture "…slightly disabled candidate who's willing to risk life and limb training an untrained dwarf miniature horse?"

"Yes, I know how to train the VSE, and I have mentors who are as close as my phone. Yes, I have found my human helper. Thank you for your *support*, Doctor." Anne shoved her chair back, took her coffee and stalked off toward her cottage to get ready for today's problems.

As she brushed her teeth, she glowered at the mirror. One of these days—and soon—she was going to throttle that man. Unfortunately, he had a point. She needed two things. Very soon when she had done the preliminary work she needed to visit someone who was training minis as helpers. Second, she needed a willing candidate to train with a beginner horse. If she could train one, she could train others.

"VINCE PETERSON, YOU may be a good doctor, but you can be a royal pain with people," Victoria said.

Vince raised his hands chest-high in a gesture of surrender. "I'm just sayin' someone has to keep a hold on reality. It's too soon to be talking about bringing in someone to work with an untrained horse worked by an untrained trainer."

"Anne is not untrained. She was working with a riding for the disabled program in Memphis very successfully until they lost their grant. That was a bad enough blow to her self-esteem. Now here she is trying to do something really good, and all she hears from you is that she's not smart enough or..."

"Hey, I never said she wasn't smart, Victoria. From what I've seen, she's smart and conscientious. She just hasn't proved she knows how to train the animals. We've barely begun teaching these guys to behave, much less do any of the behaviors they need to aid an owner. It's not supporting the people who need help, and it's likely a waste of effort."

"Then it behooves us to stand behind her any way we can, Vince. She told me you didn't like her. I can certainly see why she would believe that." She glanced past his shoulder. "Here she comes. Be nice."

"I'm always nice."

"Except when you're not. So, Anne, ready to get started on the hellions?"

"In a minute." She set her coffee down and leaned on the table with both hands. "Just listen before you say no. This won't mean anything to you, Vince, but, Victoria, do you remember Becca Stout?"

Victoria nodded. "The girl who was so badly hurt at the Florida young rider finals last year? How's she doing?"

"What happened?" Vince asked.

"Her jumper crashed a fence on a cross-country three-day event course, fell on her and rolled. She was wearing a protective vest and a hard hat—otherwise I don't think she'd have survived. She's been back and forth to Atlanta for rehab for the past year. Her leg's healed, and so's her broken pelvis, but the doctors say she's never going to be completely free of her balance problems. She had a bad concussion. They induced a coma and kept her in it for nearly a month."

"So she'll never be able to ride again?" Victoria asked. "Oh, dear, she's a senior in high school, isn't she?"

"Actually, somehow, with tutoring she managed to graduate two weeks ago. Her horse, Aeolus, boards at the barn I worked with in Memphis. I was exercising him for her before I came here."

"She can't ride him?" Vince asked.

"She says she's like the White Knight in *Alice Through the Looking Glass*. She can't stay in the middle of the saddle. I just got off the phone with her. Her horse, Aeolus, has been sold, and it's killing her. She doesn't want to be around to see him leave."

"I don't blame her," Victoria said.

"Before I got laid off, I was working to move her to carriage driving, but she needs help keeping her balance. She's a perfect candidate for a helper horse."

"Anne, dear." Victoria patted her knee. "We don't have a helper horse yet. Heaven knows whether we will ever have a horse that is completely safe for a disabled owner."

"That's the beauty part," Anne said. "I've been working with Becca at my old barn ever since she came home from rehab in Atlanta. She's been doing yoga and tai chi. Her balance is better, but the doctors say it will never come back a hundred percent. She's a real horseman, and she's desperate to do something that will keep her involved with horses, even if only as a groom. She wants to learn along with a mini."

"Can she drive a car?"

"She can drive in town, but she's not comfortable on the highway yet. I talked to her mother after I spoke to Becca. She's on board and enthusiastic. Her dad is dead set against Becca having anything to do with horses. He's scared she'll try to ride when the doctors forbid it. Her mother says if we don't find something she can do and fast, she may wind up doing something crazy. It's not like she's a beginner. She was in line for a big sponsorship to send her to Germany to train after she graduated from high school. She's dying to start ASAP. She wants to come up this afternoon. She can stay in the cottage with me. Her mother will drive her up. I'll take her home Monday morning. See how it goes."

Victoria ran a hand down her face. "So soon? Will her mother sign the same hold harmless statement all of my clients sign when they come to board and ride here?"

"Absolutely. The state of Tennessee says that working with horses is intrinsically dangerous and that the client understands that. So unless we are negligent—which we won't be—Martin's Minis is legally safe from a suit. I learned the law when I set up classes at my old barn. If this weekend isn't successful, we'll still have learned something."

"That you have no idea what you're doing?" Vince said.

Victoria glared at him.

Then Anne glared at him, too. "Among other things."

"Which horse are you going to use?"

"Who else? Tom Thumb."

CHAPTER EIGHT

FRIDAY AFTERNOON, ANNE and Victoria watched Becca and her mother park near them at the top of the hill.

"This is so lame," Becca said as she climbed out of the front seat of her mother's Lexus, took a step away and then reached a hand behind her to brace herself against the roof of the car. "Look at that thing in the pasture. That's not a horse, it's a skin growth."

"It can kick, bite, paw, buck and run away with you. Of course it's a horse," Anne said. "Hey, Mrs. Stout. Thanks for driving Becca up."

Willa Stout nodded, but kept her eyes on her daughter, who still leaned against the side of the car.

Becca rolled her eyes. "You'd have to be a doll to actually ride one of the things. Actually, most of the dolls I still have would be too big. This is stupid. I'm going home. Oh my gosh, there's another one."

Out of the shadows under the sycamore tree in the corner of the paddock, Tom Thumb trotted toward Becca.

"He wants a treat. Have a baby carrot." Anne handed Becca a truncated carrot. Tom Thumb skidded to a halt and reached across the fence with his lips puckered. "Well, give it to him."

With a look of disdain at the stubby little horse, Becca handed the carrot to Tom. He took it gently between his lips, chewed and swallowed, then ducked his head and batted his brown eyes at her. As she turned away from him, he bumped his nose against her forearm and nickered softly. She glanced down at him and whispered, "I swear he's smiling. Horses can't smile."

"When Tom wants a treat, he can. So give him one." Anne handed several more miniature carrots to Becca. "He should carry a sign that says, Will Work for Food."

Molly joined Tom at the fence and shoved him to get out of her way. She was larger, but his center of balance was lower to the ground, so he didn't move.

Becca handed Molly a carrot as well and received a tiny nip from Tom. "Hey! Cut that out." Tom blinked innocent eyes at her. She reached across the fence and scratched between his ears. For Tom an ear scratch was not as good as a carrot, but it would have to do, so he sighed in momentary ecstasy. Becca snorted.

"Want to go into the paddock with them?" Anne asked.

"I guess," Becca said, then sighed. "Not a good idea. I might fall on my face. She leaned close to Anne and said softly, "I don't see how this can work. One of those little things can't hold me up when I start to fall over."

Anne whispered back. "You don't generally go all the way, do you?"

Becca pulled her shoulders back and spoke in a normal voice. The others were walking back to the patio. "What I do is stumble, then go into this little sideways two-step until I find something to grab hold of. Everybody thinks I'm drunk or stoned. It's why I don't drive on the highway. If I got stopped and had to walk one of those lines, I'd wind up in the drunk tank."

"Do you get dizzy when you drive?"

"Never as long as I'm holding the wheel."

"So what's the difference between holding on to the wheel to keep your equilibrium and holding on to a horse's training harness?"

Becca frowned. "I... I don't really know. You think it might work?"

"That's what we're going to find out. We've barely started this training, and frankly, I'm darned near as much an amateur as you are, but Tom Thumb is wicked smart, loves people. So far he figures out what we want from him quickly, then goes ahead and does it."

"He looks different from the little mare. She's taller and prettier. His legs look funny."

"He's actually a dwarf. It's a genetic anomaly. Mini breeders have been trying to get rid of it from the gene pool, but it still crops up. Tom is lucky. Frequently endocrine and heart problems go along with the condition, but Tom seems to be totally healthy. He's just short and stubby."

Becca had been avoiding looking at either horse, but now she peered down at Tom Thumb, then Molly. From the slow smile she gave the two, it was obvious that she was hooked.

Anne nodded. Becca had cleared the first hurdle.

"How many of these things are here?" Becca asked.

"Eight total. Then there are the regular-sized horses that board here."

"Did you bring your guy with you?"

"Yep, I brought Trusty, plus there are several boarders' horses, and Victoria's Morgan, her driving horse. We plan to teach the minis to pull a carriage, if they aren't suited to be helper horses."

"What makes the difference?"

"I'm not certain yet, but I know that Tom Thumb will be a helper horse. He already seems to understand what is wanted from him, and he likes people. Molly—the little mare who came over with him—maybe, maybe not." She waggled her hand. "She should be able to pull a mini carriage…"

"They have tiny carriages?"

"For tiny horses. Yep. And tiny harnesses and tiny shoes and…"

Becca snickered. "Okay, I get it. So maybe they're not exactly a skin growth. Can we go see the others?"

"Let's get you settled first. You have your own bedroom in my cottage, but I do not do maid service."

"Neither does my mother. While I was in rehab, I tried to learn to cook. I'm limited, but not bad so long as you don't want beef Wellington or coq au vin."

"Pity. I love beef Wellington."

"Who can afford it? Hey, my mother's waving at me. I think she wants to find out whether or not I'm staying."

"Are you?"

Anne heard the catch in Becca's voice.

"The horse movers were coming after lunch to pick up Aeolus. He's going to Virginia. I didn't want to be there when he leaves." Her shoulders hunched. "I know it's the right thing to do. The girl who bought him loves him to pieces. But…" She began to sob. "He's *my* horse."

Anne opened her arms. "Oh, Becca, I'm so sorry."

"I said goodbye this morning before we left to drive up here. I'll never be able to ride him again, and I just can't *stand* it." She moved into Anne's arms, laid her head against Anne's shoulder and sobbed.

Anne patted her and rubbed her back.

She was crying, too. What a hard thing for Becca to have to suffer. Aeolus would be happy, but he wouldn't understand why his human, his person, had gone out of his life. And he'd remember. Anne had met one of her old school horses two years back at a horse show in Atlanta. She heard him nicker before she saw him. Happy, content, the idol of the girl who rode him. Still, she felt as though she had to walk away from a member of her family.

When Becca encountered Aeolus, and the chances were that she would, they would know one another and remember. Just as she and Trust Fund would always have a special bond, even if they never saw one another again. There was no sense of communication like the one between horse and rider. Feeling the horse respond to the slightest change in balance or leg pressure was glorious. When it was right, it was as though the two became one mind. How could Becca get past the longing for that feeling?

"Becca, honey, are you all right?" Willa Stout was trotting down the gravel path toward them with her arms outstretched, her face a mask of concern.

Becca caught her breath, sniffed and stepped away from Anne. She ran her fingertips under her eyes to brush away the tears without smearing her eyeliner, gulped and said without turning to face her mother, "I'm fine, Mom. Little tired is all. Can we go take my stuff into the cottage?"

"Sure," Anne said. "You hungry?"

"We had lunch in Williamston at that diner

you recommended on the phone," Mrs. Stout said. "So, Becca, honey, I guess that means you're staying for the weekend."

"I guess. Can you bring my duffel? I'll probably stagger if I try to carry it down." Becca strode past Anne and her mother and down the hill to the cottage with no sign of balance problems.

"Sure," Anne said, and picked it up.

"This has been a really hard day for her," Mrs. Stout said. Her voice quavered. "Saying goodbye to Aeolus…it liked to have killed both of us. I'm so glad we could come up here on such short notice. I tried to explain to her father what giving up riding means to her. I said it was like telling a seventeen-year-old Tom Brady that he could never throw a football again because he'd had too many concussions."

"Did he get it?" Anne asked.

Mrs. Stout shrugged. "Maybe a little. He's just afraid she'll ride anyway. That's why we desperately need some kind of alternative that gives her at least a touch of horses without the risk of riding."

She took a deep breath. Her eyes followed Becca's long-limbed body until she shut the door of Anne's cottage behind her. "Should I stay for a while?"

"I'd prefer that you didn't," Anne said. "Like leaving your kid on the first day of school. It's tough, but it's better."

"Do you know what you'll be doing today?"

Anne walked beside Mrs. Stout toward the cottage. "Probably just playing around. Maybe trying on harnesses. Bits and pieces. Just get her comfortable with the idea of trusting an animal again."

"Have you picked out her mini?"

"I think so, but it's not a hundred percent settled. I may harness up Victoria's Morgan gelding to her carriage and let Becca get the feel of the reins behind a big horse that's trained to drive already. She'll be using reins to control her mini initially." She held the door of the cottage open for Mrs. Stout. They could hear Becca in the spare bedroom. She'd already set up her sound system. The walls were thin, so the music came through at top volume.

Anne dropped Becca's duffel beside the couch and blinked at the noise level. "Boy, does that make me feel old. It's no wonder some of the kids I taught already have hearing issues."

"Becca, turn that down," Mrs. Stout called. "Becca, now!"

Something slammed down inside the room, but the music stopped.

"At least she's not tethered to her cell phone the way most of her friends are," Mrs. Stout said. "She couldn't use it in the hospital. Against the rules. Besides, reading the numbers made her sick to her stomach. Now I think she's outgrown it." Mrs. Stout sank onto the blue denim sofa in front of the fireplace. "She lost all her horse friends and most of her nonhorse friends. Hard to keep up with your acquaintances when you're in a coma." She wiped the tears from her eyes just as Becca had done.

"She'll be going to college in the fall if she can get around campus without falling, but she'll still be living at home. We can't trust her to manage dorm life on her own." She leaned across and took Anne's hand. "You have to help her, Anne."

"I warned you both this is our first experiment. We'll do our best, but we're going to make mistakes. I don't want Becca to pay for them."

"I can look after myself," Becca said from the doorway to her bedroom. "Go home, Mom. I'll be fine."

Anne noticed that Becca kept one hand on the doorjamb.

Willa pasted a smile on her face. "See you Monday."

Anne and Becca stared at one another for a long moment after she left. Then Anne said, "You've marooned yourself."

"I can always steal the farm truck and drive home."

"You said you can't drive on the highway."

"Not can't, just don't."

"What happens if you take your hand off the doorjamb?"

"I've been in position long enough for my equilibrium to stabilize. Nothing should happen. What tees me off is that I never know *when* it'll happen. Some days it's nothing. Others, I'm doing the sideways shuffle a dozen times."

"What do the doctors say?"

"That it will probably keep getting better. Fewer episodes, shorter duration. They don't think I'll ever be back to a hundred percent. So no foot in the stirrup or butt in the saddle. Ever. But hey, what do they know?"

"What, indeed. Come on. Let's go get Tom Thumb—that's the dwarf—and see if we can find a harness that will fit him."

CHAPTER NINE

TOM THUMB SEEMED delighted to have his very own person. He transferred his allegiance from Anne to Becca in the first fifteen minutes of following her around the arena. Anne walked on Becca's right side to catch her if she started to fall.

After a couple of circuits of the arena, Becca leaned on the fence. "Man, I've got the stamina of an earthworm." She closed her eyes and took deep breaths. "I used to be able to ride all day and party at night on the weekends after horse shows."

"Takes time to get your strength back."

"How would you know?" Becca snapped.

"I missed my thirteenth birthday party because I was in the emergency room with a minor concussion after going through the jump standard helmet-first," Anne said. "That was before I got Trust Fund."

Becca turned away from her. "I still can't talk about Aeolus. I'll never forget him. The feeling when he went over a big jump and we were together—it was like flying, like we were one creature."

"I know," Anne said. "Doesn't always happen, but when it does, it's magic."

Becca turned to her with her eyes wide. "I try to tell people, but, like, my parents don't get it, you know? Daddy keeps telling me to take up golf. As if."

"I had my share of falls. Comes with the territory."

Becca snapped at her. "You had one little concussion. Big deal. I was in a coma and then rehab for a year."

"It was an accident, Becca. Could have been me."

"But it wasn't. You didn't have to stop riding. I've seen you ride at horse shows. You're fearless. I couldn't go over a five-foot jump on my best day before the accident."

"That's not fearless. I'm always scared. I know Trusty can take the fence if I get out of his way, but that's not to say that he won't slip on a wet patch or trail a fence pole under his hind legs. It's a dangerous sport."

"Ya think? Come on, Tom, little guy, let's see if I can walk right across the arena back to the barn."

Anne fell into step beside her. She could tell Becca was tired and kept a close eye on her. A dozen steps from the door to the stable, she listed to her left. Before Anne could grab her arm to keep her upright, she stepped sideways. She dropped her hand on Tom's withers, the spot where neck met shoulder.

Anne reached for Becca, but missed and grabbed the tail of her T-shirt. She expected both horse and girl to collapse into the sand.

Instead, Tom braced all four of his stubby legs and took the weight of Becca's outstretched arm and hand on his shoulder. She leaned her hip against him, stabilized her balance and grabbed Anne's hand on her other side.

It seemed to Anne as though they stayed that way for an eternity, although in reality it was probably no more than a few seconds. She hooked her fingers through Becca's belt and hauled her upright.

Tom didn't move until Becca took a tentative step away from him. He swung his head and cut his eyes up at her as if to say, *Okay, we good?*

Neither Anne nor Becca said a word until Becca sat on a couple of hay bales stacked in the aisle inside the barn.

Then Becca grabbed the cheek pieces of Tom's halter and pulled him close to her, where she could nuzzle his face. He lifted his front legs onto the edge of the lower bale of hay and laid his head in her lap.

Anne watched her scratch between Tom's ears and croon to him.

She turned away so Becca wouldn't catch her sniffling and spotted Vince's silhouette at the front door of the barn.

Anne went to him. He took both her hands, leaned over and whispered, "Congratulations."

"It worked. It really worked." She looked back over her shoulder. Neither horse nor girl had moved, but remained cuddled together. "Come on, leave them to it."

Outside, Anne leaned against the wall of the barn and gulped air. "I have never been so scared in my life as when she started to fall. I was planning to grab her before she went down. I expected Tom would walk out from under her. Instead, he just stood there. Nobody taught him to do that—I haven't had time yet. It's as if he knows instinctively."

"Doesn't mean Molly would, or any of the others. You might not have been able to catch her with Molly or Grumpy."

"I do not need any more thunderstorms on my parade, thank you, Doctor. It was a success, however it came about. The point is, it's possible. Don't you scientific types say you have to be able to duplicate an experiment to prove its value?"

"If you can't?"

"I can and I will."

"Admit it may not work. What'll happen to the horses with no skills when no one wants them? The people that need them will find another solution, but there is no solution for the minis."

"If I can't train them, I'll find somebody that can. Is that what you wanted to hear? I'll give up? I won't abandon them even if I have to go back to bartending full-time to pay for them. Now I have to look after Becca and start working the other horses." She glared up at him. "Why are you here? I thought you weren't scheduled for today."

"Just checking on any possible overnight disasters. When I saw what you were doing I wanted to watch. Now I'm on my way to give eighteen piglets their first shots."

She shoved off the wall and grinned at him. "Couldn't happen to a nicer guy."

IN HIS REARVIEW MIRROR, Vince watched Anne standing outside the barn, hands on her elegant hips in their tight britches. He seemed to appeal to clingy women, which was probably why he didn't appeal to *her*. He doubted she'd cling to him if she was about to be thrown into Kilauea volcano.

She was about the most stubborn woman he'd ever met. Maybe that's why they seemed to butt heads. She wanted to do things her way. He knew better.

He hadn't really grown up with horses, not the way she had—training them to jump fences and ride with a foxhunt. She also had experience working with disabled kids and adults. In Wyoming he found he had a talent for getting horses ready to work cattle, but that was a far cry from what Anne did and planned to do.

He didn't want to see her fail. Maybe she'd succeed. He'd be the first to applaud her efforts. He might not agree with her, but he liked her. She'd give this horse thing her best shot.

At home in Mississippi there were always horses around for riding the fields and working the cows, ponies for the children and their friends, and his father's beloved grand champion walking horse mare. His father loved that mare in a way he had never loved his sons. He was more demonstrative with her than with any of them.

Vince had practically lived on a horse during the summer after he graduated from Mississippi State. At the Wyoming ranch where he'd taken a summer job, he had broken horses to ride and taught them basic roping and cutting commands. Nothing fancy. Pretty didn't matter. Utility and trustworthiness did. They were the work vehicles on the ranch. Good working quarter horses, the ones with talent, seemed to take to herding cattle instinctively. The most talented flat-out hated cows and enjoyed shoving them around.

It was still better to use horses to work cattle than ATVs. At least in Wyoming. Too many hills, too many prairie dog holes, too much bad weather from tornadoes to hail to blizzards. He hadn't been there long enough to encounter the blizzards, but his ranch buddies told him horror stories that were probably no more than ten percent fantasy. He had learned to judge how to keep the mustangs healthy and how to know when they were too tired or hot or being worked too hard. He'd carried that skill home to vet school with him. Checking and measuring his clients' horses had become second nature. He thought Anne was conscientious as well, but he would still keep an eye on the minis she was training.

There were times when he still missed Wyoming. He had loved it. Before Tiffany, the owner's spoiled daughter, had decided she wanted to marry him, he had considered staying, settling down and buying some range land. Wyoming was definitely far enough away from his father.

But he couldn't let go of his dream of vet school, and that was in Mississippi. He certainly did not want to marry Tiffany, no matter the pressure she put on him.

Not that marriage to Tiffany had ever been an option for him. He'd already made up his mind not to marry, ever. His family did not have a talent for it. His father was a terrible example of what a husband and father should be and the single example he'd grown up with. His brothers were trying to overcome Daddy's legacy with only partial success.

So far not marrying hadn't been a problem for him, because he'd never been in love. He'd always been willing to walk away from his current—what? Girlfriend?

He checked his rearview mirror, but he could no longer see Anne. He experienced a fleeting sense of loss. That was crazy. She was not even a friend. Barely a colleague.

Then why did he miss the sight of her when she disappeared from his mirror?

He checked his GPS to see if he was headed for the pig farm. It was on the edge of the territory he and Barbara covered, but he had never been there before. He wasn't looking forward to the procedure. He was fond of pigs. They were smart and clean. But piglets made an unholy racket whenever anybody picked them up.

He liked most of the animals he served. You could trust them to act in character.

Human beings? Not so much. Human females? Never for one moment.

Back on the ranch in Wyoming, Tiffany was beautiful and bright and would be rich. She was the boss's daughter, after all. She was also the most spoiled woman he had met in his life. Vince had grown up in Mississippi, the home base of the Daddy's Girl, so to call Tiffany worse was saying something. When Tiffany wanted something or someone, all she had to do was crook her little finger, maybe shed a tear or so, and Daddy would get it for her.

Hadn't worked with Vince, mostly because he was too busy and too blind to see what she was trying to do. She'd never forgiven him for passing her up.

He still had no clue why she'd wanted him.

Maybe after he'd graduated from vet school he could have seen it. At that point he'd have career prospects, be able to afford a wife and children. That summer he was just another saddle bum working for her father, two years younger than Tiffany, naive, unformed and not simply wet behind the ears but downright sopping.

If he ever did consider marriage, he had no intention of living off his wife's money, or his father's, either. *If* he ever did decide to marry. But in that summer between his graduation from Mississippi State and his matriculation in their veterinary medicine program, he had nothing to offer. She was already once married and divorced. The woman jetted off to New York to get her hair cut, for Pete's sake.

He'd heard from the other hands who had stayed on the ranch after he left that she had married a real estate tycoon she'd met on one of her New York trips. She was living in an apartment on the Upper East Side. No broken heart there. On either side.

He'd been nothing but another saddle bum come to Wyoming for a summer of breaking broncs, working cattle and sowing a few wild oats. The other hands envied him. They thought Tiffany was a catch. He'd rather have hooked a barracuda.

He'd come to Wyoming in the first place to get away from his family and to make enough money to pay for his first year at vet school.

His father had made it clear that unless he agreed to come home to practice after he qualified as a vet, he would not foot the cost of tuition. If Vince accepted family support, he would be indentured for life. Not going to happen.

He spotted the sign with a silhouette of a Duroc boar beside a pair of fancy iron gates. Most farmers hesitated to boast about raising hogs, so the sign was unobtrusive. He turned in and drove up the long gravel drive past the farmhouse and parked beside three red metal barns. The place was immaculate. The sort of place his father might have offered him. He climbed out, leaned against the hood of the van and waited for someone to come get him.

When he came back home from Wyoming at the end of the summer after avoiding Tiffany, he discovered his daddy had picked out a wife for him in Mississippi.

He'd gone to kindergarten with Cheryl, known to her family as Sugarpie. He loved her like a sister. He did not want to attempt to love her like a wife. The problem was that Sugarpie was slightly more agreeable to the marriage idea, although *he* knew she only loved him as a friend. She wanted him to come home to do what his father wanted. She didn't want to leave *her* family to move away. When he said no, he'd lost her as a friend. He hated that.

Since he'd taken his new job at Barbara's clinic, he figured he was back to the way he lived in Wyoming. No time, no women.

"Hey, Doc," called a gravelly voice from the shadows under the overhang of the nearest barn. "Got your earplugs in?"

Vince grinned. He was ready.

Two hours later he drove back out the gates and left behind a satisfied client, and a bunch of vaccinated pigs.

He looked at his watch. Shoot, it was early yet. He might as well drop back by Martin's Minis to see if Anne had managed to dodge disaster without him.

Why did the woman tread on his last nerve?

Something about the look of her with those long legs and that smooth stride stirred him. Something about her fair skin made him want to stroke her cheek. Something about her lovely, wide mouth and sensual lips made him want to kiss them to see if they were really as soft as they looked.

The rest of her wasn't bad either.

But for the foreseeable future, women were out. Probably a good thing she didn't like him. Made keeping his distance simpler. Anne deserved a man who knew how to love her. He didn't. All his life he'd watched his father bully and demand so much from his wives that they left. His own mother had walked out eventually, even though she abandoned Vince as well. He had no point of reference for what made a good husband, built a good marriage. That kind of thing was born in or trained in early. Too late now.

CHAPTER TEN

"WHO IS THAT man getting out of the van?" Becca whispered. "He's gorgeous." She turned from brushing little Grumpy, who stood half-asleep on the cross-ties.

"Him?" Anne looked toward the parking lot. "Oh, that's Victoria's vet, Vince Peterson. He's in practice with Barbara, my stepmother. He's helping with the minis."

"Is he married?"

"I have no idea." She'd assumed because he wasn't wearing a wedding ring that he was single, but many medical and engineering types did not wear rings because they could get caught in equipment.

It suddenly struck her that she did not want him to be married. What did it matter? She'd already classified him as having too high a "jerk" rating. "He's too old for you, Becca. Put your eyes back in your head."

"Nothing that looks like that is too old for

me. I'll bet he's got six-pack abs. Yum, yum. You have dibs?"

"Good grief, no. We have a very prickly professional relationship. He thinks I'm an idiot. I think he's a pompous jerk."

"Then let the games begin." Becca actually smacked her lips.

"Oh, no, you don't. Your mother would kill me. You're barely eighteen."

"I've always liked older guys. I was madly in love with one of my doctors in Atlanta, but he blew me off after he told me his wife was expecting their second child."

"Good for him."

"Besides, no guy wants to go out with somebody who could fall on the floor without warning."

Anne caught the change in Becca's voice. Studiedly casual. This was the first time she had let slip that her disability bothered her more than she admitted.

"You're not going to fall. Not with a helper horse. You didn't have a problem with Tom, did you?"

Becca shrugged. "That's because Tom didn't move away, and you grabbed my belt. A whole lot different from crashing in the fruit aisle at the grocery store and knocking a humongous stack of watermelons on the floor. I can't take Tom Thumb into the store."

"Sure you can. He's no different from a see-ing eye dog. He can go with you into stores, on airplanes, to class in the fall."

"I want to move into the dorm this fall. My stupid parents won't let me."

"Keep talking to them. Maybe you'll be ready."

"So what am I doing this afternoon?"

"Working with one of the other minis."

"Why not Tom Thumb?"

"Don't forget you're a test case. We're going to see which minis we can train as helpers and which to drive carriages. You need to learn to drive a carriage, as well. You may not be able to ride a horse over fences at a horse show, but you can certainly drive a mini in carriage driv-ing. Plenty of classes for VSEs."

"But…"

"Since you're only going to be here until Monday this time, we have to shoehorn as much as we can into the schedule. We can plan what to work on when you come back for more. Tom Thumb can lag behind in his lessons and catch up fast. The others—not so much. How about we put Grumpy back in his pasture and get ready for lunch?"

"With Mr. Handsome?"

Anne laughed. "That's Dr. Handsome to you."

As they walked up the hill toward the patio and swimming pool, Vince came out of Victoria's kitchen door carrying a tray piled high with sandwiches. He set it down on the wrought-iron table and nodded to the two women. "Ladies," he said, and flashed them a smile that made Anne's heart leap. Heaven only knew what it did to Becca.

Anne introduced them. Becca reached out and took Vince's hand. He pulled away before she did. Anne had never mastered the Southern simper, but Becca was a genius at it, complete with fluttering lashes. Uh-oh.

Anne hoped she wouldn't have problems with Becca over Vince. The difference between eighteen and thirtysomething was substantial, but not insurmountable. As her mother had told her, older men played by different rules. Their idea of a relationship did not stop with sharing a chocolate malted after a movie, then parting at the front door with a good-night kiss. 'Course, from the stories she heard around the horse shows, girls Becca's age were also playing by grown-up rules.

Not under Anne's care, however.

She and Becca had both grown up in the horse show world. There tended to be fewer boys than girls riding. Add in the time spent in rehab after her accident, and chances were good that Becca had never had a real boyfriend.

Anne had once asked her father if he had any idea why there was such an imbalance between boys and girls in the horse world.

He told her not so much since Title IX—the law that tried to equalize sports for girls with sports for boys. But before that, boys had more access to *team* sports—baseball, football, soccer. Girls tended toward individual sports like tennis and golf that their parents paid for. "Girls fall in love with horses in a way boys don't," he said. "It's as if they get infected with the equine plague. Some of them never recover."

Anne hadn't. Becca obviously hadn't either.

"Victoria's fed me half my meals the last couple of days," Vince said. "Thought I'd reciprocate with lunch from the snack shop down the road."

Becca flashed him a killer smile.

Anne was surprised when he took a step backward and gave Anne a *help me* glance.

Throughout the rest of the lunch, he talked

mostly to Anne and Victoria. He didn't actually snub Becca, but he avoided her eyes and moved his chair out of touching range.

"So, how did it go?" Victoria asked as she reached for a roast beef sandwich and another can of diet soda.

"Remarkably well," Anne said. "We'll take a break after lunch, and then we're going to fit Molly with a VSE harness and see if we can drive her with the reins but without the cart. She needs to respond to rein signals without a rider or a cart behind her."

"How do we do that? Becca asked.

"We walk behind her using pressure on the reins to point her in the right direction. Once she can do that, then we give her a bit of weight behind her to actually pull. A small trailer tire, for instance. After she's comfortable with that, then we try to harness her to the little carriage."

"It's unfortunate that I don't have a VSE that's already trained to drive," Victoria said. "Putting an untrained horse to a carriage beside a trained horse turns the old pro into a teacher."

"Are *you* going to be here to help?" Becca asked Vince.

He leaned back in his chair and laid his half-eaten sandwich on his plate. "Sorry, no can do. I've got a list of appointments that will take me past office hours all over Williamston County. Even across the bridge to the south side of the river."

"I'm going to be a vet like you," Becca said.

Anne raised her eyebrows and caught Victoria's surprised glance. This was the first time Becca had mentioned the possibility.

"I'd love to ride along with you on your calls," Becca said. "I'd love to watch you. I could help."

That's all they needed.

"Sorry, I don't take ride-alongs. You're here to work with Anne. Aren't you going home Monday? Not much time to get in everything you all want to do, is it?"

Becca pouted. Anne figured the teenager thought she was pouting "prettily," but the expression turned her into a spoiled toddler.

Anne had to fight a smile when Vince rolled his eyes at her. Obviously he was used to being the recipient of crushes, was uncomfortable with them, but definitely knew how to defuse them. No worries there. Still, it was a good thing Becca planned to go home to Memphis on Monday.

Victoria took Becca down to the barn while Vince and Anne cleaned up after lunch.

"She's got a crush on you," Anne said.

"I'd rather have a water moccasin fall on my head." He reached down to pick up a plate that Anne had just rinsed to put in the dishwasher. Their hands touched. For a second neither moved. His fingers laced into hers while the warm water flowed over them.

"Anne," he said softly and turned her toward him. Their eyes met and held.

The plate clattered in the sink as he moved his fingers to the back of her neck. She swayed against him, unwilling or unable to look away.

As he bent toward her, the screen door to the patio opened, followed by footsteps.

They sprang apart and turned back to the still-running water.

"Come on, slowpokes," Victoria said. "What's taking so long?"

Vince cleared his throat. "Just doing a good job. We can go now. I'll walk the two of you down to the barn."

Victoria looked from one to the other with a slight frown on her face. "Sure," she said.

FITTING ONE OF the VSE harnesses Victoria had acquired on Molly took Vince's intervention.

"I can stay long enough to give you a hand," he said.

Anne felt herself blush.

Molly had no intention of allowing all that rig to be buckled on her small body. She spit out the bit on the little driving bridle half a dozen times before Vince managed to get the bridle over her head.

When Anne lifted her tail to place the crupper—the piece that buckled under her tail and kept the harness in the center of her back—Molly lashed out with a foot and would have connected with Anne's shin if she hadn't jumped out of the way and against Vince's chest.

He caught her. "Careful, sport," he said with his lips against her hair.

She moved away quickly and checked to see that neither of the others had noticed that second's hesitation.

While Becca buckled and snapped and fed the reins through the round metal eyelets called turrets that held them in place between bit and carriage, she did not show any sign of losing her equilibrium. So, Anne thought, physical concentration and hands-on labor might keep Becca's stumbling and dizziness to a minimum. If so, then the more Becca was occupied in a task outside herself, the better she might be.

"Looks like you've got everything under control," Vince said. "Anne, mind walking me up the hill?"

"Sure. Don't do anything, Becca. Be right back."

As they strolled to Vince's truck, he said, "I wasn't kidding about being careful. Becca can't get out of the way as fast as you can."

Anne stiffened. "I had noticed." *Back to: you doctor, me peon.*

They had reached his van. He took her arms. "Don't let anything happen to you. That girl adds a whole new element of danger."

She relaxed. "I promise I'll watch out. Thanks for helping with the harness."

She waited there until he drove out. What had almost happened in the kitchen? She could still feel his hands on her arms. They'd been about to kiss when they were interrupted. She *wanted* him to kiss her. Some old comedian used to say, *What a revolting development this is.* That about summed up her feelings. Feelings she definitely did not want to develop for Vince.

By the time Molly was in harness, but still nowhere near the little carriage that stood in the aisle behind her, Anne stepped back out of kicking range, took the long carriage reins in both hands, and clicked to send Molly forward.

The little mare did her bounce up/kick out routine to the front of the barn before Anne tightened the reins and stopped her. Or at least stopped her forward motion. She stood in one place and danced, ready to explode all over again.

"Stand." Anne said as she kept Molly in one place. She continued to bounce, but then moved off in a straight line when Anne asked her.

Anne realized she was not in as good physical shape as she'd thought. After one circuit of the arena leaning back on Molly's long lines, she was puffing. Becca and Victoria hung over the fence and watched.

"Let me," Becca said as Anne walked by her.

"I don't think so," Anne said.

"I can walk around behind that bitsy mare and avoid being kicked. Aren't I here to try?"

Anne looked over at Victoria, who said, "Your call."

"Okay, but I walk with you."

"Deal."

The initial stages of the transfer of lines was

chaotic. "She knows there's someone else in control," Anne said. "Try to keep a gentle feel of her mouth on both sides."

"How do I turn?"

"Loosen the outside rein a little. Tighten the inside rein a little. Lay the outside rein against her side like a barrier. She'll turn."

"Wow," Becca said as they moved around the corner of the arena. "It works."

Twenty minutes later, the three women plus the mare were all soaked with sweat as they went through the reverse process of taking the harness off an annoyed Molly.

"Why do they wear blinkers on the sides of their bridles by their eyes? Our riding horses don't," Becca asked.

"So they don't freak out when they become aware that there is a carriage with a person in it chasing them. The more they run away from it, the faster it follows. With the blinkers they don't see what's behind them, so they are less likely to be scared."

"But they feel it," Becca said.

"That's why they have to learn to drag a weight—like a trailer tire—behind them before they try to pull a carriage."

Becca rolled her eyes. "Like that will be fun.

She'll run away. The tire will fly up in the air and slam into my head."

"Not if I can help it," Anne said. "That's for tomorrow. For your first day, we've done a lot, right, Victoria?"

"Remarkable," she said. "As a treat for good work, how about a swim before dinner?"

"Mrs. Martin, you don't have to cook," Becca said.

"I'm not cooking. Edward, my husband, does the cooking when I have people staying. You and Anne clean up. So how about the swim?"

Becca didn't stagger on her way to the cottage to change. So exercise did help.

Anne might actually be able to help the girl and prove the value of the program to Vince.

She couldn't keep her mind off him. What had changed? It was as if he had suddenly looked at her as a woman and not just "Anne who disagrees with him." She suspected they'd slip right back into their previous roles. He'd get annoyed. She'd get defensive. They'd snap at one another.

But his hand felt so warm. His arms so strong...

Good thing she could cool off in that pool. She needed it.

CHAPTER ELEVEN

VICTORIA'S SWIMMING POOL at the side of the patio was big for a private pool and free-form with a fountain and a waterfall. Victoria had softened the area around it with hot-weather plants like yucca that made it look even more natural. Anne loved the feel of the warm water over her muscles.

Becca wore a very small bikini. Anne hadn't worn one since she came home from horse camp her senior year in high school.

Victoria whispered, "I should warn Becca that she's skinnier than she'll ever be in her life again. She should enjoy it."

Anne looked over the top of her sunglasses at Becca as she flashed through the water like a tetra fish in an aquarium, chasing dinner. "Should she be swimming?" The thought had only now occurred to her.

"Her mother said she could. She only staggers when she's walking."

"I'm going to bring Tom Thumb over from

the pasture. We need to see if he's afraid of the water and how he reacts if Becca holds on to his mane and asks him to pull her."

Tom Thumb was delighted to be on the patio with human people.

"Becca, see if you can lead him down the steps at the shallow end and get him to swim with you," Anne said. "You feel secure enough to attempt it?"

"Sure. Come on, Tommy Baby, come to Mama." Tom made a tentative approach into the water, then stood with his hind hooves on the edge of the pool and his front ones submerged on the top step. He looked bemused at having his rear end higher than his front.

Anne joined Becca in the water to help guide in case the little horse wanted to turn around and hoist himself back onto dry land. They let him stand and figure out the problem by himself.

After several minutes of looking at the water in confusion, he glanced over his shoulder at Anne and gave a hesitant nicker.

"I'm sure he's been in the lake at his home farm," Victoria said. "It was the only source of clean water they had, and probably the only place they could get cool and keep the flies away."

"Come on, Tom," Becca crooned.

He took another tentative step, launched himself and promptly sank under the water.

"Anne, help! He'll drown," Becca squealed, but Tom's wet face surfaced. He snorted and swam toward her.

"Told ya," Anne said. "Grab hold of his halter, and see if he'll pull you through the water."

Tom decided Becca had invented a new game, one that involved his trying to swim away from her while she held on and swam beside him. He paddled through the water from the shallow end to the deep end. It was all the same to him—even in the shallow end his legs didn't touch the bottom of the pool.

"All we need is a beach ball," Victoria said. "I know they play polo with elephants, but water polo with minis—what a concept." She entered the pool in a flat dive that barely disturbed the surface and swam over to join the group. "Tomorrow we'll try Molly and Grumpy."

"I don't imagine they'll be quite so sensible," Anne said. "Tom doesn't seem to care what we ask as long as we're around when he has to do it."

Becca treaded water with her left arm across his withers. The three women and one horse

seemed to be involved in a four-way conversation. "All he needs is a voice box to be able
to talk," Anne said. "He'd be happy to instruct
us about the best way to teach him. Becca, can
you swim away? See what he does."

Becca let go of him and launched herself toward the far end of the pool. Tom gave a single glance at Victoria and Anne. Then, having
made his choice, he swam after Becca.

"It's almost as though he feels as responsible for her as if she were a foal or yearling
he needed to instruct," Victoria said. "Think
that's enough swimming?"

"For the first time, absolutely. Horses use
the same muscles when they swim as when
they walk, but it's still exercise, and he's Mr.
Tubbo at this point. Come on, Becca, walk up
the steps and out of the water. See if he can
figure out how to get himself out or whether
we'll have to pick him up."

Becca crouched on the side of the steps after
she climbed out and clapped to him. "Come
on, Tommy Baby. You can do it."

He managed to put his front feet on the step,
but going up one hoof at a time seemed con-
fusing. The three women let him puzzle it out
for a couple of minutes. Then Anne swam
over and lifted one front foot to the next level.

He shifted his weight. She'd trained plenty of horses to hop up into a horse trailer, but never tried steps under water. Victoria got behind him and shoved his rump forward. He leaned back against her. Then he put his other front hoof down and climbed up and out of the water.

"Good boy!" Becca said and hugged him. He shook water off his coat and swept his wet tail across Victoria's face.

"Hey! That hurts," she said and spit out the horse hair.

Anne and Victoria climbed out beside him. All three women sat on the patio while Anne tried to convince Tom to lie down.

Amazingly enough, he did. He laid his head in Anne's lap and went to sleep.

"I don't think it's supposed to be this easy," Becca whispered.

Tom answered with a soft snore.

"I doubt that it will be with the others. He's remarkable," Victoria said. "If I didn't know better, I'd swear he'd done all this before."

"Could he have? I mean, could the man who owned him have taught him?"

Victoria leaned back on her elbows. "Mr. Amos, who owned them, hadn't been capable of that kind of thing since before Tom was born."

"I think he just likes people," Anne said.

"Good evening, y'all," said Victoria's husband, Edward, as he strolled from the kitchen. "What y'all got there?"

"We've been teaching Tom to swim," Victoria said.

"He looks like a little sultan dozing in the middle of his adoring harem."

Tom opened one eye, snorted, pulled his legs under him and rolled to his feet.

The three women stood as well, and then Anne began to lead Tom Thumb back to the pasture. "This good little boy needs treats."

"And some brushing. Becca," Victoria said, "there's a bag of carrots on the table over there."

Becca took two steps and stumbled. Victoria grabbed her and shoved her into one of the iron chairs around the table. Becca dropped her head on her forearms. "Every time I forget, it gets me. It's not fair."

"Nope, it's not. You sit there," Anne said. "You didn't have any problem in the water or sitting on the edge of the pool."

"But I want…"

"You've done a bunch. Let me handle this."

"Without Tom, how do I get back to the cottage by myself? I'll stumble and land on my rear. Can we get Molly or Grumpy to let me hang on to them?"

Anne and Victoria glanced at one another. "Okay, we can give it a shot. I'll bring Grumpy back with me from the pasture," Anne said. "He's quieter than Molly. I'll be right beside you. I won't let you fall."

Twenty minutes later, Victoria, Grumpy, Becca and Anne proceeded down the hill to the cottage. Becca stumbled once and held on to Grumpy's mane. He shoved against her hip, but didn't miss a stride.

"Is he trying to knock me out of his way?" Becca asked.

"Not at all. Horses lean into pressure, not away from it. He's following his instincts."

After they settled Becca in her bedroom, Victoria took Grumpy back out to the pasture for his dinner.

Anne's phone rang while she was waiting for Becca. Vince.

"So?" he asked. "How did it go? You still in one piece?"

"Went surprisingly well. Molly gave us some high kicks, but she settled down. That's only the beginning."

"Uh-oh. I told you it was dangerous. Did Molly get hurt?"

Anne leaned back against her pillows and chuckled. "Ask about the horse first?"

"You already said you're okay. So, Molly?"

"Fine. We took Tom Thumb with us into the swimming pool."

"You what? He could have drowned you." He took a breath. "Or Becca."

"We all loved it. He swims better than I do. I keep telling you, *Doctor*, I know what I'm doing."

"You're moving too fast and taking chances. What if…"

"It worked. And we plan to do it again tomorrow. If you're so all-fired concerned, come over and watch us." She hung up the phone.

Same old, same old. Why did she think otherwise?

BECCA CAME OUT of her room twenty minutes later, showered, shampooed and freshly made up. Her eyes, however, were suspiciously red and puffy. She wore short shorts and a black T-shirt that read, Out of My Way, I'm the Boss Mare." She sank into the other armchair and leaned her head back. "I refuse to cry."

"No reason you should. You've done an amazing lot today."

"I almost fell on the way back down here. Maybe you need to get another guinea pig. Maybe a blind person. They use horses to lead blind people, don't they?"

"More and more. For one thing, miniature horses live much longer than dogs. I can't imagine the pain of losing a beloved guide dog after eight or nine years and having to start all over. With good care, a VSE will be going strong after thirty."

"With good vet care like Dr. Vince around. Yeah."

Anne suspected she was considering the vet rather than the horse.

Anne handed her a tall icy glass of lemonade from the tray on the coffee table beside her. "You're our first test case. We wanted someone who needed help, but with some personal control and knowledge of large horses. You and I and Tom are a team."

"Tom's already doing it all."

Anne laughed. "We've barely gotten started. We're also collapsing the time spent training. We've been told by one of the older groups in North Carolina who are already doing this sort of training that it can take anywhere from three months to a year before the clients are ready to take their horses home for good. We're aiming to team you with a horse before you go off to college this fall. Three months. We may not make it. You could still be coming back here during school holidays."

"I should go on home and give up the whole idea."

"Sure, if you want to."

Becca sat up and gripped the arms of her chair. "You'd let me quit? Honestly?"

"Not without a fight. Now, if you're up for it, how about we drive into Williamston to eat at the café? It's a real cultural experience. Everybody in town goes there. I warned Victoria that we wouldn't be home."

"She's okay with it?"

"I suspect she and Edward don't get to spend enough time alone as it is. I think they appreciate their time together. Now, why don't you relax, take a nap. I've got chores to take care of in the barn, and my horse, Trusty, has forgotten he's my horse. I want to give him a brush and a kiss."

She'd hoped to fit in another trail ride on Trusty, but so far there had not been enough time, and she still didn't know the property well enough to be certain she wouldn't get herself lost in a neighboring farmer's bean field or drown in the swamp.

Did Vince ride? Now, why on earth would she care?

For Becca, watching Anne trot off on Trusty would be like rubbing alcohol into an open wound. She'd wait until Becca had gone home to Memphis. Then she'd persuade Victoria to show her around the land some more.

When Anne came in from her chores, Becca was asleep in the armchair with her empty glass lying in her lap.

Anne snuck by her to have her own shower and shampoo. During the summer, she needed two a day if she planned to go anywhere in the evening.

"HEY, VELMA," ANNE greeted the waitress as she ushered Becca into the Williamston café. "Can we have our usual booth?"

"Sure, honey. Where's Victoria and Edward?"

"Having some alone time." Anne introduced Becca.

"You helpin' with those little bitty horses? They are so cute. Don't know what you can do with them, though."

"You'd be surprised. Before long we'll

be bringing one with us when we eat here," Anne said.

Velma shook her head. "Can you do that? Dogs, I know you can. But horses?"

"The disability regulations say so long as a VSE is a companion or helper animal, he can come in."

"So what do you do with him while you eat? It gets crowded in here. What if it has to go potty? Eeew."

"Trust me, Velma. By the time we bring one of our guys in with us, he'll be potty-trained. He'll probably curl up under the table and take a nap."

"Or just stand by the table and wait until we finish," Becca said. "That's what a big horse would do if it were tied to a hitching post outside."

Anne nodded her approval.

"If you say so, I guess it'll be okay."

"If they can ride on escalators and fly on airplanes, I'd say so. Now, what's the special today?"

"Fried pork chops, turnip greens and salad with our own tomatoes. Peach cobbler for dessert."

"Becca?" Anne asked. "You can have a

menu if you like. I'll have the special and iced tea."

"Me, too," Becca said. "Unsweet tea. No sugar. If I ever do get a chance to ride again, I don't want to be blown up like a bowling ball."

"They blow up soccer balls," Anne said. "Bowling balls are solid."

"Whatever."

Becca scarfed down her dinner, then eagerly moved on to dessert. As Becca devoured the peach cobbler and ice cream, Anne said, "I thought you were off sugar."

Becca answered between bites. "Get real. Who's gonna turn this down? I'll work harder with Molly and Grumpy tomorrow. Aren't you having any?"

Anne patted her flat midriff. "I wish I had your metabolism. I have to sweat to keep the bowling ball effect at bay."

"Do you get to ride much?" Becca carefully chased the last of the peaches around her dish.

"Not as much as I'd like. Trusty is a big warmblood from Germany. He gets along fine with less exercise. If he were a Thoroughbred, at this point he'd be high as a kite without daily outings. What is…" She stopped herself. She was going to ask about the breeding of Becca's

Aeolus, but the wound was too fresh for her to mention his name.

"It's okay," Becca said. "I can talk about him. I've been emailing the girl who has him now up in Virginia, giving her tips, you know. Like, he likes those little baby carrots, not the big ones." She turned away and surreptitiously ran her fingers under her eyes.

Not okay, Anne thought. *Still hurts.*

"But, hey." Becca gave Anne a sunny smile. "I've got Tom now. Horse is horse, right?"

Anne laughed. "Always has been for me. Maybe when you're little, it's being in control of something that's so much bigger. My father still has a picture of me, age three, leading a big gray warmblood gelding from the practice ring to the stable. I am trucking along with this humongous creature beside me that could smash me into a pulp. I'm lit up from inside like a Christmas tree. Don't forget, we're going to work with Molly and Grumpy, too. Not just Tom."

"How about the stallion? What's his name, anyway? I don't think you said."

Anne chortled. "His royal littleness is registered as Martin's Born for Glory."

"You're joking."

Anne shook her head. "Known as Glory."

"Who's boss mare?"

"Guess," Anne said.

"Molly. Got to be."

Anne nodded. "I'm not telling, but you'd be surprised."

"When can we take Tom to the grocery store?"

"The next time you come up to Victoria's, if he goes on the way he's been going. I don't think I'd start with the grocery store. Imagine Tom with a whole table full of lettuce just his height? When are you coming back?"

Becca shrugged. "I'd just stay if I could, but Daddy says I have to come home during the week. He's scared if I spend too much time up here I'll get on a horse like Trusty and break my neck. He does not trust me."

Should he? Anne wondered. Becca wanted what she wanted. And more than anything that was to set her foot back into a stirrup.

"He'll only let me come if you act as my jailor." She looked up from under her eyelashes to check out Anne's response.

"It's a country club prison with a swimming pool, not Devil's Island. Be grateful."

"Hey, lookie who's here," boomed a voice by the front door. "Good evenin', Miss Anne, and who might this sweet thing be? I don't think I know you, honey."

Anne stood quickly and reached out both hands. If she was avoiding a hug from the honeydew-shaped middle-aged man heading for their table, the ploy didn't work. He flung his arms in their Egyptian cotton shirt around her and nearly broke her ribs. He smelled of warm starch and some expensive French cologne for men. Anne couldn't identify it, but she knew it cost a fortune.

"Good evening, Mr. Mayor. Becca, this is Williamston's mayor, Sonny Prather. Sonny, this is Becca Stout. She's up here from Memphis to spend a weekend learning to drive minis."

"Well, good evenin' to you, too, Miss Becca. I do believe I have seen you a time or two showing hunter horses over fences at the Williamston horse show, am I right?"

Anne saw Becca's shoulders stiffen, but her Southern training held true. She was charm personified, although only when the mayor moved away to the next table to schmooze, did her shoulders relax.

"At least he didn't remember I tried to get myself killed," Becca whispered. "Oh my gosh, he looks like Tweedledee."

"He ought to put that on his campaign posters. 'Vote for Tweedledee for Mayor of Williamston.'" Anne spread her hands the width of a banner. "He'd win. He never has anybody running against him. Are you about ready to go? We should get to bed early and go to work first thing tomorrow."

"Might as well. What else do you do for fun in this burg? Watch the grass grow?"

Both began to slide out of their booth when another voice from the door called to them, this time a soprano. "Yoo-hoo, Anne. You can't leave yet."

Becca's head came up, and she swiveled to check behind her. Her lips split in a broad grin and she ran her hands over her shining hair. "It's Vince with somebody." She wriggled like a puppy waiting to be patted.

Oh, man. Actually, it wasn't only Vince, but Barbara Carew MacDonald with Anne's father, Stephen. Barbara had been the one calling out to them.

Anne introduced Becca to her father and stepmother and nodded to Vince. He gave sort of a deer-caught-in-headlights glance at Becca and pulled up a chair so that he could sit at the end of the booth where he did not have to slide in beside either Anne or Becca. Becca's pout increased when Barbara sat beside her, forcing her to the inside away from Vince, and Stephen slid in beside his daughter on the other side.

"To what do we owe the pleasure?" Stephen said with a smile for Becca. "Anne told me you were in town, but I assumed you'd be eating with Edward and Victoria."

"We decided to give them a break," Anne said. She glanced at Vince. "We've got to stop meeting like this. My husband's getting suspicious."

Becca said, "You don't have a husband."

"Old joke," said Stephen. Then, with a smirk at Anne, he said, "Very, very old joke. Pay no attention."

Some casual remark. Anne knew she was blushing. The café was shadowy, so chances were Vince wouldn't catch her, but it had been a stupid thing to say. She turned to him. "Are you coming back Monday morning to work on Molly's hooves? She's still a little lame. I'm not sure you got the hoof abscess completely cleaned out. She may need you to do some more digging."

"If I can fit it in, it will have to be late afternoon. I've got to drive to Memphis Monday morning to pick up my new portable X-ray machine from the shipper. They refuse to take responsibility for carrying it from the airport to Williamston."

"Monday?" Becca said. "This Monday morning?" Her senses were on high alert like a bloodhound that had spotted a possum in a sycamore tree.

"Yeah." He sounded suspicious.

"Wonderful. Anne, Vince can drive me back home to Memphis Monday morning. You won't have to." She turned a glowing face toward Vince. "We can have lunch before you leave to drive back to Williamston. I know this wonderful new barbecue place down on Mud Island I've been dying to try..." She stopped midsentence. "What?"

"Sorry, Becca, I can't drive you. I have to take the van, and there isn't room for you, Anne, and all my equipment, plus the new X-ray machine."

"Anne? No, you don't understand. If *you* take me, Anne can stay here and work horses. You'd prefer that, wouldn't you, Anne? See, Vince, if she doesn't go, you'll have plenty of room for me."

Anne caught the look on Vince's face. Becca was glaring at her. Good thing she wasn't watching Vince, since his face said, *Rescue me.*

She kept her own features composed. "I'm

afraid I have some things to pick up at the tack store in Germantown before I drive back to the farm," Anne said. "If Vince is going anyway, it would be a help to ride along with him into Memphis. Vince, we can fit Becca into the back seat of your van, can't we?"

She heard rather than saw his sigh. "Yeah, okay. I can shift some stuff. But no time for lunch, Becca. Sorry. Won't be too comfortable in the back seat, but you won't have to make the return trip with the machine and whatever Anne picks up."

Becca looked at Vince as though he had just canceled Christmas, and at Anne as though she were a water moccasin.

Anne had a feeling the argument wasn't over. She was surprised at Vince's reaction to Becca's suggestion. Knowing the teenager's crush, however, Anne could see his point. He did not want to be trapped in a car with Becca. Did that mean he wanted to be trapped in a car with Anne? When she glanced at him, he looked away from her. She could feel her face flush and turned away from him as well.

Velma laid Anne and Becca's bill on the table, greeted the newcomers, handed out menus and proffered ice tea. Anne picked up the bill without looking at it and slid it to her father with a grin. "Thank you for our dinner, Daddy."

"Oh, Mr. MacDonald," Becca said, "I can't..."

"Yes, you can. That's what fathers are for," he said as he reached for his credit card. "Here you go, Velma." He walked Anne and Becca to the car and saw them both safely inside. "Good night, ladies, drive carefully," he called as he headed back to the restaurant.

WHEN STEPHEN MACDONALD gave his daughter a kiss on the cheek as she bent over him to say goodbye, Vince recognized the easy affection between them. Stephen had said, "That's what fathers are for." An alien concept to his own father, for whom the smallest kindness demanded payment in guilt. Vince couldn't take the chance that he would evolve to be like the old man. It was the only frame of reference he'd had growing up. No wife, no child deserved to have to pay for affection, but each generation learned from the ones that came before. He'd been secure in his decision to stay alone until now, but watching Anne's taillights as she drove out of the parking lot, he felt empty.

Anne had been raised by loving parents. Now her father had found another love. Anne deserved nothing less. For the first time in his life, he wished he were capable of that kind of love.

ANNE LAY IN BED, thinking how lucky Barbara and her father had been to find one another. Her parents had a wonderful marriage until her mother died of cancer much too young.

Now her father had found Barbara Carew and married her. He'd lucked out a second time, when Anne couldn't seem to catch a break even once. He and her stepmother Barbara—boy, did that sound weird—were supportive, loving and working toward the same goals. They had their separate lives, but they had one another's backs, too. Her father respected Barbara—her career, what she had accomplished and would continue to accomplish. She respected him in return.

For Anne, that she wanted to love and be loved was a given. She had seen the love her parents shared, and the love that her dad and Barbara had found. She wanted nothing less than to feel that connection, that intimacy. Surely it was out there waiting for her somewhere. Happy marriage was possible. She'd seen it. Two people who wanted success and happiness for their partner even more than for themselves. Someone with whom you shared memory. Someone you could trust to keep your counsel. To respect you.

How come she couldn't seem to find someone who respected *her*? Oh, the few guys with whom she'd been serious started out acting as though they did. But they quickly slid her into second or third place or even lower in their lives.

Maybe she asked for too much.

Heck, no, she didn't.

Most of all, she wanted someone who listened to her and understood what she was talking about. They might not agree, but they should at least value her opinion.

Boy, did that respect part leave Vince Peterson out. Every time she thought he was starting to treat her as a colleague, he snapped at her.

Not that he could ever be more than a colleague, of course. He heard one voice in his head, and it was his own.

But what about that almost-kiss in the kitchen? How would they deal with one another after a kiss? The relationship would change, but from what to what?

Her cell phone on the bedside table blurped its nasty blurp. She really ought to change the ring tone to one she didn't loathe. It was nearly midnight. Something was wrong.

"Hello? What's up?" she said.

"Whoa. It is late. I apologize," Vince said. "Nothing's wrong. I wanted to thank you for tonight."

"What on earth for?"

"You picked up on my signal back at the café. I'd rather not drive to Memphis alone with Becca. I'm glad you're coming with us. And don't forget to sit in the front seat of the van."

"Sure."

"And thanks." He hung up.

Anne lay back on her pillows. For some reason she felt hot all over. Residual embarrassment, no doubt.

VINCE HUNG UP the phone and laid his head back against his recliner. He ought to be falling asleep on his feet, but he couldn't seem to get comfortable. Maybe a beer would help him relax. No. The effect of even that small amount of alcohol at this time of night would slow down his responses. When seconds could mean life or death for an animal, he couldn't risk being less than on top of his game.

He really shouldn't have called Anne Mac-

Donald at midnight. He'd been taught better than that. Of course, she would assume that something was wrong. Now that he knew her better, he had revised his opinion of her from down to up. He still considered her what his father would have called "uppity," but she was conscientious and capable, if prickly. He did know how to dig an abscess out of a hoof, and he was darned sure he'd gotten all the infection from Molly's without her input. He chortled at the memory of their skirmish with the hose— both times. The pair of them must have looked pretty funny all wet.

She was definitely beautiful. Whoa! Where had that come from?

He sure didn't need any nonprofessional contacts with any female at the moment. Becca was going to be trouble enough, and she was only a kid.

Anne was already a woman, not in any sense a kid. She was—he tried to think of a suitable word—*luscious*. Like a shining, sleek mare certain of her position as leader of the herd.

He'd watched her tonight with her father. She trusted his love. Vince could never let down his guard around his own father. He never knew what would set his vicious temper off, but the old man invariably knew the buttons to push to make his family cringe. He drove his wives away one after another, and each time, he'd blame them for leaving him.

Every time he let his temper loose, Vince could hear the echo of his father's voice. He fought it, but he could never trust his control. He would not treat any woman as his father treated his wives. Certainly not Anne. She deserved a darned sight better than a man with "issues."

CHAPTER TWELVE

MONDAY MORNING VINCE arrived at the farm early. Becca was already packed, and both she and Anne were waiting for him. Apparently, none of the three was a morning person. Victoria came to the van to deliver three cups of coffee. She barely got a thank-you in return.

Anne was afraid there would be a battle for the front passenger's seat, but Vince held the door and handed Anne in before Becca could react. She slid into the rear bench seat behind Anne. Good thing Becca didn't have laser vision. She'd have bored a hole in Anne's backbone before they pulled out of the parking lot and headed to Memphis.

The trip was nearly silent. Becca had her headphones on, probably cranked up to maximum, but her presence deterred conversation between Anne and Vince.

Vince dropped Becca off at her parents' big house outside Collierville in the late morning, saw her to the front door and waited until a maid opened it. Becca flounced in without a goodbye.

As they drove away, Vince said to Anne, "Wasn't that special?"

"Cut her some slack, for Pete's sake. She has every right to the sulks. I don't know whether you ride horses or simply work on them, but if your whole life was centered on a saddle, you might be pretty miserable too if in one second it got snatched from under you. Okay, example. How would you feel if you were a candidate for the Heisman trophy and a multimillion-dollar contract with a pro team, and then they said you could never play football again because you'd twisted your knee?"

"Point taken. Actually, I do ride horses at home. Although he's mostly stuck in a wheelchair, my father still rides his old walking horse mare around the property occasionally. She's well past twenty, but I've kept her sound so far. Then there are quarter horses for me and my brothers and their wives, and a couple of Welsh ponies for my brothers' kids. They're not fancy show horses. They wrangle cattle. The only time one of our horses ever took a fence was when some idiot cow got stuck in the barbed wire and had to be rescued before it cut its leg off."

"You don't foxhunt? I know you have two good hunts down there. I read about them in the horse magazines."

"Galloping over unfamiliar countryside full of armadillo burrows, following a bunch of nutso hounds over tall obstacles, is not my idea of fun."

"What do you *do* for fun?"

"*Fun?* Not a word I am familiar with. Is it English or some strange ancient foreign tongue? Becoming a qualified veterinarian does not leave much time for fun. I'm on call 24/7 to fill in for Barbara when she needs backup. I work every weekday and a half day Saturdays at the clinic. I can't tell you when I last saw a movie. I don't dare drink more than the occasional beer, because I may have an emergency to tend to. I spend my days mostly dirty and often bloody. I get stomped by bulls and butted by goats…"

Anne held her hands up in front of her. She was laughing. "Whoa, there. Admit it, you flat-out love it, don't you?"

He shrugged and grinned back at her. "Darned straight. Why do you do it?"

"I got bit by the horse bug the first time my father held me on a pony at the zoo. I love the feel of them, the smell of them, the way they respond when I do things right and ignore me when I don't. I love the big draft horses and the VSEs equally. It is humbling when a whole other species shares the kind of connection with human beings that we do with horses. Is that good enough for you, Doc?"

"Good enough. Here's The Tack Stall. Got your list of stuff Victoria needs?"

"In my purse. You coming in?"

"Absolutely. Can't pass up a tack store."

The young woman behind the counter looked up from the dressage magazine open in front of her and smiled a welcome. "Hi, Anne. I thought you'd moved to middle Tennessee."

"Hey, Dee. Not quite that far. Williamston, up by the Tennessee River."

Then the woman's eyes and smile widened. "Vince! Vince Peterson, as I live and breathe." She came out from behind the counter, threw her arms round Vince's neck and kissed him soundly before she let him go.

Anne leaned back against the counter and chuckled at the blush his tan couldn't conceal.

Dee Nash slipped her hand through Vince's arm and leaned against him. "Haven't seen you in donkey's years, sugar. Heard you were up in Williamston too working with Barbara Carew. What brought you down here?"

"Running errands, picking up an X-ray machine. Anne's working with Victoria Martin these days.

Dee giggled. "I heard Victoria got stuck with a bunch of crazy minis."

"She brought me in to try to add some sanity," Anne said. "Y'all catch up. I've got a bunch of stuff to pick out for Victoria. You got a basket I can use?"

"Right here," Dee said and handed Anne a wicker basket. "Now, Vince honey, bring me up to date. How's your family? Any changes? New additions?"

Anne stooped behind a tall shelf to grab a gallon of shine shampoo. Obviously, Dee was attempting to discover whether Vince was still single. Dee was twice divorced with a six-year-old daughter who already rode her Shetland pony in lead line classes at horse shows.

She couldn't make out the murmurs of their conversation, but Dee kept giving out with a squeal that was supposed to be girlish laughter, but could etch glass.

Was Vince a chick magnet or what? Even Velma, the waitress at the café in Williamston and a happily married grandmother, had simpered when she poured Vince's iced tea. Anne vowed that she would not be trapped in his aura. He was good-looking, certainly, although not handsome-handsome. His nose was too big and his jaw too square. He'd probably go bald at fifty. Not that she disliked bald men. They were kind of sexy. The man had a great body, but he was working hard for Barbara six days a week. His schedule would help him hold on to all those muscles. On top of everything else, he had an ego as big as Mars and a head as hard as a rough diamond—emphasis on the rough. She'd had her share of bossy men, and he was definitely bossy.

Anne filled her basket to overflowing, took it to the counter and waited while Dee rang up her purchases and bagged them.

"You want this on Victoria's account, right?"

Anne nodded.

Before they had a chance to walk out the front door, Dee came from behind the counter again to hug and kiss Vince on the cheek. She couldn't get close, because Vince had taken Anne's bags to carry to the car.

Once they were on their way again, Vince said, "Now for the airport to pick up my machine, and then we find somewhere for a decent lunch before we drive back."

"You told Becca we didn't have time for lunch."

"I lied. I'm hungry. It's a long way since that cup of coffee."

"Is that all you had for breakfast?"

"Yep. And a can of tomato juice. Nothing in the house to eat, and I didn't have time to drive a dozen miles either to Williamston or the twenty-four-hour snack shop down by the lake."

"Victoria would have fed you when she fed Edward."

"Okay, here's the turnoff for the shipper."

He pulled into a parking spot. "Shouldn't take but a couple of minutes to pick up the X-ray machine. You staying in the car?"

Anne nodded and pulled a horse magazine out of Victoria's bags.

It might have taken only a couple of minutes to get the X-ray machine. It took at least twenty for Vince and the loader to situate the cumbersome box in the van to their satisfaction, then another ten for Vince to go back inside and sign paperwork. After he had climbed back into the van and they were on the road again, he said, "I don't know about you, but I am spittin' cotton."

"Me, too. Where can we get a sandwich and some iced tea?"

"You like Mexican?"

Anne nodded.

"Then do I know a place. Doesn't look like much from the outside, but their seafood fajitas are killer."

Vince was right that the restaurant did not look promising from the parking lot. Except that it was only eleven thirty in the morning and the lot was full of pickup trucks. The restaurant was nearly full as well, but after only a five-minute wait they were seated.

Anne decided that they were the only customers chatting in English. The salsa and chips were homemade, and the iced tea was fresh. Anne was surprised when Vince placed their order in fluent Spanish.

"Sorry, I didn't ask you what you wanted," he said.

"Your restaurant—your menu, your order."

They both practically inhaled their first servings of iced tea and half of the second.

Anne sat back. "I forget how hot it is in Memphis in the summertime."

"Williamston's only a degree cooler."

"But you get more breeze from the Tennessee River. Is your family's farm in Mississippi even hotter?"

Vince leaned back. "My daddy says that it's probably cooler in Hades than it is in the Mississippi Delta in summertime. He calls it 'simmertime.' He says he's not worried because he's already served his time in the hotter of the two—Hades versus Mississippi."

Anne laughed. "He sounds like a funny man."

Vince pulled his napkin through his fingers and said seriously, "As funny as a rattlesnake coiled on a rock and ready to strike. Think of some almighty conquerors like Genghis Khan or Attila the Hun. My daddy could give them chapter and verse and leave them standing in the dirt when it comes to psychological massacres. Sometimes he's happy with a bloodless coup where he destroys his enemy's spirit without messing up the carpets."

Anne was surprised to see that his blue eyes had turned the color of the North Sea in December. Cold.

"The only reason to get divorced is if you screw it up the first time. My daddy is on wife number four. Guess why I'm not into marriage. I learned at my daddy's knee."

The fajitas arrived. Anne was glad to get back to casual conversation. She'd thought Vince was altogether too sure of himself, when he was actually pretty fragile. You never knew with people. Everybody had a secret place where they hurt.

"These are marvelous," Anne said after five minutes. "How'd you find this place? It's not exactly in the middle of Memphis."

"One of my clients recommended it. He breeds Nubian goats for the Hispanic market. These folks roast a whole goat for every holiday."

"I've never eaten goat," Anne said, "but I'll try anything once. I like octopus and eel, why not goats?"

"I'll find out the next time they're roasting. Maybe Stephen and Barbara would be interested, too. Possibly even Victoria and Edward."

"Daddy and Barbara are nearly ready to move into their new house on the clinic property," Anne said. "Barbara swears she's going to have a gigantic garage sale, clean out tchotchkes and have a big barbecue."

"What about your family house here in Memphis?"

"Daddy sold it lock, stock and barrel—minus the books and the stuff we treasured—to my older sister, Elaine, and her husband, Roger. He's a corporate lawyer. They entertain a lot. The house is perfect for them. I was living there for a while in an apartment on the third floor and looking for another place when Victoria offered me a job with her in Williamston. A blessing, really, since my previous job had just collapsed. I jumped at the chance, although I had no idea what I was getting into."

"Why were you looking for another place? You and your sister don't get along?"

Anne rolled her eyes. "If you knew Elaine you wouldn't ask that question. Elaine thinks working with horses isn't an actual job and that I should grow up. She keeps telling me I ought to get a decent job in an office." She rolled her eyes. "Nine to five. Eeew. To hear her tell it she was born into royalty and snatched away by the fairies from her cradle. She is still seeking to return to her throne. In the meantime, she treats the rest of us like serfs. You should have seen the commotion she made when Barbara and Daddy said they were planning to get married."

"I heard some about that. Didn't you all chase them all over west Tennessee to try to keep them from getting married in such a rush?"

"Tennessee and northern Mississippi," Anne said. "In the end, they managed to be lawfully wed. Got to give Elaine credit. She is now crazy about Barbara. Since she's just gotten pregnant, she's looking forward to having Barbara as a grandmother. Barbara is the only grandmother whatever-it-is will have. Roger has practically no family. Is your family all in Mississippi?"

"I don't know about you, but I want some flan and some more iced tea. Can I seduce you with dessert?" He caught his breath. Anne dropped her eyes.

They went on as though nothing had happened, but the word lingered in the air between them.

"Absolutely," Anne said. "I love good flan."

He placed their order again in excellent Spanish, and turned back to her. "My family has major problems. My brother Cody says my current stepmother is thinking about leaving. Cody thinks she and Daddy really care for one another, but with Daddy it's tough to tell."

"Oh, my."

"I have two brothers, Cody and Joshua. We all have different mothers, so I guess we are actually half-brothers. One of them is on his second wife. I have four nephews—two for each brother. My stepmother, Mary Alice, is a perfectly nice woman, but my father is driving her what the Brits call "barking mad" with his constant bad temper and demands for attention. He waits until she's sewing or cooking to demand she bring him a glass of water that he could get himself. It's a control thing to keep her focused on him. She's a full-time caregiver when they could easily afford to hire somebody. She doesn't even go out to lunch with her girlfriends any longer."

"Was he in a wheelchair when she married him?"

"He's actually officially not in one now. When he's feeling feisty, he walks around the barns and drives his old truck to town. He's had a series of small strokes. He can walk when he chooses to, but he can wield more power being an invalid."

Anne realized that Vince seemed to want to dump all his baggage on her at once. In hindsight, he'd hate that he'd opened up this way, but she had no idea how to head him off so he wouldn't regret what he was telling her. Instead she sat without moving, her hands in her lap, and avoided looking him in the eye.

"What about your mother?" Anne asked.

"She took off one night when I was five. Even then I understood it was a nasty divorce. Daddy could afford the best lawyers in Mississippi, which is not noted for looking with favor on women who leave their husbands and children. One day she was there, then it was as though she'd evaporated. I realized eventually that Daddy must have known where she was in order to divorce her, but he swore he didn't. He told me more than once that it was obvious she didn't want me."

How could any father tell his son something like that? Maybe the old man was hurting himself, but that was no excuse.

She wanted to put her arms around Vince, say something comforting, but she decided if he was intent of telling her, she wasn't going to stop him whether he regretted his words or not.

"They tell me I kept running away to try to find her. Daddy threw out all the pictures we had of her, so I can't even remember what she looked like..."

"I was nine when my mother died. Old enough to have memories to hold on to," Anne said. "I grew up surrounded by photos of her, of us together. Otherwise I probably wouldn't be able to remember her face, either. How could he do that to you? Daddy still reminds me that she loved us and never wanted to leave us." No wonder Vince was damaged.

"I don't know whether she ever tried to get custody of me," he continued. "If she did, she lost. For years I got Christmas cards and birthday cards from her—always from different places. A partial antidote to Daddy's story. When I turned eighteen and had unfettered access to the internet, I tried to find her. No luck. The cards stopped—never a return address, by the way. I tell myself she must be dead."

As the waiter set his flan plate in front of him, Vince laid his napkin across his lap. "It would be nice to know one way or the other. Every year on the Fourth of July we have a big reunion at the home place. I used to hope maybe she'd show up for one of them, but she never did. It's dangerous to love somebody. The first thing love does is hurt."

Anne had no idea what to say, so she reached across the table and laid her hand on his. She felt his fingers tighten, then he drew away quickly. He couldn't accept even so small a gesture. Shoot, no wonder he wasn't married.

"That's enough drama for one lunch," he said. "Eat your flan or I will."

"Try it and lose a hand," Anne said. Spell neatly broken. Back to preconfession status.

Pain made both animals and people bad-tempered. His pain was deeper than physical. It might not show on the surface, but it was there just the same. He might not ever heal.

CHAPTER THIRTEEN

BACK AT MARTIN'S MINIS, Anne unloaded Victoria's purchases and organized everything in the cupboards of the tack room while Vince pulled Molly out of the pasture and led her to the wash rack. She wriggled and attempted to walk over him. Vince simply picked her up and set her down with her rear end against the back wall. Before she realized what had happened, she was cross-tied. He gave her a peppermint from his jeans pocket to appease her, then picked up her off-front foot and began to poke it with his hoof pick as he searched for the telltale black spot that would indicate there was still infection in the sole.

Molly stood still at first, although she was unhappy at being off balance. She tried to wrench her hoof out of his grasp, but he was much stronger than she was and held on.

He was sure he'd opened the abscess completely on his last try. He was only making this gesture to appease Anne.

Actually, to prove her wrong.

Without warning Molly squealed, reared and struck out with her near forefoot. She caught him a glancing blow on his hip as she landed.

"Hey! That hurt, witch," he said. Another bruise to add to the ones he already had. Good thing he wasn't keeping score. He dropped the hoof and ran a handkerchief over his sweaty face. Skin-deep bruises faded. The bruises inside that he had revealed to Anne never went away.

What had possessed him to open up to her at lunch? The more she knew about who he was, what made him tick, the more power she had. He hated that. One thing he had learned from his father—never let on who you really were. People would use your vulnerabilities against you.

He continued to grip Molly's pastern just above her hoof until she settled down. "Hang on. Nearly finished."

He felt a trickle of moisture in his palm, glanced down at the sole of her hoof and saw a thin line of blood seeping from a pinhole in the sole. A pinhole he had not dealt with before.

Anne had been right. He had not dug all the infection out the first time. With such a tiny opening, the hoof did not need to be bandaged after he cleared it. He disinfected the hole, packed it with cotton and more disinfectant, unhooked Molly and walked her off the wash rack.

With the pressure relieved and the infection cleaned out, she walked without a limp. He considered not telling Anne what he'd found. As a gotcha game it had backfired just when he needed to feel superior.

"Hi, find anything?" she said as she walked down the aisle toward him.

Would he tell her?

Of course.

He expected her to gloat. Instead, she simply nodded and took Molly's line from him.

"I'll put her back in the pasture," Anne said. "We can work her tomorrow. Without Becca here, I'll concentrate on simple commands like *forward*."

He fell into step beside her. "When will Becca be back?"

"She may not come for a couple of weeks, depending on what her father says and whether her mother will drive her up here again. Her dad's afraid she'll get hurt. I can teach the minis simple commands on my own, but I can't put Molly or Grumpy or even Tom into a harness and attach them to the driving cart by myself."

"Maybe Victoria can help."

"She has lessons scheduled with her regular students. She says they may stay to go swimming afterward." She let Molly into the pasture and turned her loose.

Molly trotted off to join her buddies under the trees.

"We'd better head up the hill before all of them come over and try to mug us for treats. I'm not carrying any. How about you?"

"Used my last peppermint on Molly," he said.

Victoria walked out of the kitchen and onto the patio. "Ready for a beer, anyone?"

"I'm not on call this evening, unless Barbara runs into an emergency she can't handle, so I could murder a beer," Vince said.

"Anne?"

"Yuck. I'll stick with iced tea. Victoria, have you been able to hire any summer help yet? With Becca not here, I could definitely use it."

Victoria sank onto one of the chaise longues beside the pool and took a deep swallow of her beer. "I made a couple of calls. One of the boys I generally use is on his way to a summer program in Oxford."

"England or Mississippi?"

"England, I'm afraid. The other one, Calvin—you know Calvin, don't you, Vince?"

Vince nodded.

"He's home from Florida State and is starting work here tomorrow. He's really good with horses, Anne, big and little. A nice boy. Hardworking family. I've known him most of his life. I put him on his first pony."

"I don't suppose you know anyone, do you, Vince?"

"'Fraid not. I haven't been working for Barbara long enough to know local teenagers who might need summer jobs."

"Then let's hope Calvin works out and has a friend who needs a job as well." Victoria set her empty bottle on the patio table beside her chair and asked casually, "There's always you, Vince."

"Me what? You know I'll be here to work on the horses' health, but I have a more than full-time job as it is."

"I wasn't expecting you to clean stalls, but you might help drive the carriage some. Safer and easier for Anne with someone else around."

"No doubt, but not me. There aren't enough hours in the day to get to all my calls as it is.

I did some horse-breaking in Wyoming the summer I spent up there as a saddle bum, but that doesn't count as actual training, and I have never learned to drive a carriage."

"We're talking rudimentary commands and manners. The arena is lighted. No reason you couldn't come over and help Anne with our little imps then when it's cooler. Anne can manage most of the command training alone, but getting the minis accustomed to wearing harness is better with two people— one in the carriage, one on the ground."

"One to pick up the pieces," Anne whispered. She caught Vince's eye. She was willing to bet that they were both thinking the same thing. Why couldn't *Victoria* pitch in in the evening after dinner? Edward generally handled the cooking and the cleaning up. Anne had noticed that Victoria was good at getting out of real labor and always seemed to have somewhere else to be. Even though she was paying Anne, Anne had not been hired as a stable hand, but as a trainer.

"Barbara and I have already talked about your spending some extra time over here. Your regular rate while you were helping here would go on my monthly bill. I can't afford much of your time," Victoria continued. "I'm only paying Calvin minimum wage and pool privileges. I have enough horses on full board to be able to afford the extra until fall. What do you have to go home to but microwave dinners and television? You're all alone living in Barbara and Stephen's rental house."

"It's comfortable, and I'm only there to sleep most of the time. Once Barbara and Stephen move to their new house, I'll take over her apartment in her barn. It's plenty homey."

"I'm a much better cook than your microwave is."

"You said Edward does the cooking."

"So he does. You have to do a follow-up check of Molly's hoof tomorrow, don't you?" Victoria asked. "If you're here, you can help Anne hitch up the carriage…"

Anne rolled her eyes at him.

He did not need to check Molly's abscess tomorrow, but Victoria was a valued client. Of course, he would come, but not necessarily when she needed him.

"I'm on clinic duty tomorrow," he said. "How about I give you a couple of hours after work and you feed me. No charge. In an emergency, all bets are off."

"And I'll throw in a swim. Deal." Victoria stuck out her hand.

He shook it. "Okay, Anne?"

"Sure, why not. All assistance gratefully accepted, so long as we agree that when we're training, I'm in charge."

He came to his feet. "Right, boss." He gave her a salute. "Only while you're training."

Anne lifted an eyebrow. How would he react the first time she gave him an order? This was one instance when she was the pro and he was the amateur.

"Stay for dinner tonight," Victoria said. "We always have enough for at least a couple of guests."

"Thanks, but no. I'm going to have an early night. Been a long day." He stuck his hands in the pockets of his jeans and sauntered up the hill to his van.

VINCE WALKED PAST the stallion's paddock. The little horse gave a long, lonely call and finished it with a series of grunts that sounded more leonine than equine. He trotted over to intercept Vince by the paddock fence.

Vince stopped to give him a face rub. "You don't take orders from females, do you little guy? Not sure I can take orders from Anne. If I disagree with her technique I know I'll interfere. Better hope I do agree with her."

The stallion gave an exasperated snort, whirled away, cantered to the end of the paddock closest to the mares and whuffled to them seductively. They ignored him.

"I get you, brother," Vince said. "Females drive me nuts, too." He glanced back at the patio where Anne lounged with her long legs stretched out in front of her. "One of them does, at any rate."

CHAPTER FOURTEEN

VINCE TURNED THE air-conditioner in his van on High on the drive back home. He'd be glad when the heat wave broke, but with global warming that might not happen until October. Hard on the horses, hard on him. Extra hard on Anne. She did need help. Even so, he should never have been conned into helping her. Working with her would make his long days even longer. Tired vets made mistakes. He didn't allow himself mistakes. He'd have to remain sharp somehow.

His primary responsibility was to Barbara and the clinic, but she'd already told him he should help with the VSEs. He'd have to maintain his emotional distance from Anne. She was becoming a distraction rather than an annoyance. She was too easy to talk to.

Why on earth had he told her all that stuff when they were having fajitas? He should learn to keep his mouth shut about his family.

They weren't all bad. He considered his

current stepmother, Mary Alice, as kind of a present-day Katherine Parr, Henry the Eighth's last wife—the one who outlived him. Old Henry couldn't have been easier to deal with than his father Thor Peterson. The main difference between the two was that Henry chopped a couple of his wives' heads off. Thor divorced his.

King Henry had produced one sickly boy child who barely lived to maturity. He never thought the girls counted. Thor had produced three strapping males, then spent his time interfering in their lives and treating them like undervalued servants.

Vince turned on his radio, listened to the beginning of a news story about the latest disaster and turned it off again. After a day spent pregnancy-checking fifty cows in the oppressive heat, he relished the quiet.

At last he turned into the driveway of his cottage, across the street from Seth and Emma's house. Inside their living room warm light glowed and spilled out onto the front porch. Through the window Vince could see that Seth, who often worked late, was home on time tonight.

Emma came in from the kitchen carrying their baby, Diana.

Vince was close to crossing the line between neighbor and peeping Tom, but he couldn't turn away.

Diana reached out her arms to her father. He took her from Emma and cradled her against his chest. Emma sat beside him and leaned against his shoulder. Vince felt a stab of jealousy. Without a wife, he would never have a chance to hold his own child. He could hope that he'd be a better parent than his father had been, but the odds were stacked against him.

He hadn't realized that his father's parenting tactics could be viewed as child abuse until his freshman psych class at college. The professor harped on the generational thing—one generation of abused children became the next generation of abusers.

His father had never raised a hand to him or his brothers. He hurt with words. Those wounds went deeper and bled longer.

In the darkness of his own front porch he fumbled with his house keys, got the door open and turned the lights on.

He'd shared dormitories and student apartments in college, and a bunkhouse in Wyoming. Here not even a cat or dog greeted him. He could feel the emptiness.

Since he didn't plan to marry, and didn't

like the idea of sharing living arrangements with a woman to whom he was not committed, he'd probably never enjoy the kind of closeness Seth shared with Emma. No divorce meant no marriage.

Hadn't mattered so much up to now. He thought he'd made his peace with lonely, but tonight as he'd watched Seth with Emma and their daughter, he'd realized that he would always be outside looking in on someone else's happy family. He'd never before known a special woman to come home to with a special pair of lips to kiss and special arms to hold him. Now, for some reason he didn't understand, it was Anne's face he wanted to see when he walked through his door, her arms reaching out to him.

He sank onto the couch, leaned his head back against the sofa and closed his eyes. Her face was there in his mind.

He was tired, that was all. A good night's sleep, and he'd have his perspective back. He would make a lousy husband and a worse father. If he truly cared about Anne, he couldn't take the chance of hurting her as his father hurt the women he married.

He hauled himself up from the couch and slid a frozen dinner into the microwave. Victoria had been right about that. He would have eaten better at her house. He opened a long-neck beer—the one he allowed himself after work most nights—and turned on the TV. He needed human voices even if they were only in the background.

The microwave dinged. He burned his fingers pulling the carton out and almost dropped it on his tray. "Dumb," he said. He wasn't paying attention to anything, not the TV or his dinner. He pulled a chair out from the dining table, sank into it and removed the plastic cover from his dinner.

Neither the smell nor the appearance of the food appealed to him. He wasn't certain what it was supposed to be. Limp broccoli, watery mashed potatoes and some kind of mystery meat? He shoved it away and considered getting another beer.

No way. He'd watched his father drink his meals every time he was between wives. He had no intention of going the same way. He emptied his dinner down the disposal and cranked it. Might as well go to bed and read until he fell asleep.

He did not want to dream about Anne, but he probably would. He'd been dreaming of her regularly. In his dreams she was generally annoyed with him. Just like real life.

Why had Anne's face become so endearing? He even looked forward to their arguments. When he saw her, he came alive in a way he'd never before experienced.

He wanted to kiss those lips, hold her… He hit the wall beside the refrigerator. "Ow, that hurt, you idiot. Get over her, man."

He had no intention of falling in love with anyone and certainly not with Anne.

DRIVING TO THE clinic the following morning, he tried to work out how he'd wound up so opposed to having a family. First, he had been raised hearing that old Southern saying that a man was not a man until his daddy told him he was. That meant all three of the Peterson boys were doomed to permanent childhood, because their father would never validate their manhood. He grappled his sons and their families as close to him as possible, not for love, but for control.

Vince's cell phone rang. He had a handsfree attachment, but he still pulled off the road and stopped when he saw his brother Joshua's name. He couldn't talk to his brother with half a brain. "Hey, bro, what's up?"

"When you comin' home?"

"You sound frazzled, Josh."

"I'm finishing up the quarterly taxes. The old man's telling me I have to stop working for my best-paying client to finish his. He says as long as I'm living in his house, on his land, he gets first dibs."

"Tell him no."

"Then he wants to take off the entire cost of the new baler in one lump sum rather than amortizing it the way we're supposed to. He treats me like I'm six years old and can't add two and two. What does he think that CPA on my wall means? I can't even get loose from here long enough to go pick up the boys in Jackson. The divorce settlement says they're supposed to spend half the summer vacation and alternate weekends during the school year here with us, but I barely see them, Vince. I need you to come down here and knock some sense into Daddy's head."

"What makes you think I'd do any better than you?"

"The difference is, bro, that you would actually *do* it. I owe him too much. He may have built me this fancy house, but he's the one that holds the mortgage."

"Move out. Move to Jackson. Take a job with one of the brokerage houses."

"I'd never get a job with one of the big companies."

"Then open your own office."

"I owe too much alimony and child support. He's got me, Vince. Just like he's got Cody. You're the only one who ever got out and stayed out. Come home to visit at least."

If he went home even for a short time, his father would try to reel him in like a catfish.

"You warned us, Vince. You said if we let Daddy build us houses in the compound, we'd never get away."

"Daddy offered to build me a house, Josh, and a clinic, too. Complete with the wife of his choice."

Joshua snickered. "He's never forgiven you for turning him down. He probably had the names for your two-point-five children all picked out."

"He won't kick you out if you tell him no, Josh. Get Cody to go with you. He's there, I'm not."

"Cody's no help. The man actually *wants* to live here. He loves cattle farming. As long as the operation makes money, he can ignore Daddy."

"What does your Nell say about this?" Vince asked. "She married you knowing you have an ex-wife, two children and a family like ours..."

"We waited less than a year after the divorce. I'll bet she wished she'd waited longer. She's kept her job as librarian and she runs half the civic committees in the county. I tell her it's so she can go out to meetings three or four times a week away from family dinners. Woman's a saint, Vince. She thinks I'm a wuss. I wish I could sic *her* on Daddy."

"Do it. Do it together. I'd put Nell up against the old man anytime. Get Mary Alice to help. Heck, get Cody and all the wives together. Get your ducks in a row, all of you, and take back your lives."

"Easy for you to say. You're not here."

"And I don't plan to be in the near future, either."

"How'd you get the gumption to run off and break horses that summer you graduated from Mississippi State?" Joshua asked.

"Daddy wouldn't pay the tuition to vet school. I had enough money to pay for my first year after three months in Wyoming. I vowed never to live at home again."

He didn't need to marry. His brothers had already provided heirs. He wanted to stay where he was in Barbara's clinic, become a partner and build a bachelor life a four-hour drive from his father. Truth was, he'd have preferred the other side of the world—Australia, say, or New Zealand.

Too far from the new friends he had made in Williamston. Too far from his brothers and their children.

Too far from a woman with blue-green eyes and an attitude.

BY EIGHT O'CLOCK Tuesday morning, Anne had already fitted Molly into her training reins before the sun turned the arena into a heat sink.

"Forward," Anne said. Molly looked back over her shoulder, but didn't budge. "Forward," Anne repeated patiently. She flicked the reins.

Molly took one grudging step.

"Good girl. Forward."

Victoria sat on the arena fence and watched. "She thinks you want to lead her."

"That's what I'm trying to get across to her. When she's tacked up this way I'm no longer *her* leader. She must stay by her person's side and stop quickly in case someone like Becca loses her balance and needs to brace herself. If she was leading a blind person, she'd be wearing one of those harnesses they use on guide dogs. Ideally, she'll track a tiny bit ahead, but not way out in front as if she were pulling a carriage. She's almost got it. She's comfortable with guide reins instead of a single lead line. Come on, Molly, once around the arena, then I'll work Grumpy until we take an iced tea break."

"Ah, I think that's Calvin pulling his truck into the parking lot," Virginia said and climbed off the fence. "He's the boy I hired to groom for you. Down here," she called to him.

"Yes, ma'am."

The young man walking down the hill wore tight, faded jeans bunched at the ankle above dusty boots. A V-neck cotton T-shirt showed plenty of muscle on a hairless tan chest, and he wore a baseball cap instead of the usual cowboy hat.

"Good, he's taller than Becca," Anne whispered.

"And cute," Victoria whispered back. "Killer smile. Beautiful eyes."

"Hello, baby horse," Calvin said and scratched Molly's back. She batted her eyes at him.

Victoria introduced him to Anne and strolled off toward her house with her hand under his arm. "Paperwork," she called to Anne.

"Right. Calvin, come back down here as soon as you can."

CALVIN WAS A fast learner, but not much of a talker. Anne figured he was shy. He and Anne settled into a routine in which he groomed and tacked up the next mini in line to be trained, swapped the fresh horse for the one Anne had finished working, rinsed the dirt and sweat off that one, returned it to the pasture, then started grooming the next on the agenda. Somehow, he managed to clean stalls and sweep the aisle as well.

After seeing him off at the end of the workday, Anne sprawled on the patio with Victoria and a pitcher of iced tea. "That was a very long day. Calvin's going to do fine," she said. "He's a hard worker even in the heat. Doesn't say much, but I didn't have to tell him anything more than once. I can probably work all the horses that need it in one day since he'll be doing the grunt work. Should speed up the training considerably."

"That's a lot of work for a young man."

"Yes, he does still have a bunch of kid in him. Not that he'd believe that."

Now, Vince was a man. Nothing of kid in him. He might be happier if there were. He didn't seem to have enough joy in his life to let the kid part come out.

Vince had said he would come by this evening for dinner and a swim unless he had an emergency. There was no medical reason he should check in. None of the horses had health issues now that the regular farrier had taken over hoof trimming from Vince. Anne was growing used to ending the day in his company. She missed their usual verbal skirmish.

Thinking about him raised her temperature, and it was already close to a hundred. "I could use that swim," she said. "Be right back after I change." Why should thinking of Vince make her blush? She could not possibly be interested in him. He was an irritant, nothing more. Irritants caused rashes on contact and were to be avoided.

She'd hoped they could at least become friends after he'd opened up to her. Actually, he'd backed off, gone quiet. Poor man. He had never known parents who loved each other and wanted what was best for their children.

Ten minutes later she slipped into the deliciously cool water of Victoria's pool, grabbed one of the inner tubes and allowed herself simply to float with her eyes closed. Not as efficient as a cold shower at cooling her blood, but it was close. She needed something to settle her inside as well as out.

"Uh, Anne," Victoria said softly, "you're not asleep, are you?"

Anne opened her eyes.

"I have to tell you something. Mrs. Stout called this afternoon. Becca wants to come back on Sunday."

Anne rolled over in the water. The inner tube rolled with her and dunked her. Sputtering, she surfaced to see Vince slipping out of his shirt by the deep end. He was already wearing trunks.

Up went her temperature again. For such a big man, he was slim with long muscles and narrow hips. So many big men were either muscle-bound or running to fat. Not Vince.

He might be an inappropriate crush for Becca, but Anne couldn't fault her taste. She'd have to warn Vince that Becca was coming back. Calvin didn't know it yet, but he was about to be offered up as a sacrificial lamb.

"Sonny Prather called me this afternoon," Victoria said casually. Much too casually. Sonny was always after something. To hear him tell it, whatever he wanted was for the good of the community. Mostly it was.

"Uh-oh," Vince said under his breath. He had not yet gotten in the water, but now he made a shallow dive and surfaced beside

Anne. He shook the water out of his hair and ran his hand down his face to clear his eyes.

Victoria sat down on the edge of the pool and kicked her legs gently so that the water swirled in eddies around Vince and Anne. "He's well aware of all we've been doing to train the minis. He's offering us a chance to take an experimental field trip."

"Meaning what?" Anne asked.

"Offering? Like a gift?" Vince grinned. "I'll bet."

"One of the ladies at the Williamston County Assisted Living home is celebrating her hundredth birthday. They're throwing her a party, of course, and the newspaper will be there to cover it. Maybe a photo along with the story. Sonny wants to do something special for her."

"He wants us to bring over a mini for her party, right?"

"Is that possible? That kind of publicity we can't buy. Apparently, the birthday girl loved riding when she was younger and keeps telling everybody how much she misses it."

"She's not expecting to ride, is she?" Anne asked. "She does know we raise miniatures?"

"Of course. Sonny did mention possibly driving one of the mini carriages."

"No way. Even if we could take a carriage

and harness, not even Molly is ready to be driven off-site." She hesitated., then pulled herself out of the pool and sat on the edge. She reclaimed her lemonade from the patio table and drank half the glass. "But, you know… maybe we could take Tom Thumb to visit. Let her feed him some carrots. Nothing fancy. He doesn't know any skills like opening doors yet. He's months away from being a real helper horse."

Victoria pulled her legs out of the water. "Her daughter says that just being able to pet one of the minis would be the best gift she could get." She looked away and said casually, "I told Sonny you'd be delighted to come. The party is this Thursday afternoon."

Anne choked on her drink. "*This* Thursday? Like the day after tomorrow? Indoors? We're not ready to mount an expedition anywhere, much less to an assisted living place."

"Tom Thumb can do it," Victoria said. "You keep saying how fast he learns."

"Not that fast. He's only tried that old pair of sneakers once and they weren't cut to fit him properly. We have to fit him and teach him to walk in the shoes without bucking or running away.

"Will he have to walk up stairs? Ride an

elevator? Heaven forbid, an escalator. Call Sonny back and give him a rain check—maybe a month from now."

"I can't break my promise. I bought a dozen pairs of children's sneakers this afternoon. At least a couple should fit Tom. You and Vince can fit him in his little shoes this evening after dinner. Vince, you will stay, won't you? I think Edward is bringing Chinese home from the office. He's been running some sort of financial planning seminar for retirees all day and has no desire to cook. Heaven knows I don't want to. He always buys too much, so there will be plenty for you."

Vince lifted his eyebrows at Anne. "I agree it's too soon, but it has to be your call. You keep saying you can do this. Here's your chance to prove it."

"Is that a challenge?" Anne said. She walked to the edge of the patio and stared into the paddock where the horses were contentedly munching grass. "Oh, what the heck. As long as everybody understands things could go wrong, we'll do it."

Victoria clapped. "I knew you'd say yes. Tom can practice walking on the tile floors in my living room. Vince will help at the nursing home, won't you, Vince? You can pick Tom up and carry him up the stairs if you have to, can't you?"

"Victoria, he weighs darned near as much as I do, and he has four legs to my two. No, I can't carry him upstairs."

"I told Sonny he might have to bring the patients down to the main floor for the visit."

"If we can get him upstairs, we will, but he needs a Plan B if we can't," Vince said. "Plan on bringing a pooper scooper too just in case. He's barely begun to understand holding it indoors."

"You will help us at the home, won't you, Vince? Anne and I can load him into the SUV and unload him when we arrive, but we may need backup with muscles. Barbara can handle the clinic for the few hours you'll be gone."

"You've already talked to her, right?" Vince heaved a deep sigh. "Okay, but first we need to fit him properly in tennis shoes and watch him walk."

AFTER DINNER, ANNE brought Tom Thumb to the patio. As always, he seemed delighted to be with his human beings and made a beeline for the pool. She stopped him before he could dive in. "Not this evening. You have work to do."

"I have some show forms to fill out for the

Williamston Horse Show," Victoria said. "I'll be in my office. You don't need me."

As Victoria disappeared into her house, Anne and Vince locked eyes. "She ought to join the magician's guild," Vince said. "Never saw a better disappearing act."

"She's right. We don't need her watching, trying to second-guess. She already raided the discount children's shoe store before I got here and brought home several small sizes. The boxes are stacked on the shelves in the mud-room. I'll go get a couple of pairs that ought to be the right size. Then it's trial and error."

By the time they had finished dinner on the patio, everyone had largely dried after swimming. Time to fit Tom for his sneakers.

Anne had read articles on how to create sneakers for horses, but she had not tried fitting them yet.

"How do we do this?" Vince asked Anne. Tom stood beside the round table on the patio and seemed bored with what his humans were doing.

"First we measure his hooves and draw an outline on paper. We can use the cardboard box lids from the shoes."

Tom didn't like having Anne lift his foot and attempt to set it down solidly on the paper.

"The cardboard won't eat your foot, I promise. Leave it down."

By the time they had four hoof outlines, Vince and Anne were both hot and sweaty, while Tom was threatening to do his dance routine again.

"The heavy shears should work," Anne said. "We cut the back third of the sneaker off, slip the front end of the shoe under Tom's hoof, lace it up tight in front…"

"What keeps him from walking out of it?"

"Hook-and-loop tape. I feed the tape through the top eyelets at the front of the shoe and fasten it behind."

"You are aware that we have to make slippers for four hooves?" Vince asked.

"I did actually notice that Tom has four feet, thank you. Shall we get started?"

After an hour, even Tom had about reached his limit. He had begun to fidget and stamp as they fastened the last sneaker around Tom's right front foot.

Anne sat back on her heels. "There. I'm not certain I can get off the floor without help. I lost contact with my legs thirty minutes ago."

"Here." Vince took her hand, waited while she got her feet under her, then pulled her up.

She came up fast. Tom snorted and danced out of her way.

Vince caught her around the waist with his free arm. "I've got you," he said.

He pulled her tight against the length of his body.

Their eyes met and held a moment too long. For Anne, the oxygen seemed to have been sucked out of the atmosphere. She felt her own heart thudding in her chest and Vince's echoing hers.

He bent to her and brushed her lips with his. When she didn't back away, he pulled her closer and deepened the kiss. She slid her arms around his shoulders. She could have stayed within the circle of his arms forever...

"Hmmmmmmmm," Tom nickered and shoved his small body between them.

Vince released Anne instantly and turned away from her.

"I swear he's jealous," Anne said in what she hoped was a normal tone of voice. Tough to do when she couldn't seem to draw a breath.

"Just impatient," Vince answered. His voice sounded tight as well. "What say we see if he'll walk in his shoes."

Tom's first few steps looked ridiculous. He picked up each foot, shook it, and set it down as though he worried that it did not actually belong to him.

He didn't buck, and he didn't try to run away. He seemed simply bemused at the crazy things his people asked of him.

"Come on," Vince said, "let's see if he can manage to walk on Victoria's tile floor."

Tom was hesitant, but once he figured out that he wouldn't slip, he began to walk around the kitchen as though he had been wearing sneakers all his life. He looked quite proud of himself.

Victoria came out of her office and stood in the kitchen door watching. "Edward, come look at this."

Reluctantly, Edward muted the Major League baseball game on the television, but kept his eye on the screen. "Uh-huh," he said. "He seems fine with them. Hey, home run. Y'all excuse me." He went back to his game.

"I think that's enough for tonight," Anne said. "Calvin and I will do more work tomorrow."

"See, I told you we could take Tom to that party on Thursday," Victoria said. "Have faith."

CHAPTER FIFTEEN

WEDNESDAY AFTERNOON AFTER Calvin had left, Victoria intercepted Anne on her way to feed the boarders' horses in their stalls.

"The TV station just issued a severe thunderstorm warning," she said. "Straight-line winds, a couple of tornado watch boxes. It'll be past us in an hour or so. In the meantime we need to get the horses into their stalls. The lightning strikes on the radar look like the Milky Way."

"Great," Anne said. "I've about had it with this heat. A big ole thunderstorm should cool us off for a couple of days."

"It's the first big storm we've had since I brought the minis home," Victoria said. "I don't know how they'll react."

"They'll turn their tails to the rain and wind and hunker down together like regular horses."

"I hope so. They were left outside in pasture where they were before, but I worry about the lightning hitting a tree and dropping it on their heads. Glory hates being alone in the stallion paddock when he can't see his mares. I already know he freaks when there's lightning and thunder. We need to get him into his stall fast. We can bring the others then."

"Uh-oh. Look over yonder," Anne said.

The bright arc of the setting sun on the western horizon disappeared as black clouds rolled across it, turning late afternoon into late twilight. The wind tore at the trees and blew sand from the arena into eyes and mouths.

Anne grabbed Glory's heavy stallion halter off his gatepost and called him. She hadn't handled him much, but she'd made friends with him. He tossed his mane and neighed loudly as he cantered toward her—definitely upset. In their pasture, his mares bounced around in obvious distress. They were affected by his antics as much as by the weather. As lead stallion, he was supposed to stand between them and trouble, but he couldn't head off a thunderstorm. If he was concerned, then they were, too.

"They can feel the drop in barometric pressure," Anne said. "Makes them antsy."

"According to the radar it's not a deep storm. A single narrow band, but it's moving fast. It's already on this side of the Mississippi. Should pass us quickly. But they think it's going to be a bad one when it hits. Hand me the stallion halter. I'll take Glory inside to his stall. He can be a handful when it's like this. I know how to handle him."

Victoria clipped on his halter, then slipped the heavy leather lead line across his nose to give her more control. "You start haltering the others, but wait until Glory's in the barn where he can't see them before you bring them out of their pasture. I don't want him to break away from me and run back to them."

"Drat it, I've got a mouthful of sand."

"They should come over to the gate when they realize Glory's in the barn. Start with Big Mary. If she comes, they'll all come. Oh, good, Vince just drove in. I wasn't expecting him. He can help."

"Heard the forecast," Vince called as he trotted down the hill toward them. "I was in the area and thought you might need a hand."

"I'll go get the halters and lead lines," Anne said and jogged off to the tack room to collect them. The big horses like her Trusty were already in their stalls, munching their evening oats.

On her way back to the pasture gate, Anne passed Victoria leading Glory in. He was squalling and humping his back, fighting to get to his mares.

"Stupid horse, stop that," Victoria snapped as she hauled him forward. "We'll bring them in for you. Shut up and behave yourself." She disappeared inside. "Stallions are almost as much trouble as men," she called over her shoulder.

Vince opened the gate to the mares' pasture a couple of feet and slipped inside. "Here, Anne, pass me a halter."

Big Mary led the others over to him at a trot. With the exception of Tom Thumb, who as low horse in the herd waited patiently at the back of the group, they were tossing their heads, bouncing and pawing the ground as they pushed toward the head of the line. So far as they were concerned, if Glory was not there to protect them, they were at risk. Going to Glory was their protection when there was danger.

As she reached Vince at the gate, the herd bully, Big Mary, all thirty-two inches of her, decided she'd done enough waiting. She lowered her head, knocked Molly aside and charged straight at Vince. She hit him hard in the sternum, knocked the wind out of him and shoved him and the gate out of her way.

Before he could catch his breath, she thrust by him and tore off at a dead run for the unfenced acreage west of the barn.

The others did what their instincts and their mothers had taught them to do—they followed her.

Tom Thumb hesitated just long enough for Anne to grab his halter to keep him inside the pasture. "No, you don't." Anne shoved him back, pulled Vince out of her way and shut the gate behind him. Alone, Tom butted the gate and neighed miserably for his companions.

"The horses are loose!" Victoria shouted as she ran up the hill to Anne and Vince. "How on earth…"

"My fault," Vince gasped as he tried to catch his breath and regain his balance.

"We have to get them back before the storm," Anne said. "Victoria, where would they go? They started off in that direction." She pointed toward the south west.

"You've been down there with Trusty. That's the way to the creek. In a rainstorm it floods and turns into a swamp. If they get stuck in the mud, they could drown."

To complicate the situation even more, the heavens opened. In seconds the barn was invisible behind sheets of water cascading down the roof and over the sides.

Victoria started after the horses, but Anne stopped her. "Call Edward. Tell him to bring heavy-duty flashlights and the boots out of the mudroom. Vince, can you drive the ATV?"

He nodded. "Sure. Keys in it?"

She nodded back. Vince ran toward the equipment shed.

"How close can we get to the swampy part?" Anne asked Victoria. She had to dash her hands across her eyes to keep from being blinded by the driving water and sand.

Half a dozen streaks of lightning flashed out of the dark clouds to the west where the Mississippi River flowed.

"One, Mississippi, two, Mississippi, thr…" Anne jumped as thunder crashed, crashed, and kept crashing. "Too close—less than three miles away."

Victoria spoke into her ear. "Remember, the gravel road ends just before you hit the swamp. I had Calvin put a pole across it to mark the end so you don't drive off into the mud. Easy to spot in daylight. In the dark, not so much."

"If we're lucky, Molly or Big Mary will stop them before they get there. She's too fat and lazy to gallop far."

Vince swept up in the ATV. "Get in."

Anne hopped in beside him.

"There are a couple of big hand lanterns behind the seat," Victoria shouted. "Go. Edward and I will follow you on the motorbike."

Vince hit the gas. "Hold on."

The narrow road curved back through the thick copse of pine trees past the pasture. Anne might have ridden this way on Trusty once with Victoria, but in the rain and the wind it looked different. The ruts in the road had already filled with water. Vince splashed through them too fast and barely held the ATV on the road.

Anne screamed and held on tighter.

The farther from the barn, the less they could see.

"How far to the swamp?" he shouted over the rain.

"Not sure. Looks different."

"The rain's already slacking. Should improve the visibility."

"But the sun's going. It's getting really dark."

The sky lit up again, but this time the lightning struck north of them. Anne counted. Five seconds. Going away. She heaved a sigh of relief just as Vince drove into an exceptionally deep pothole. A wave of muddy water rode up over the floor of the ATV and drenched her from the knees down. She wiped her sopping shirt across her eyes and mouth, reached into the back seat and picked up one of the hand lanterns.

"Where are the headlights on this thing?" Vince asked.

"Here." She hit the switch. The windshield wipers, such as they were, couldn't keep up with the water sluicing down the windshield, so Anne leaned out the side and focused the flashlight ahead of them.

"That helps," Vince said. Without taking his eyes off the road, leaning forward with his forearms on the steering wheel, he said, "This is my fault."

"The horses suckered you." Anne swiveled to look at his silhouette in the little light that remained. She could barely see the outline of his jaw, but it looked as though it belonged on Mount Rushmore.

Vince was right, Anne thought. *This was his fault*. He knew better than to wade into a spooked herd in the middle of a lightning storm. Or to leave a gate partially open and basically unguarded except by his body. The minis were small, but as Vince had said, they were heavier and tougher than a man, especially when they were in a group. He was lucky he had stayed on his feet. They'd have tried to avoid stepping on him, but in the chaos, he might have been trampled.

"Stop!" Anne shouted. "I remember that split tree from my trail ride with Victoria. This is where it gets gooshy." She waved the light ahead. "There's the pole marking the end of the road. It's fallen off one side. We could have driven right by it and *splat.*"

Vince picked up the other hand lantern and swept the area ahead of them at the level of a mini's head.

"Look," Anne grabbed his arm. "Over there."

Both knew the problems of locating horses in pasture at night. Their instinct was to stand still so predators would not see movement. Often the only clue to their location was the reflection of a flashlight beam off a pair of equine eyes.

"Turn off the motor," Anne whispered. He did.

"Yoo-hoo, Molly?" she shouted. "Grumpy? Is that you? Big Mary, you come right on here. Dinner's waiting. Little Sammy. Harriet. Time to go home. Storm's over." She waited. They both listened. No response, but Vince's light caught flashes from at least two other sets of eyes.

"Time to bring out the big guns," Vince said. "Treats! Come get your carrots." He dropped his hand on Anne's knee. "Quiet."

Ahead of them came a tentative splash and then another.

Anne assumed Molly would be the first to reach them and was surprised when Big Mary loomed out of the shadows and into the light. Interesting. The boss mare's job might already have passed from Molly to Big Mary.

Close to Molly's rear end came Grumpy.

"Stay here," she said to Vince. "I'll go stand at the front in the headlights so they recognize me. If I can get halters on Molly and Grumpy, the others should come. Right about now they'll be feeling pretty embarrassed. They know they screwed up."

"And they're hungry."

She pulled a couple of small carrots out of her britches pockets.

She held a carrot out to Molly, and when she reached for it, snapped the halter closed under her chin.

"I'll take her," Vince said. He eased out of the ATV and made his way quietly to the front between the headlights.

Anne repeated the process with Grumpy.

"I am up to my knees in mud," Anne said.

"Me, too. Let me have the lines. I'll walk them back behind the ATV. I don't want to tie them to the bumper. If they try to jerk away they could spook the rest of the herd. See if the others will come."

The minis took their time, but they came.

"It's all right, girl," Anne said as she fed Harriet a carrot and snapped her halter on. She turned to Vince. "Now what do we do? We can't stand here all night holding these horses. Can you see to turn the ATV around?"

"Not in the dark with all this water. If I had my phone, I could call Victoria to explain the situation. She was going to bring the motor scooter down, but they may be stuck up the road. They'll have to bring the truck."

"In this mud? I can't see but one way out of this, Vince. Each of us takes half of the lines and we walk the horses back to the barn."

"Do I carry a flashlight in my teeth or use my third hand?" Vince asked. "In case you hadn't noticed, the headlights are pointing over the swamp, not up the road behind us. Once we're out of reach of the lights, it'll be too dark to see the ditches beside the road. I'd rather not fall in or have to pull a drowning mini out."

"Grumpy, sweetie, come here," Anne took his line from Vince. "This is your new lesson, Grumpy. How to carry a flashlight tied to your halter. Vince, you're going to have to hold them all until I get this done. If it works. There's bound to be at least one Bungee cord in the ATV." She handed her lines to Vince and scrounged in the box of supplies behind the seat. "Found one. Let's see if I can make this work."

After several tries, Anne managed to attach the flashlight to the top of Grumpy's halter so that it pointed slightly forward rather than straight up. "Not great, but better than nothing."

Grumpy went to sleep during the process and only woke when he felt the flashlight jiggle against his forehead. He wiggled his ears and snuffled, but didn't attempt the kind of solid shake that would have knocked it loose. He took a tentative step forward, then decided the thing was not a ravenous leopard on his head and walked with Anne.

"Let me turn the headlights on the ATV off," Vince said. "They're doing no good. No sense in running the battery down. I can hold one of the hand lanterns as well as a lead line.

Should provide enough light until we hit the pine trees. Ready?"

"Ready," Anne said. "Good thing they don't mind being ponied together. I am really learning to love these little guys, you know?"

Their progress was slow. They stumbled into puddles and had to keep forming and reforming their little equine cadre as the outsiders tended to pull away from the insiders.

As fast as it had descended, the remnants of the storm passed to the east. As the clouds fled, an anemic moon peeked beneath the remaining scraps of cloud, but cast little light on the road.

As they rounded the last bend before the pasture fence, they were struck by the beams of two large flashlights.

"Anne, Vince," Victoria called. "Are you two all right? Did you find any of the horses?"

"We found all of them," Vince said. "Come get them."

"Where's the ATV?" Edward's voice rose out of the darkness.

"Back on the edge of the swamp where we found the horses," Anne said. "We couldn't quite manage to bring it back with us. We were otherwise occupied."

"Here," Victoria took Anne's lines while Edward took Vince's. "Let's get the mud rinsed off them and put them in stalls. You missed dinner, didn't you, you bad children?"

"What caused this in the first place?" Edward asked. "Who the heck let them out?"

"I did," Vince answered.

"You really didn't," Anne said. "Molly and Big Mary ran over you. You're lucky you didn't get stomped."

He glanced at her in surprise. She could easily have thrown him under the proverbial bus, but she supported him. Through all the chaos, they had worked together without a cross word between them. He had grown accustomed to taking one step forward, then one step back in their relationship. This was a big step forward. Maybe they could maintain it.

"Now we know how they react in a thunderstorm," Victoria said. "Another lesson learned. We'll have to desensitize them to storms as well as crowds and escalators."

"Fine," Anne said. "Once you figure out how to create a thunderstorm on command."

"Good luck with that," Edward said. "This is why I don't mess with Victoria's horses any more than I have to."

"How's Glory?" Anne asked.

"Settled down. My word, you're dirtier than the horses. There are plenty of leftovers from dinner we can feed you, but not until the horses are rinsed off and so are you. Vince, do you need to borrow a pair of Edward's jeans and a shirt?"

"I've always got clean clothes in the van, although if I keep coming over here I'm going to have to add to my backup wardrobe. Thanks anyway. After we get the horses clean and put away I'll rinse off on the wash rack in the barn. Won't be the first time. No sense in getting your house muddy."

"Don't be silly," Anne said. "There won't be enough hot water for you and the horses both."

"The cold water spigot in the barn comes straight out of the aquifer," Edward said. "It's freezing all year long."

You can use my shower in the cottage," Anne said.

"I'll track mud all over."

"Like I won't? The cottage is more or less dirt-proof. Go grab your clothes out of the van while I start rinsing off horses."

"Edward and I will do that, won't we, darling?" The emphasis on the "darling" carried more than a hint of command.

Edward shrugged. "Yeah, sure. You two, come on up to the house for something to eat when you're clean."

ANNE AND VINCE dropped sodden paddock boots and socks inside the front door of the cottage. "Use my bathroom," she said. "That way I won't have to scrub mud out of Becca's bathroom, too." She brought him a stack of thick towels the color of peach meringue, opened the first door off the hall and flicked on a light. "That's the door to the bathroom through there. There's shampoo and stuff already. Not necessarily the scent you normally use, but at least you'll be clean. You actually carry another set of boots as well as extra clothes in your van?"

"When I get dirty, I get filthy. Try pulling a calf out of a cow without getting blood on your boots. Don't you want to go first?"

"Company goes first. Want a beer? Wine?"

"I'd kill for some sweet tea with a ton of ice."

"You got it. Here, better take your clean clothes with you." She pointed to the clothes folded on the back of the sofa.

"Oh, yeah."

"Yell if you need anything you don't see."

Vince was a connoisseur of showers. Anne's

measured up well. Plenty of jets, plenty of hot water.

As he soaped up he drew in the fresh scent of Anne—lavender, maybe, with a hint of something spicy—onto his skin and into his nostrils. Edgy, like Anne. He closed his eyes and leaned back against the tile. He felt wrapped in the essence of her.

He wanted to fill all his senses with her.

Even when she was covered in mud, he enjoyed looking at her. He liked the way her blue-green eyes snapped at him when he annoyed her. Or more often when *she* annoyed *him*.

She could easily have cussed him out in front of Edward and Victoria for letting the horses escape, but she hadn't let him take the blame.

He deserved whatever she dished out. He should have gone straight home after dehorning those goats this afternoon. He'd been cross-eyed with exhaustion. That contributed to his screw-up, but it was an excuse, not a reason.

The whole day had been murder. He'd been met at the clinic door first thing by a Great Dane unable to deliver what turned out to be seven puppies without a C-section.

He hadn't taken a break the rest of the day.

He'd never even stopped to grab a candy bar out of the clinic vending machine.

After he'd clipped the horns from the last goat and started his drive back to the clinic, he'd heard the weather report. He hadn't made a conscious choice. He'd turned right instead of left and headed for Victoria's place. To help Anne.

Some help he'd been.

Stumbling like that against the partially open paddock gate and knocking it open was a mistake that nearly had nasty consequences. He'd never expected the usually calm minis to make a break for freedom because of a couple of lightning strikes. Big mistake.

He did not make mistakes. If Anne had been responsible for the breakout, he'd probably have yelled at her. If she'd cussed him out right that minute, he'd have deserved it.

She hadn't. Now that they were alone, she might yell at him, but she hadn't done it in front of Edward and Victoria. He was grateful for that. It galled him to admit that she'd taken the lead in getting themselves and the horses back unhurt, while he followed her orders.

He normally would not have taken orders from anyone but a more experienced vet.

Pretty darned arrogant. Time he started listening more and talking less.

He rinsed the shampoo out of his hair and let the water cascade over his head and shoulders.

Anne was getting to him.

Heck, she had gotten to him the first time he met her. That was unfortunate for both of them. She wasn't the kind of woman any man could walk away from. He was beginning to worry that *he* definitely couldn't. Better to return to their prickly semiadversarial interaction. Safer that way for both of them.

Wanting a woman who wasn't interested in him was a new experience. He thought he'd be happy about that, but he didn't like it. Anne didn't even want to be around him much. He should be grateful. Instead, he was surprised that he was a little hurt.

OVER AFTER-DINNER DECAF, Anne pleaded exhaustion and walked back to her cottage to sleep. "Tomorrow is 'take a horse to the nursing home' day. Good night, everyone, and thanks for your help, Vince."

"If help is what you call it. See you tomorrow in time to load Tom and get to the nursing home on time."

He didn't really want to stay for an extra cup

of decaf, but Victoria said she needed to tell him something.

Like most men, he figured "we have to talk" from any woman was a lead-in to a notification of impending disaster.

He sat back down as Victoria filled his cup yet again and said, "What now?"

"Becca's coming back on Sunday to stay until Friday."

His shoulders tightened. "Let's hope she likes Calvin and leaves me alone."

"We can't count on her leaving you alone. Calvin's younger brother, Darrell, is going to start working here three afternoons a week. I didn't realize how much extra trouble eight small horses could be. If Becca doesn't like one of the boys, maybe she'll like the other. Darrell is only a year older than she is. Nice boy."

"She'll think he's too young."

"He's a sophomore at Middle Tennessee State in their rodeo program." She heaved a sigh. "He rides bulls."

"Oh no."

"When you were in Wyoming breaking horses, did you ride bulls, too?"

Vince shook his head. "One of the few pieces of usable advice my daddy ever gave me was to stay off bulls. He says it is crazy to climb on a ton and a half of animated steak, hand him eight seconds to try to kill you, then let him keep trying after he's thrown you in the dirt. He says good bucking bulls are demons. I say it takes one to know one."

"Oh dear, you're still not getting along. Barbara hoped that once you were up here…"

"That I'd mend fences at home? Not gonna happen."

"We certainly don't want to lose you to your family, but Barbara and I both wish things were better for you at home." She patted his thigh. "You know us Southern women—we like things smooth for our men. She and I both have happy families. We'd love to see you happy, too. Surely your daddy has mellowed."

Vince laughed so hard he spit his decaf across the table. "Thor Peterson? Mellowed?

"My daddy has so far married four women. He divorced two for adultery. They may or may not have been guilty, but if they were, I don't much blame them. My mother ran away from both him and me in the middle of the night."

"Oh, Vince, I'm so sorry."

"It's a long time ago." He shrugged. "Gives me an excuse for being screwed up. His fourth wife, Mary Alice, used to spend a lot of time in Mobile with her girlfriends to get away from him. My brother Joshua says recently Daddy fusses if she wants to meet a girlfriend for lunch away from the farm. Wouldn't surprise me if he kicked her out too, but not until he's got number five on his horizon. What's that old saying about the triumph of hope over experience? His hope is that he'll browbeat one of them into total submission."

"Obviously that doesn't work," Victoria said.

"Not so far. He keeps marrying strong women. He says the battle for control isn't satisfying unless he has a worthy opponent."

"How does he manage to get any woman to give him a second look, much less marry him?"

"He's rich. He can be charming when he puts his mind to it. My sister-in-law Nicki, Cody's wife, says he's good-looking for an old guy. I wouldn't know. My brother Joshua is divorced once and has separated from his second wife Nell several times. So far, she's come back. She says she loves him. Cody has kept it together with Nicki, but then, she's a saint. Joshua says divorce is too expensive, but he would say that. He's a CPA."

"And you?"

"Bachelor for life. The only thing I know about marriage is that I never learned to do it."

"How about love?"

"Don't believe in it. Not for me, at any rate. People get married because it's economically advantageous or physically enticing. Whatever love is, it goes away faster than it comes."

"Uh-huh."

"You don't sound convinced."

"We'll see," Virginia said. "Your father is not getting any younger. I had some problems with my mother, but we made up before she died, thankfully. Not a day goes by I don't miss her, wish I could hear her laugh or smell her corn bread baking. Don't wait too long to make up with your daddy. I promise you, Vince honey, you will regret it if you don't."

"I figure I've got a while yet. That lady at the nursing home we're going to see tomorrow is a hundred. I'm expecting Daddy to celebrate his nine-hundredth like Methuselah. He'll out-live all of us."

"Running a cattle operation that size in the present economy must be terribly stressful on his health."

Vince leaned back and stretched his booted legs in front of him. "My brother Cody runs the cattle operation and my brother Joshua handles the business end. With Daddy's constant inter-ference, of course. Thor has very little stress in his life, but he's a powerful carrier. Like Ty-phoid Mary. She didn't come down with the disease, but she gave it to everyone she met."

Victoria laughed and coughed when her cof-fee went down the wrong way. "Your father's given name is actually Thor? In the South?" She picked up the carafe and lifted her eye-brows at Vince.

He shook his head. "No more, thanks, even if it is decaf."

"How on earth did your people wind up in Mississippi?" Victoria asked as she topped off her own cup.

"I had a Norwegian emigrant ancestor who served in the civil war to procure citizenship. After Appomattox he decided he preferred Mississippi summers to Minnesota winters, so he moved his family down here."

"A real carpetbagger."

"You got it. People were poor, land was cheap. Some folks still consider us foreign-ers, even though we've been here since 1867." He set his cup down and stood. "I really need to get home. I've got to wrangle Tom Thumb tomorrow, remember?"

"See you at twelve thirty to load Tom," Victoria said. "Thank you for getting the horses in this evening."

"Least I could do. I let 'em out."

CHAPTER SIXTEEN

"OFF YOU GET, little guy," Anne said. Tom poked his head out the van's open tailgate, took a tentative step down the ramp, then tiptoed the rest of the way to the ground. He was still not completely at ease wearing his cut-back sneakers. When he stood on the concrete of the parking lot outside the nursing home, he lifted and shook each foot in turn before trusting himself to stand on it. He gave Anne a reproachful stare, but walked forward when she held one of his favorite apple treats too far in front of his nose for him to reach it by stretching his neck.

"He'll be okay in a second," Anne said. She moved away from the van, clasping the reins to her side. He gave up shaking his feet and walked beside her.

"First bridge crossed," Vince said as he cut the engine and headed back to the ramp. "Good boy, Tom."

The wide glass door into the nursing home

opened before they reached it, and a small dapper man in a starched seersucker suit came forward with outstretched hands.

"Welcome, welcome. I'm Beau Caldwell. I manage our assisted living. This will be such a treat for Mrs. Hamilton and the others. They're waiting in the day room. I told them we had a special visitor coming, but not who it is." He reached out and brushed Tom's neck with his fingertips, then drew back as though he'd been scalded.

Tom butted his hand.

"Oh," said Beau. "I've never seen a horse this small before. I figured I shouldn't touch him without permission. We've had companion dogs visit—our clients love them—but this is our first companion horse. He's not very big, is he?"

"Big enough to do the job," Vince said.

"I'm sure, I'm sure. Are you ready? Shall we go?" He kept wary eyes on Tom as though expecting him to blow up into a Clydesdale. He held the door until Tom and the others had passed through, then stood in front of it as if to keep them from running back out before Tom had fulfilled his commitment to the residents.

Anne cut her eyes at Vince and held up crossed fingers. "Ready as we'll ever be."

"It's only your first test. Remember you've got over three months before Becca goes to school and six months minimum to have him ready to try out as a real helper horse for a total stranger."

She was afraid that Tom would be nervous and misbehave when he heard the chatter of voices and clink of china and silver coming from the dayroom, so she concentrated on keeping her own nerves under control. He'd take his cue from what he felt from her. So long as she stayed calm, he'd stay calm. At least, that was the idea.

They waited outside in the hall while the manager went in to the day room, shushed everyone and announced the arrival of their special guest.

He flung open the doors as if he were pulling a rabbit out of a hat and ushered them through. The moment the patients saw Tom, they all began to chatter and applaud. Loudly. Anne tightened her hold on Tom.

He stood stock-still and leaned even closer to Anne. His ears were waving like semaphores, but he didn't back up or attempt to escape. He was curious, but not frightened.

"Where's the birthday girl?" Vince asked Mr. Caldwell.

A tiny lady in a wheelchair that nearly swallowed her lifted an arthritic hand from the blanket that covered her knees. She had shrunk to child-size—almost small enough to ride Tom. She clapped softly while she whispered, "Oh, oh, oh."

Tom had never seen a wheelchair, let alone been close to one, but when Anne walked him to it, he came with her willingly. He reached the old lady and did what he always did when he could manage it—he laid his head on the blanket that covered her lap and gazed up at her as though she were the fount of all treats.

She stroked Tom's cheek. He sighed and blinked at her.

Anne blinked to keep from crying as she saw the sheer joy in Mrs. Hamilton's eyes.

"My goodness, he's so little," Mrs. Hamilton said. There was nothing childlike about her voice. It was raspy, possibly from a lifetime of smoking cigarettes. If so, she'd still managed to make it to the century mark. Her body might be failing, but her voice and spirit were still strong.

"Put a saddle on you, horse," she said, "and I swear I could ride you right on out of here and back home, small as you are." She giggled. "When I was a girl I had a Shetland pony not much bigger than this. Rode him to and from school, rain or snow, almost lived on him. After we married, my husband bought me a chestnut walking horse, but I never forgot little Posey." Tears rolled down her wrinkled cheeks, but not in sadness.

"We never forget our first pony," Anne said. "My Brownie is still teaching kids to ride and is as ornery as ever."

Mrs. Caldwell chortled. "Did he ever throw you off?"

"Did he ever. After a while I lost count of the times he dumped me. If I tried to ride him into a creek, even a deep puddle, he'd walk us out into the middle, lie down and roll. I learned to jump off him at the first sign he intended to go down."

The entire room had gone quiet as the others listened to their conversation.

"Gertrude, don't keep him to yourself," called a male voice from somewhere in the room. "We all want to pet him."

"Oh, pooh, I'm the one who's a hundred years old. I get to do whatever I like." She hugged Tom as though she couldn't bear to stop touching him.

"You can't hog the horse," said a female voice from the other side of the room. "Bring him on over here and let me scratch his ears. He got a name?"

"Tom Thumb," Vince said. "We'll get around to everybody."

"Promise?" A third voice. They all began to speak at once to demand a turn petting Tom. He seemed content to give them their chance.

Vince raised his eyebrows at Anne. She nodded and took up the slack on Tom's harness.

The three of them began a royal procession through the room, not only from resident to resident, but to nurses orderlies, and the rest of the assembled staff.

"Look at his little shoes," one woman cooed. "How does he keep them on?"

"They lace up the front and have hook-and-loop closure around the back," Anne told her.

"He likes them," another lady said. "Does he have different pairs to match different halters?"

"Zelda, don't be a soppy idiot," said a blousy woman who stood well back from contact with Tom's furry body. "I, for one, think it's appalling to coerce these poor dumb animals into wearing painful shoes and tiring themselves out working for *people*." She made *people* sound like a swear word. "They can't possibly enjoy it. They should all be running free in the grass."

"Uh-oh," Vince whispered.

"What can they do anyway? Dogs are smarter. A horse can't protect you from gangs. It won't take a bullet for you."

Anne glanced at Vince. He seemed to be swelling. At six-four, he was a powerful-looking man, but when he drew himself up and tightened those muscles, he was downright scary. "I assure you, madam, he is happy and well taken care of."

"Piffle," said the woman. "Let him go, bet he'll run away."

"Lucy," said a man close to her, "shut your mean mouth. Nobody wants to hear a thing you got to say. Look at this boy. Why, you can tell he's having a whee of a time, aren't you, son?" He scratched along Tom's back. The little horse shivered with pleasure. "You ain't ruinin' this party like you always try to do, Lucy. Shut up or I'll tell Beau Caldwell to shut you up."

Where is the manager anyway? Anne wondered.

She laid her hand on Vince's arm and shook her head. "Leave it," she whispered. "Let's move on."

Vince's jaw remained set.

Anne felt certain he would snap back if Lucy kept on.

As he opened his mouth to reply, Tom stamped on his instep. Hard.

Anne took hold of Tom's reins and moved to another group of adoring fans. Massaging his instep, Vince limped after them.

The rest of the visit went smoothly after Lucy stormed out of the room. Several people applauded.

After a long visit that included carrots for Tom and carrot cake for Anne and Vince, Anne thanked everyone, gave Mrs. Hamilton a final opportunity to hug Tom, then said their farewells.

"Will you come back again when it's not my birthday?" Mrs. Hamilton asked. "I may not be here, but everyone else will be."

Anne caught Vince's eye.

"We'll be back," Anne said and waved to the room.

Everyone began to applaud. Tom wriggled, but stayed put.

"I think he's about reached his limit," Vince whispered. "Potty break before we leave?"

"If Beau can provide a patch of grass."

Beau filed in beside them. "There's a place

under the trees." He chuckled. "All manure happily accepted. My rosebushes love it."

She stood with Tom in the shade of an aged oak and said, "Go time," in a firm voice. Tom regarded her as though she had grown a second head, then he began to paw.

"He's still got on his sneakers," Anne said to Vince in a quiet voice. "He won't know what to do."

Tom lifted his tail, gave her an *oh, yeah?* glance and took care of business.

Anne pulled off his sneakers and filled his water bucket from the gallon jugs she carried. She waited while he drank. Then she and Vince walked him up the ramp and shut the doors on him.

"We did it!" Anne raised a palm for a high five.

"No, *you* did." Vince grasped her hand, swept her up and kissed her hard.

She threw her arms around his neck and kissed him back. His lips were hot and demanding against her mouth.

She relished the taste of him, the feel of his muscular body against her, the scent of him. One kiss with him brought her alive in a way no other kiss—no other man—had ever done. She didn't want to let him go. It was as though

Mrs. Hamilton had blessed them with a bit of her joy,

Vince lifted Anne off her feet and swung her around. She held on and buried her face against his shoulder, and when he let her feet touch the ground again, she was looking past his shoulder to where a bemused Mr. Caldwell stood smiling at them.

"Oh— Not here," she whispered.

From the back of the van came an importunate neigh. "Tom's impatient," she said. "We need to go."

They said their goodbyes and promised to come back. When they were finally on the road back to Martin's, Anne said with a casualness she did not feel, "The timing of Tom's stomp on your instep when that woman was so mean has to be a coincidence. Horses can't read minds."

"Coincidence or not, my foot hurts like the devil." Vince reached behind him and scratched Tom's forehead. "Didn't want me making a social gaffe, did you, Tom, my man. You knew I was mad, didn't you?"

"What was that woman's problem?" Anne asked.

"There are some people who would rather see an animal suffer than interfere with Mother

Nature. Personally, I have found Mother Nature to be low on compassion and dead set against innovation. Companion horses are a relatively new concept, and therefore they're against nature. There's somebody like that woman in every crowd. She'll probably post a nasty email to all her friends tonight saying what evil people we are because he's not running free where the coyotes can eat him. Lucky Tom stopped me. I would have said something impolite and we might have ruined the party. Thanks to Tom's sharp hoof, we didn't."

"So are you beginning to think what I'm trying to do might be worthwhile?"

"Lady, I never doubted it was a worthwhile concept. I just didn't think you had the skills to do it."

"How well did you neuter your first cat, Doctor? Or stitch up your first cut on a horse's rump? Or put back your first prolapsed uterus in a cow? Or even clean out your first hoof abscess? You learned how, you practiced, then you learned some more. That's what I'm doing. Learning and practicing. Six months from now I'll know a bunch more and have better skills. And both the people and the horses will benefit. Count on it." She wrapped her arms across her chest and glared out the window.

Vince dropped a hand on her thigh. "This afternoon you did a great job. Maybe you'll convince me yet."

"But don't count on it?" She laughed.

After another few miles, he cleared his throat. He'd learned that his best choice was to act as though their previous conversation had never happened. Nor had that kiss.

"You and Tom made that lady very happy," he said quietly. "You made her feel young again. You should be proud, and I should keep my mouth shut."

"You said what you believe. Eventually, I'll convert you to my way of thinking."

"I hope you're right."

She turned in her seat so that she could see his profile. "If I can find someplace in Williamston to practice, I need to teach Tom and Molly to walk up stairs and ride escalators," Anne said. "We won't be so limited in the places we visit."

He relaxed. This was the closest thing Anne offered to an olive branch. "Call Sonny Prather. He knows every piece of real estate in Williamston County and beyond. Now that you've broken the ice, Calvin can go with you instead of me. I haven't been holding up my end at the clinic. Barbara needs me."

Anne felt a sudden pang. So much for that kiss. Was she the only one whose hands had been shaking? That was no simple congratulatory kiss—not for her, at any rate. But he was ignoring the entire episode. They were talking as though there had been no kiss.

Would he back off? Leave her to Calvin's care? She'd gotten used to seeing him at odd hours of the day and nearly every evening. He was coming to see the horses, of course, but the result was the same. She would miss him. Miss more kisses, miss his strong arms embracing her.

Just miss *more*.

The cell phone plugged into the van's console rang. "My phone. 'Scuse me. Gotta take it." He pulled to the side of the road before answering. "Peterson. Hi, Barbara." He listened, then said, "Anne's with me. We're on our way back with Tom. Yeah, went great. Tom was his usual charming self." He listened again. "How far? That close." He turned to Anne. "Horse with a bad cut a couple of miles from here. Barbara's busy and can't go for a while. Can you ride along? You can graze Tom while I stitch."

"How bad?"

"No idea. Probably won't take too long, but you never know."

"Of course, we'll ride with you. Tom won't mind."

The call came from a shiny new and very ritzy boarding barn with elegant stables, a regulation-sized dressage arena and a separate indoor jumping arena set with freshly painted jumps. A glassed-in viewing area for clients had been built above the arenas. "Talk about posh," she said.

Anne had seen the trainer coming toward them at several horse shows with his students, but had never ridden against him and did not really know him.

Vince didn't seem to know him personally, either, but they all quickly introduced themselves.

"I have a VSE in the back of the van, Mr. Able," Anne said. "May I walk him around while Vince stitches your horse?"

"You're that girl's been working with Victoria, aren't you? Sure. I've seen VSEs in carriage classes at shows. You make yourself at home. There's an empty turnout paddock behind the barn with a water trough in it. Take him in there and let him loose. Come on,

Vince. Glad you came when I called your office."

"Lucky Anne and I were already close. The sooner we treat the injury, the better."

"When he didn't come up with the others for the evening meal, chow hound that he is, I knew something was wrong. I sent one of my boys into the pasture to find him. He did, all right—standing in the shadows under one of those big pin oaks and pouring blood out of a gash on his left flank."

"How'd you get him into the barn? Could he walk?"

"I drove the trailer down and picked him up. We did manage to get him on the wash rack. Gave him a shot to take the edge off his pain. Been running cold water on the cut. He's mostly stopped bleeding, but the gash is a good six inches long and deep. I can see muscles."

The edges of the cut were ragged, as though something had ripped the flesh rather than sliced it. Vince numbed the area, and trimmed the edges of the cut to fresh tissue.

Vince hunkered down beside the horse's flank.

Able leaned over him. "What're you doing? What's happening? What do you see?"

"Making sure he doesn't have part of a tree

limb stuck in him." Vince glanced over his shoulder and pointed. "Step back. You're in my light."

Anne appeared from settling Tom in the paddock and took the man's arm. "Come on, Mr. Able. Dr. Peterson likes to work alone. We can wait in the aisle."

"You left your minihorse in the paddock?" Able craned past her to see what Vince was doing.

"Tom's fine in your paddock. This is a marvelous place. When did you move in?" Making conversation might divert Able from hovering over Vince.

"What? Oh. We've been here a little more than a year. Moved down from Illinois north of Chicago. Taxes were running me out of business."

"You started from scratch?"

Able tried to slide in closer to Vince but Anne edged him away. "Yeah. Sold my place in Illinois to a developer. Made enough to build this place and have some left over. What's he doing now?"

"Blast!" Vince snarled. "I don't believe this."

"What? What, man?" Able crowded in once more and leaned over Vince's shoulder.

Vince sat back on his heels. "Look at this.

It's a miracle he didn't slice a tendon." He held up a bloody six-inch piece of rusty barbed wire. "You've got PVC fence all around this place. Where'd the barbed wire come from?" He surged to his feet and brandished the wire in Able's face like a sword.

"I—I don't know. Folks who owned the land before us had cows. They had barbed wire. It was all tangled with wild roses and love vine and such, but we pulled it all out when we put the new fence in."

"Not quite all, boss," said a gnarled gnome of a man wearing old-fashioned jodhpurs and cracked brown paddock boots. He'd approached so quietly that Anne hadn't even noticed him. She bet he'd been a jockey. There was something about his bowed legs that was as revealing as a tattoo.

"What barbed wire? We pulled it all."

"Where was it?" Vince asked.

"Couldn't be." Able frowned and pushed the old man aside.

"Tell me now," Vince said. Then, since Able stood with his mouth open, he turned to the old man. "Well?"

"We ran out of PVC fence posts with no more'n fifteen, twenty feet left to go across the back of the property."

"You left barbed wire?"

"It was tight and new," Able said. "Grown full of wild roses and poison ivy. Wasn't going anywhere. Lately, we've been busy working up the arenas. We figured the horses would stay away from that area until we got around to finishing it. Needed the arenas first."

"*You* figured," the old man whispered.

"We were planning on getting to it next week sometime."

Vince was doing that red-faced, hard-eyed thing again. Anne had kept him from cussing out the lady at the nursing home. She hoped she'd be able to do the same thing with Able. In this case, however, Vince had more reason to lose his temper—a horse was hurt, and it was a human being's fault.

She caught the old jockey's eye. He gave her a tiny nod. He could tell how close Vince was to exploding.

"You'll be lucky if your horse heals sound," Vince said in a deceptively quiet voice. As though he couldn't look at Able any longer, he turned to the old man. "Name?"

"Jimmy."

"Okay, Jimmy. He's going to need heavy antibiotics for at least ten days. Then we'll see if he needs another go-around. I'll leave you enough medication, and I'll be back tomorrow. I've sutured the skin tears inside and trimmed off the necrotic edges, but you'll have to let it heal from the inside out. Flush it with cold water every two hours, then flush it again with antiseptic solution."

"Stall rest?"

"Keep his stall extra clean. Pick out the manure as needed and add clean shavings. Hand walk every couple of hours. Take his temperature when you give him his antibiotics. If his temperature goes up, or if he shows any signs of colic, call me at the clinic. Don't wait and hope it gets better. Give him some analgesic for the pain and try to keep him on his feet. Ought to know something in forty-eight hours."

"Yessir. I'll get him through it if he can be *got*." The old man had not taken his eyes off Vince. Now he spared a small smile for Anne. "Thank you, ma'am, Dr. Vince."

Vince turned to walk out without saying a word to Able.

"Vince," Anne called after him, "would you load Tom? His lead line is hanging on the gatepost by the paddock he's in. I'll be right after you."

No doubt Able felt Vince had treated him like some kind of criminal. In Vince's eyes, he was. Although she agreed with Vince, she needed to pour some heavy oil on troubled waters if the clinic intended to keep Able as a client. Nobody liked to lose new clients. His horse needed Vince even if Able didn't.

"You know horses always figure out ways to get into trouble, Mr. Able. You're so lucky to have an experienced man like Jimmy caring for him. I know he'll do his best."

"Yeah, okay, right." His head came up. "That blasted barbed wire's not my fault. I ought to fire the whole lot of 'em."

"No, you shouldn't. You'd have to train a whole new crew. Jimmy is a blessing. You'll finish that new fence first thing tomorrow, won't you?"

He answered her with a grudging nod and went back into the barn.

She ran to the van. Vince had already loaded Tom and was revving the engine as he waited for her.

Before she'd buckled her seat belt he said, "What'd you say to that numbskull Able?"

"That I felt certain he'd replace the fence tomorrow and how lucky he was to have Jimmy."

"Not what a tyrant I am?"

"He got that on his own. I was afraid you were going to deck him, and I'd have to bail you out of the Williamston County jail on an assault charge."

"I considered it. Scared if I got started I wouldn't stop."

"You've had two close calls today, Vince. You kept your temper both times. Congratulations. I know how much you hate people who hurt animals through sheer stupidity, but all that does is upset you. Why don't you try turning something like this into a teachable moment? Some good might come out of it. Who knows?"

Ten minutes later Vince parked the van at Martin's. He and Anne unloaded Tom and walked him down to his paddock, where the other horses waited at the gate.

Anne removed Tom's sneakers. They were dirty, but they were washable. Vince removed Tom's halter and turned him loose with the rest of his herd.

"Here's your wandering boy child," Anne said. "Home safe."

They stood side by side as Anne latched the gate. "You, Doctor, stink."

"Comment on my competence or my odor?"

"Definitely odor."

"Can I borrow your shower again? How about driving into the café after we're clean?

That carrot cake was a long time back. I'm hungry."

"I really don't want to drive into town, but I have the makings for a killer Western omelet. It's one of the few things I can cook. My big sister, Elaine, is the gourmet cook. I wear the badge of the horse show rider, the cold cheeseburger."

"I need to get another change of clothes from my van, and I should tell Victoria about Tom's triumph."

"And Able's wounded horse. I should be clean and beating eggs by the time you finish with Victoria. I'll leave the front door open. You know where everything is in the shower."

AFTER DEBRIEFING VICTORIA and gathering fresh clothes and boots from his truck, Vince started down the path to Anne's cottage. For Tom's visit, he'd put on pressed chinos and a starched shirt. Both were now caked with blood and probably unsalvageable. He might have to start leaving a couple of extra sets in the tack room.

Behind the open curtains, Vince saw Anne, her hair still damp from her shower, standing at the kitchen counter, beating eggs for the omelets.

When he had looked into Seth's lighted windows, he'd envied the man his warm, glowing home. Envied him the beautiful wife waiting for his kiss, the child cuddled against him.

In the event he did marry at some point, he'd come home bloody, dirty and late to a cold wife, a cold stove and a screaming child who wanted no part of him. He had no frame of reference on how to build a happy family. What did it even look like? Growing up as he did, all he knew was anger, chaos. Disruption. His father talked about wanting peace and harmony, but every time harmony reared its head, Thor Peterson poked it until it withdrew and left only recrimination and hard feelings.

This afternoon had been a small triumph for Anne's training, but it drove home to Vince how much like his father he was becoming. Irascible, impatient, annoyed with the smallest infraction.

His father's first rule was, "Do as I say and be quick about it. Never mind what I do." For as long as Vince could remember, he'd always been on edge around his father. He never knew what word or action would set the old man off. His sons came in for the worst of it, but he could tear a strip off his employees as well.

No child should have to grow up under those conditions. Whenever his father brought home a new wife, Vince assumed she was temporary. He never expected any of the wives to love him, so he never took the chance of loving them.

As the middle child, he'd been pretty much ignored anyway. He'd been able to fly under the family radar a good bit of the time, read his books, work with the farm animals and periodically fight with his brothers. Josh, as the eldest, had the toughest time. Cody, the youngest, never seemed to do much wrong in his father's eyes. For one thing, he loved cows.

Vince opened the door of Anne's cottage and heard her in the kitchen humming an old folk song. He recognized that's what it was, but couldn't recall the words. Probably something about a tragic love affair. They usually were.

He slipped past her and into the shower. How easy would it be to finish that omelet and slide into her arms?

Too darned hard, as a matter of fact. Once he held her, he was afraid he'd never be able to let her go.

So he must never hold her in the first place.

CHAPTER SEVENTEEN

"Looks great, smells great," Vince said as he sat down at the small kitchen table that served as Anne's dining table. He tasted a forkful of his outsize omelet. "Most important, tastes great. If this is what you call not being able to cook as well as your sister, she must have a dozen Michelin stars."

"Elaine cooks fancy. She reads gourmet magazines and actually makes the recipes turn out looking like the ones in the photos. Doesn't hurt that she and Roger, her husband, had the kitchen updated after Daddy sold them our old house. Elaine believes that entertaining important people is the path to making Roger important."

"Is it working?"

"Seems to be. He's made partner in his law firm. Not named partner yet. He's not printed on his firm's letterhead, but Elaine thinks her committee work and inviting people with influence to dinner parties will put Roger over the top." She buttered an English muffin, poured honey on it and took a bite. After a minute, she said, "Now that she's gotten pregnant, either she'll slow down, dump her committees and morph into the perfect mother, or she'll double her efforts to get Roger's name on that letterhead."

He took a second muffin and followed Anne's lead with butter and honey. "What's your best guess?"

"No clue. I have never understood my sister and she doesn't understand me. Other people's opinions matter terribly to her."

"Not to you?"

"I want to be thought of as honest and competent. I don't sweat the small stuff."

Vince put down his muffin and shook his head. "You sure sweat the competence part. Whenever you think I'm stepping on your toes you launch a preemptive strike."

"You grew up on a farm. I grew up in the city. Even my father thought the horses were a phase I'd grow out of. For him, people ride horses as a hobby, not as a career. And I do respect your ability as a veterinarian."

"In public. When nobody's around, not so much."

"You can be downright arrogant. If you

don't stop snarling at clients, you won't have them long. Poor Mr. Able. I was afraid you were going to deck him. That would not make Barbara happy."

He set his fork on his plate. "When people do stupid things that put animals in danger, they *should* be snarled at."

They glared at one another across the table. After a long moment, both took a deep breath.

"Sorry," Anne said.

"Yeah. You're right. Whenever I start to lose my temper I hear my father's angry voice come out of my own mouth. Thanks for helping me shut him up. We had a successful day. How about we change the subject. How 'bout those Bears?"

She burst out laughing. "I presume you're referring to a team. My answer to your question is who are the Bears?"

"This fall I'll show you. Assuming Barbara hasn't fired me for running off her clients."

"She tells Victoria that you are a godsend and a superhero. She's just scared you'll heed your family's call and move back home to Mississippi."

"No. Not now, not ever. Thanks for dinner, but I need to get home. I have an early day tomorrow."

"You want some coffee? Or a brandy? After the day you've had, I think you deserve it."

He shook his head and started to get up.

She stopped him. "Okay, what is it with you and your family, *Doctor*? They put you through vet school…"

He rinsed his empty plate and placed it in the dishwasher.

"Where's that brandy?"

She pointed to the cabinet over the sink. "The snifters are right beside it."

He poured himself a splash, leaned back against the kitchen counter and took a sip. "Good stuff."

He didn't ask if Anne wanted some, too.

"First off, I paid for vet school," he said. "My father refused to give me a dime unless I promised to come back afterwards to be the farm's exclusive veterinarian. I inherited some money from my grandmother about that time and made some lucky investments, but I still didn't have enough. I worked two jobs, and spent my first summer after college breaking horses in Wyoming."

"Only one summer? Why didn't you go back the next year?"

"There were—problems."

"VICTORIA SAID YOU have two brothers. Older or younger?"

Now that he had opened up a little about his family, she planned to learn as much as she could before he shut down again.

"One of each. My younger brother, Cody, runs the cattle operation. Man's born to raise cattle. Loves them. My older brother, Joshua, is a CPA and handles the farm finances with constant interference from my father. They each have a house on the family compound built for them by my father as a bribe to keep them close. Like 24/7 close."

"He didn't offer to do the same for you?"

"Sure he did. A house, a clinic and marriage to the girl he'd picked out for me. He's never forgiven me for saying no to all three."

"WHAT WAS WRONG with the girl?" The moment the words left her mouth, Anne could have bitten her tongue. Talk about a Freudian slip. She got out another snifter and poured herself a tiny puddle of brandy. The small sip she took burned all the way down.

"Nothing is wrong with Cheryl," Vince said. "Her family lives across the road from us. We've been friends since kindergarten. I love her like a sister. Couldn't see myself ever loving her like a wife."

"Oh."

"Daddy doesn't give up easily. Nicki, my brother Cody's wife, just emailed me that Cheryl announced her engagement to an internist from Hattiesburg." He chortled. "Bet Daddy's working on ways to break them up before the ceremony. Man never gives up on what he wants whether it's good for other people or not."

"You talk as though your daddy was some sort of monster."

Vince finished his brandy and poured himself another.

Anne didn't say anything, but if he finished it, she intended to take his van keys away. He could sleep in Becca's room or on the couch. As tired as he was, she suspected he wasn't conscious that he was drinking more than his one beer.

He set the snifter on the kitchen counter. "He's not a monster. He's the product of a long line of patriarchs who believed in ruling their roosts. My grandfather was as big as me and my brothers—bigger than my father. My grandmother once told me that if he hadn't died young in a tractor accident she'd either have left him or killed him, and she'd have preferred killing."

"Wow."

"She never admitted he beat her, but I think he did. That's one thing Daddy never did. He can be mean as a snake. You think my temper is bad? Daddy makes me look like a day-old kitten. As mad as he gets at us, he has never raised a hand to any of us, not even when his marriages were on the rocks and he was battling his wives for custody. I think it's because he saw my grandfather hit my grandmother."

"Psychological abuse can be almost as bad," Anne said. She had firsthand experience with Robert before she kicked him out of her life.

"When we were growing up, Gran stood between us and Daddy as much as she could. She gave me the strength to run away from home." He shrugged. "And the money. It's easier to have principles when you're not looking starvation in the face. I always intended to be a vet. I'd have made it happen, but it might have taken me years." He closed his eyes momentarily and yawned. "I shouldn't have had that second brandy. I don't drink much as a general rule, and I'm tired. What kind of brandy was that?"

"French. I should have stopped you. I don't think you should try to drive home."

"Just feed me a couple of cups of coffee. I'll be fine."

"Fine does not pass breathalyzer tests. Take Becca's room. The sheets are clean."

"I can't…"

"Sure you can. I'm a horse show person, remember. When I was showing Trust Fund regularly, I never knew who I'd find sleeping in my guest room or on my living room floor whenever there was a horse show in the area."

"What will Victoria think?"

"That it's none of her business."

ANNE FOUND HIS note beside the kitchen telephone when she came in to start the morning coffee.

Thanks, it said. *You make a great omelet. I owe you dinner.*

She'd collect, too. She looked out her front window. There was no vet van in the parking lot. Six thirty in the morning, and he was already on the road. Away from her. Away from the revelations about his family.

Her upbringing had been so different from his. Her college professor father seldom so much as raised his voice to her and Elaine.

Her mother never did. They'd adored one another. When her mother died, it darned near killed all of them.

Anne remembered her mother as perfect. She wasn't, of course, but when she got sick, she suffered with grace. Losing her nearly killed all three of them. Her father practically disintegrated.

But his marriage had proven to him that lifelong love existed, that families could be happy most of the time, that they generally supported one another and apologized when they disagreed. When Barbara Carew came into his life, he was primed to believe that he could love again, because he knew what love felt like and had instilled in his daughters the same faith he had in love and fidelity.

Eventually, Barbara had come around to his way of thinking.

Anne supposed that was why she herself had never married the men who wanted her as a wife. What she felt for them was not deep enough to last a lifetime. She would marry for lifelong love or not at all.

Now that Robert was out of her life, it looked like not at all.

She grumbled while she stripped the sheets

and remade Becca's bed, tidied her room and bathroom, then did the same with her own.

Becca was coming for the weekend. Anne prayed that in the time she'd been gone, the teenager had reconnected with school and horse friends and had a couple of doting young men panting after her.

She'd keep Becca occupied, practicing old behaviors with the minis and learning new ones. They'd take trips to shops, with the horses, find stairs and escalators to attempt, confirm the signals that the mini needed a bathroom break. They'd harness Molly and Grumpy to the carriage, and start getting Harriet used to harness. Plenty to do without Vince.

If would be helpful if Calvin and Darrell got crushes on Becca. Even better if she were smitten with them.

Anne dressed for the day in jeans and paddock boots. No sense in pulling on britches and tall boots for work sessions in the heat. She fixed herself a glass of iced tea and poured her thermos full, toasted a biscuit in the microwave and ate it as she strolled down to the barn.

Walking into a barn where contented horses munched good oats and sweet hay always im-

proved her mood. One thing about horses—
they had no hidden agendas. Almost everyone
else she knew, including Vince, did. She called
Trusty out of his paddock and gave him a good
groom and a handful of treats. "Maybe we can
take a trail ride today," she said as she caressed
his neck. "If not, then tomorrow. I miss you,
big guy."

Trusty nickered. Anne was well aware that
affection ran second to more treats, so she gave
him a carrot, then turned him back out into his
pasture with the other full-size geldings.

BY SKIPPING LUNCH, Anne fit in a leisurely trail
ride with Trusty. She gave the minis a holiday.

Driven up by both her parents, Becca arrived Sunday afternoon. Her first greeting
was, "Where's Vince? Is he coming to swim?"

"Not here, not expected, on call," Anne said.

Becca whined, "I wanted Daddy to meet
him."

I'll bet you did, Anne thought.

Mr. Stout fitted his name. He looked sleek,
prosperous, and would be healthier if he
dropped fifty pounds.

"My wife, here, says I'm supposed to take
us all out to eat before we drive home at some-

thing called the café in Williamston," he said. He didn't look overly delighted at the prospect.

Not fancy enough for you, Anne thought.

"Becca says *wait* 'til you taste their cooking," Mrs. Stout told him.

Anne might be wrong about his being snobbish just because he hesitated about dining at the café.

"Daddy's scared of horses," Becca said. She punched her father's arm lightly. "Never been on a horse in his life."

He put his hand over his daughter's.

"Scared I'll ride again, aren't you, Daddy. He always tried to be there when I rode, and put up a big ole shelf in his den to show off my trophies, didn't you, Daddy?"

"I'll admit I didn't want her to come up here, Mrs. Martin, Miss MacDonald."

"She swears she won't get on a horse," Mrs. Stout said.

"But she's a teenager. They think they're immortal. I worry."

Anne could see the edge of anxiety in the way he looked at Becca. He loved his daddy's girl the way Anne's father loved her. That he could not have prevented Becca's accident by sheer force of will must gall him. He seemed like a man used to winning.

Becca wanted to show off the minis, so Victoria set out canvas captain's chairs beside the arena and Edward brought down a cooler of soft drinks.

"Watch what I can do," Becca said. "This is Tom Thumb. I haven't worked him for over a week, so we may be a little rusty."

"That is one small horse," Stout whispered to his wife. "Doesn't look very sturdy."

"Daddy! You'll hurt his feelings."

He rolled his eyes. "How can he possibly help you?"

Becca strode off with Tom close by her side. "Right now, I'm going to fake a fall, and you'll see." A few steps more and she began to list, then stumble sideways. Tom braced himself and stood still as she leaned her weight against his withers.

Richard Stout came to his feet and shouted Becca's name.

She laughed, righted herself, and gave Tom a minicarrot. "I'm fine, Daddy. But when I really start to fall, he does the exact same thing. He keeps me up until I get my balance back. One of the others, Harriet, is going to train to work with the blind. She's really young, and not perfect, but she'll eventually be great. Then

Molly and Grumpy are learning to pull teeny little carriages."

"Hmm… Well I'm glad it's working for you, sweetie." Richard said.

"Why don't we get ready to go to dinner," Victoria said. "Becca, help Anne feed and water. After we clean up we'll be ready to go to the café." She turned to Richard Stout. "It's ten miles away, so take your own car so you won't have to come back here on your way to Memphis. Becca, do you need a hand taking your stuff into Anne's?"

"Daddy can carry it, can't you, Daddy?" She slipped her arm through his. "Since I don't have my horse to save me, he can keep me from falling over."

ANNE KEPT A wary eye on the door of the café as they ate. On Sunday evening a great many customers came out to avoid cooking at home in the heat, so they had to wait ten minutes for a table. The café had only begun to open on Sunday evening a few months earlier but had been busy ever since.

One part of her hoped to see the silhouette of Vince's broad shoulders outside the café door. The other part hoped he wouldn't come. After last night's confessions, their working relationship might need a readjustment that she couldn't make in public.

Anne listened to the others with one ear. Every time the chime over the front door dinged she had to make a conscious effort not to check who was coming in. She would know the timbre of his voice even if she was too far away to understand his words.

If he was a grown man who could look after himself, she was a grown woman. Grown women did not check out doorways in public places for familiar faces or scan for familiar vans in the parking lot like a prepubescent girl with her first crush.

She'd never dived to answer the phone in hopes that a boy was on the line, or checked for a familiar male silhouette in whatever shadowy horse show barn Trusty was stabled in.

She did not feel empty when Robert flew off on business trips for a week at a time, or stay up half the night waiting for him to call her from whichever resort where the meeting was being held.

"I'm sorry?" she said. She had no idea what Richard Stout had asked her. Paying too much attention to her internal Vince-alarm and not enough to the other people at dinner.

"How come some of those minis look like

small horses and some look like that...Tom Thumb?"

Anne and Victoria launched into an explanation on dwarf genes in minis. They probably bored him and made him wish he'd never asked the question.

After dinner, they said goodbye to the Stouts and went to bed early after a blessedly Vince-free dinner. Who was she kidding? An evening without Vince did not seem like a blessing at all.

ANNE INTRODUCED BECCA to Calvin after breakfast on Monday. Becca treated him with complete disdain, and walked away from him with her nose in the air.

"Perfect," Victoria whispered. "She likes him."

"How can you tell?" Anne asked.

"Watch her hips. If that's not a strut, I don't know what is. Darrell will be coming after lunch to mow the paddocks close to the barn. Should be interesting with both of the boys flexing their muscles to impress her. By the way, I start with my summertime lesson schedule for the big horse owners tomorrow afternoon."

"We have to share the arena? You and the big horses, Becca and me with the minis?"

"You can work first thing in the mornings. Then I thought you might scout some places in Williamston that have stairs and escalators to practice on. Maybe a field trip to the grocery and the farmer's market. That way we won't get in one another's hair."

"We'll put Molly's harness on and take her on a trail ride in the carriage."

"You think she's ready?" Victoria asked.

"We won't know until we try. Once I'm certain Becca can handle the driving reins I may send her out with Calvin or Darrell."

She called to Becca, "Go get Grumpy and set him up on the lunge line in the arena before it gets too hot."

They worked flat-out all morning, then had sandwiches with Victoria. After lunch Becca went to take her couple of hours' siesta. She was much stronger, but she still had to replenish her energy.

While Becca slept, Anne drove to Sonny Prather's automobile dealership to ask where they could find stairs and escalators.

"Stairs, yeah. Escalators? Don't know. Williamston is a small town," Sonny said.

"We want to take the minis to the fairground," Anne told him. "I'd like to let them pull the carriage on the roads in town, but the way people drive, I'd be scared a car would run over them."

"Tell you what, Miss Anne. You let me know when you want to drive downtown. Do it early in the morning before the traffic gets bad, and I'll dispatch a sheriff's deputy in a squad car with his lights on to follow the cart, keep folks from riding up your backside."

"Mr. Mayor, is that legal?"

"Do it for funerals, don't we? You're training these squirts to help the disabled. Say, you don't want to drive in the parade on the Fourth of July, do you?"

Anne shook her head vigorously. "They don't react well to thunder and lightning yet. I doubt they'd take to firecrackers. By next year they should be desensitized. This year—not so much. Speaking of desensitization, when we get to it, can we borrow a couple of mounted policemen to teach us how to handle crowds?"

"Sure. I'll even furnish the crowd. Anybody gives you grief, you tell 'em to call me," Sonny said and patted her shoulder. "Don't nobody turn me down when I put on the charm."

She was backing out of her slot in Sonny's

parking lot when Vince's van pulled in behind her so that she couldn't leave.

Vince climbed out, left his door ajar and came to lean in the window of her truck.

"Been lookin' for you," he said. "Victoria said you'd be at Sonny's, so I took a chance. How about a piece of pie and some iced tea at the café. I haven't had lunch."

"It's three o'clock and I have."

"Then join me for some empty calories. My treat."

She knew she should get back. Instead, she shrugged and said, "I'll follow you."

Velma gave both of them extra-large pieces of Mississippi mud pie, a lusciously sinful combination of chocolate, eggs and whipped cream.

"If I can't zip my jeans after this, it's your fault," Anne told him.

"Lie down flat on your back, then zip," Velma said. "That's what I do."

"Becca's back?" Vince asked Anne.

"Last evening. We had dinner here. I thought you might show up."

"Nuh-uh. Emma and Seth fed me. I got to play with Diana. Child's gonna be walking before she's a year old the way she's going. Already trying to pull up."

"You actually like babies?"

"You don't?"

Anne waggled a hand. "I'm used to babies that outweigh me at birth and have four legs. Don't have much experience with human ones. Whenever I pick them up, they invariably squall until I hand them over to someone competent. I *was* the baby in my family. Now that my sister is pregnant, I suppose I'll have to learn to change diapers."

"That's the one thing I miss about not being home. My brothers have two sons apiece. Good kids. I don't get to see as much of them as I'd like. They're playing soccer these days. I've never seen them play. When Cody and Joshua and I were in school, we and everybody else we knew had basketball nets on their garages. We shot baskets every night after chores. Now it's all soccer."

"Big as you are, I assume you got a basketball scholarship?"

"Nope. The operative word is 'big.' Too bulky for basketball, not bulky enough for football. Too clumsy for soccer."

"You're not clumsy." Anne felt herself blush and changed the subject. Vince was one of the most graceful men she'd ever met, not just for his size. She was certain that was one of the reasons the animals trusted him. He didn't blunder all over them and hurt them.

"Why don't you drive down home and visit one weekend?" Anne asked. "Barbara would be happy to give you the time off. You never seem to take any as it is." She caught his wry expression and dropped her eyes. *Dumb, Anne.*

"Come with me."

"What? Why?"

"The other day you were talking about how much you missed your mother, plus Cody and Josh have been calling me asking me to visit. If you were along, maybe Daddy would behave himself. It's a nice drive and a pretty area. You say I should try to mend fences with my father. Having you along might keep me from killing him. I'd like to show you the place. Introduce you to the few sane members of my family. I guess that's a dumb idea. Forget I mentioned it."

Seeing he avoided her eyes, Anne was aware how much his invitation had cost him. "When?"

"I was thinking the Fourth of July weekend," he continued. "We always have a big barbecue to remind folks we're Yankees. Kind of a reunion for folks who're remotely kin to us. That's nearly everybody for fifty miles around.

Daddy stays pretty much on his good behavior, although there's no guarantee of that."

"Will there be fireworks? I adore fireworks. In Memphis I always went down to the big fireworks display down on the river, crowds and all."

"Daddy pays the local vendors to handle the fireworks. Safer than having one of us boys do it. One Fourth when Cody was about sixteen, he shot off a big rocket and started a grass fire in the pasture. That fire started a stampede that cost Daddy over a thousand bucks in fines. He's hired 'em done ever since."

"Good grief. Was anybody hurt? Did you lose any cows?"

"Nope, although we all figured Daddy would finally break his 'no spanking' rule." His shoulders began to shake with silent laughter. "There were too many people there to tell on him, but it was as close as I've ever seen him come to hitting one of us."

Neither of them mentioned her driving home with him again. She figured she'd heard the last of that. Staying in an unpleasant home with ill-tempered strangers sounded like a quick trip to hell.

So, he seemed to be actually considering making nice with his kinfolk. Introducing her to his family and showing her over his home place was a big step. An attempt to change the way he dealt with them. Had he actually been listening to her when she talked about her own family? Did he have the faintest inkling that his own relations with his father might get better?

She was developing feelings for this man, but what sort of feelings? Her entire body had never broken out in goose bumps before when a man walked into a room. And in ninety-degree heat, too. She knew instinctively that this invitation was some sort of turning point between them. What the heck. She could always turn right around and come back to Martins' the first time Thor Peterson got testy.

But only if she drove her own car.

"YOU WENT TO lunch with Vince," Becca said. "Why didn't you take me?"

"I just ran into him in town. How did you know I'd seen him?"

"You smell like you've been working with him."

"I went to see Sonny Prather about where we could take the minis. Tomorrow, we're going to load up Grumpy and Molly and go climb some stairs."

"Finally." She flounced back into the barn without the first sign of a stagger.

"Ms. MacDonald?"

"Yes, Calvin, and it's Anne."

"Yes, ma'am. Miss Victoria said me'n Darrell could swim in her pool if we hose off on the wash rack first. We brought trunks and our own towels."

"It's past quitting time. Hose away. I'm headed down to change."

"You think Becca'll come?"

"No idea, but a good bet."

The boys beat Anne into the pool. They gaped at Becca when she walked up in a minimal black bikini. She managed to splash them both when she dove in.

Anne slid in unobtrusively but soon realized that she was in the way of their horseplay. Cool enough, she climbed out, dried off and stretched out on the chaise longue beside Victoria, who handed her a diet soda without opening her eyes.

"I do believe it's working," Victoria whispered. "Listen to Becca—she sounds like one of those howler monkeys from South America."

"Which one will she pick? Darrell or Calvin?"

"At a guess, Calvin. He's prettier."

"And taller."

"So, what's going on between you and Vince?" Victoria said, still not opening her eyes.

"Nothing."

"I swore I wouldn't pry, but he stayed at the cottage the other night."

"In the other room because he was tired and inadvertently drank himself over the limit to drive. Not, I promise you, in my room. Definitely not in my bed."

"Actually, I figured, but I was dying to know for sure."

"You believe me?"

Victoria sat up and took off her sunglasses. "Of course, need you ask?" She lay back down and wriggled herself into a more comfortable position. "Were you tempted?"

Now Anne sat up. "Victoria, that is none of your business."

"You were. Bet he was, too."

Anne took a deep breath and the plunge. "He asked me to go home with him for the Fourth of July."

This time Victoria bounced all the way up to sitting. "He *what*?"

The three in the pool stopped their play and stared at Victoria.

"Go back to what you were doing," she

called to them, then turned to Anne. "I hope you said no. Why?"

"Why did he ask me? We'd been talking some about his relations with his father. All his family, actually. He said that if I go with him, they'd all have to mind their manners. They put on a big reunion with fireworks. I love fireworks."

"If you go with him, I'll bet you have more fireworks than you can handle. Anne, are you falling for this guy? Barbara said you were getting over a bad relationship. Vince is a complicated man, not into love. Certainly not into marriage. Not a good choice for a rebound."

"You can't rebound from what never was," Anne said. "I know Vince is not a keeper any more than a two-hundred-pound catfish is a keeper. He makes no secret of never wanting to marry. I want a husband and at least a couple of babies. I assume I'll like my own. That leaves Vince out. I respect his skills as a vet, and he's trying to learn not to snap at people. I enjoy his company. Anything wrong with that?"

"My goodness, you're in love with him."

"I most certainly am not."

"Are too. Listen, go to Mississippi with him for the Fourth of July, but make certain you drive down in your SUV, so you can run out if things go bad."

"I want to, but I'm not certain what kind of excuse I can come up with for not driving down with Vince."

"Your problem. We'll work out a signal on your cell phone. Call or text if you need to scram out of there. I'll call back demanding you come home because of some disaster or other. Heck, I'll come get you if I have to."

"If I drive myself down, I can drive myself back."

"Unless they take your keys or puncture your tires. Oh, I know I'm being melodramatic. I want you to know my offer stands in an emergency."

"Victoria, I will not be spending the weekend in Dracula's castle, and Vince's farm is a long drive away. So, you think I should go?"

"I think you should *not* go, no way, no how. But you're going, aren't you?"

CHAPTER EIGHTEEN

"NOT IF HE doesn't mention it again, I'm not," Anne said the next morning as she stared at her reflection in the bathroom mirror. "Your eyes look like they're sinking right out the back of your skull, woman, and as if you've been using bootblack as eyeliner. Not sleeping, are we? Tossing and turning? Do we go or do we stay? And how do I manage to drive my own truck?"

She'd have to decide before the end of June. She couldn't descend on his family out of the blue. She'd been invited to a party. Lots of people in the South drove long distances and stayed overnight for parties. No big deal. If she went, it would be to support Vince in his quest to better his relationship with his father. He wanted her for his wingman—woman. She could do that for a couple of days.

He liked his brothers, their sons, their wives and even his present stepmother. Anne could avoid the old man most of the time. If he behaved badly, she could leave.

Vince would hate that. She would be polite and courteous if it killed her. Hey, she might even make friends with Thor Peterson.

Probably not.

Vince said his family understood the old man well enough. They just didn't like him.

She really should judge for herself.

Was she crazy, or what?

She decided to tell him that evening that she would go with him for the Fourth.

Late in the afternoon, he did not stroll in from the parking lot with his bathing suit in his hand. He left the van running and the door open, jumped out and ran down the path.

Anne intercepted him. "Vince, what's wrong?"

He grabbed her arms and held her away from him. "I've got to go home. Daddy's been in an accident. He's in the hospital."

"Oh, Vince," Anne said.

Victoria and Edward ran up from the patio.

"We heard. How bad?" Edward asked.

Vince shook his head. "Don't know. Cody was freakin' out. He said Daddy's in surgery."

"What happened?" Victoria held his arm and swung him to face her.

"I don't know, but it's bad enough for Cody to tell me to come home. There's no airport close to fly into, so I'm driving down. I ought to make it before midnight. I didn't want to just call you from the road." He started back to his van.

"Should you be driving?" Anne asked as she ran beside him.

"I'm okay."

"I'll drive you."

He shook his head. "I know the road. I'll be faster."

"Call the minute you get there. Please." She hoped he heard the worry in her voice.

He started to climb in, then reached for her. "Say a prayer for the old coot. I'm sorry about all this. Listen, one thing... I love you."

He swung under the wheel. A moment later his tires kicked up gravel as he spun into the road outside the gate and disappeared over the hill.

Becca ran up from the pool. "Was that Vince? Where's he going? Did he forget his bathing suit or something?"

"He has to go home. His father's been hurt," Anne said. She clasped her hands in front of her to keep them from shaking. *Please don't let his father die. Please look after Vince.* She stared after the man she could no longer see. The man she loved.

Victoria came up behind her and put a hand

on Anne's shoulder. Anne covered it with her own. She whispered, "He said he loves me."

"Of course, he does," Victoria whispered back. "There's nothing we can do about this now. Go sit down. Becca and I will make sandwiches."

"Me?" Becca asked.

"You."

"I don't even know what's happened."

"I'll tell you in the kitchen. Edward, look after Anne. At least it's not raining. Makes the drive safer."

"Long drive down to his home place," Edward said. "Who knows what he'll find when he gets there."

"Surely somebody will call him to let him know what's going on."

"If there's time." Edward dropped his arm across Anne's shoulder.

Anne reached for Victoria's hand and held it hard. "I tried to tell him when I talked about my mother. We always think there's time to mend fences, make amends, let people know we love them. Sometimes there isn't."

ANNE HAD BEEN right as usual. Vince knew he probably shouldn't be behind the wheel of a motor vehicle in his emotional state. He set his cruise control at the speed limit so he wouldn't speed, turned on a country music station as loud as he could stand it and sang along when he knew the words. He didn't want to stop long enough to fill his gas tank and go to the bathroom, but he did. The place where he stopped carried iced coffee. He bought three large cups and headed back down the road.

He had told Anne he loved her. Where did that even come from? All he could figure was that he was so freaked that all the governors had slipped off his brain stem and let his emotions run wild.

He had wanted to bring her with him right now. She'd offered to do the driving, but he had no idea what he was getting into or even if his father would be alive by the time he arrived. He plugged his phone into the car jack so there was no chance he'd run out of battery power, but he didn't want to stop to call the hospital. He'd have to trust Cody or Joshua to call him if anything changed.

He had to keep his mind on the road, so he didn't wreck his van and add to everybody's problems. He'd never wanted another human being the way he wanted Anne right this minute, as if holding her against him would drain away all his pain.

Was this what love felt like? All he'd ever known was that love was impermanent, could not be trusted, didn't truly exist. At this moment he knew—not thought, but knew—that what he felt for Anne was as permanent as life itself.

Now, when it might already be too late, he admitted to himself that he still loved his father, whatever his flaws. He prayed he'd have a chance to tell him.

CHAPTER NINETEEN

"HE'S STILL ALIVE."

Anne had not allowed the phone to complete a single beep before she picked it up. "Vince. You got there safe." She checked the clock. "You must have flown down the road."

"Cruise control at the speed limit."

"What happened to him? How bad is it?"

"He's got a bad concussion, but they didn't have to open his skull. They're treating the brain swelling medically. His left fibula is broken, but it's a clean break. They say it should knit without pins. At his age, who knows? Bunch of cracked ribs. Cuts, scrapes and bruises."

"Have you seen him?"

"Not yet. He's in ICU. Unconscious."

"Have they induced a coma?"

"Shouldn't have to. The immediate concern is that he'll develop a blood clot. At his age, a stroke is a major possibility."

"But not so far?"

"Not so far. It could have been much worse."

"You still haven't said what happened."

"He's got a rusty old pickup he uses around the farm. He drove it out into the pasture to pick some bales of hay to bring into the barn."

"But isn't he in a wheelchair?"

"Only when he chooses to be waited on. Most of the time he just uses a cane. Sometimes not then. Big bales. They weigh over sixty pounds apiece. He's not supposed to handle them at all, much less alone, but he thinks he can do everything he could do at twenty. It looks as if he hit a flooded pothole on the side of a berm, skidded sideways in the mud. There's not a bit of tread on those old tires. No traction. The truck tipped over, threw him out and ran over his leg. Needless to say, he wasn't wearing a seat belt. Darned fool." He hesitated. "Look, about what I said…"

About loving her. Here came the retraction. Once he found his father was alive, she'd expected him to back away. The usual pattern in their relations all along—he'd tell her one important, personal thing, then step back to impersonal. This was, however, the most important thing he'd ever told her. She expected the words to be retracted or conveniently forgotten. "You were talking under pressure. I get it."

"No, you don't. No idea why I said it, but I meant it. Good night, call you tomorrow." He hung up before she could say good-night back.

What did she expect? When he spoke of love, was he speaking the same language she did, or was he simply reaching out for support, simple human warmth?

"I've MADE UP your old room," Vince's stepmother, Mary Alice, said as she hugged Vince in the visitors' waiting room at the small, local hospital where his father was being cared for. "I told Cody to tell you not to drive down. You're so busy, and it's such a long way to come when we're not certain how bad it is. Still, I'm so glad you came."

"Have you seen Daddy?" Vince asked her.

She dropped onto one of the plastic-covered hospital-green sofas. She was not that much older than Vince, but at the moment she looked every bit as old as his father. "Why, or why did he do it?" she asked.

Cody walked into the waiting room and held a plastic cup of coffee out to Mary Alice. "Hey, Vince. If I'd known you'd made it, I'd'a brought you some coffee, too."

The two men hugged and slapped one another on the back as though this was a casual meeting, then broke apart in haste and avoided one another's eyes.

"I told Daddy I'd move the darned hay bales for him from the run-in shed after I got back from driving the boys to soccer practice," Cody said. "He got mad, said I never did anything he wanted. Said he was the only one ever did anything around the place. Said I wasn't worth the air to blow me up and a bunch more. Like I'd never have a thin dime if he didn't keep me on his payroll.

"Shoot, Vince, you know how he gets. For once in my life, I told him I was not only gonna drive the boys to practice, I was gonna stay and watch them, and that we might stop for a milkshake on the way back. Then I hung up on him. It's all my fault. He was so mad he took that piece of junk truck and went out to the back pasture to do it on his own."

Mary Alice patted his arm. "Don't you feel one bit responsible. You could have moved those bales anytime in the next week. Not like you're running out of the hay already stacked in the barn."

"He wants what he wants when he wants

it," Vince said. "You did the right thing taking the boys."

"He wanted to feel put-upon," Mary Alice said. "Make you feel ashamed that you went off to play sports with your boys, when you ought to be helping your poor old father." She huffed.

"What if I killed him?" Cody wailed.

"You haven't killed him yet, boy," she snapped. "Don't let him play the guilt game with you. You probably saved his life. I didn't even think to see if that old truck was in the yard. If you hadn't spotted it on its side when you brought the boys home, he might still be lying out by the run-in shed bleeding all over creation. Now you go on home. No sense in all of us waiting. The boys need you."

"Nicki and Nell have all four of them at Joshua's house. They don't know what's happening except that their grampa is hurt. I need to stay. Joshua wanted to come, but I told him to look after the place."

"You aren't calling people about this, are you?" Mary Alice looked concerned.

"Well, Mary Alice, it's not like it's a secret," Cody said.

"It is unless you want the state of Mississippi from the governor on down calling and showing up expecting us to entertain them," she replied. "Your daddy is an important man. I've got the switchboard downstairs handling any calls except from family. Go home, Cody. Get some rest. Vince is here to take your place." Mary Alice pulled herself up to her five-foot-three and stared Cody down as though she topped his six-foot-four.

"Vince is tired, too," he grumbled.

"Not as tired as you," Vince said. "Go home, little brother. You have a family that needs you. I don't."

"We're your family," Mary Alice said. "'Until such time as you find you a decent woman and start making your own babies." She shook her finger at him. "And don't give me your usual nonsense about never getting married because we're all so hateful."

He chuckled and hugged her against him. "I never thought *you* were hateful, sweetheart."

"Oh, Vince, I don't want to lose him," she sobbed against him. "I still love the old fool, and I know he loves all of you. He just never figured out how to act like it."

Vince was finally allowed into the ICU for a glimpse of his father at two the following afternoon. He always thought of his daddy as a big man. Lying in the hospital bed amid all the beeps and lights and tubes, he looked as small as one of Cody's boys. Vince was surprised that his broken fibula wasn't elevated but was propped on pillows.

The cuts and scrapes didn't look much more serious than shaving cuts, but he had two beautiful black eyes and a gauze helmet that showed blood seepage along his left temple.

As he turned from the bed to go back out to the waiting room, Vince felt his father's fingers clutch his arm. He spun back to see the old man's eyes open and staring at him.

"Vince? Why the Sam Hill are you here? Am I dying?"

Vince felt the tears start. "Nope. Banged up pretty well, though."

His father's voice was surprisingly strong considering all the medication he was on. "Who hit me?"

"Did it all yourself with that old wreck of a truck. Fell over."

"Shoot, I remember. Cody refused to go load…"

Vince shook his head. "Nuh-uh. Not Cody's fault. Your fault. Don't even think about blaming Cody or I swear I'll break your other leg." He bent down and kissed his father's forehead. "Love you, Daddy."

"Now I know I'm dying." Thor yawned and slipped into sleep with a small snore.

As he walked back down to the waiting room, Vince considered calling Anne again. He longed to hear her voice, but she'd probably be out with the minis. When she saw his name on the caller ID, she'd be sure he was calling with bad news.

He wrapped the hospital blanket more securely around Mary Alice's thin shoulders. She had finally fallen asleep.

Why had Vince never allowed himself to love her? More to the point, why did she love his *father* after all his temper tantrums and poor treatment? Was she blessed or cursed with that lasting love? Would she have been better off if she'd left Thor as his own mother had left? As the other wives had. Did that make Mary Alice more admirable or more of a fool?

And if he loved Anne with that kind of constancy, what did that make him?

Especially since, so far as he could see, Anne didn't love him back.

How long would it be before he saw her again? For the first time in years, he considered what it would mean if he actually did move home. It was an appalling thought. His life was no longer here in Mississippi but in

Tennessee where his new-found love and his friends and his career were.

Whatever catharsis he had experienced over his father's bed, it did not include living with the man. He didn't make a bunch of money, but he'd devote every dime to providing expert caregivers for Thor as long as he needed them so he could continue to stay in Tennessee.

He lay down on another one of the couches in the shadows at the back of the waiting room. He was actually going on his second day without sleep. The couch was much too short for him.

He turned on his side and pulled his legs up, positioned the single thin pillow he had been given under his head and closed his eyes. He'd nap until another one of the family came to take over the vigil. He'd come to at least one decision. He'd considered what it would mean to move home, and he'd rejected the idea finally and completely.

What he could and would do was to get the family together and figure out how to retrain his father to act right to his family as Vince's grandmother would say. Vince included acting right to his friends, his employees, his clients and the whole human race. Horses could be retrained—look at little Molly. Why not irascible old patriarchs? The first step would be for the entire family to set boundaries. From here on, the old man would not be rewarded for bad behavior. When he acted like a jerk, no one should react. They would walk around, by or through him. It would require a miracle, but it was the only solution Vince could think of that did not require his moving back home.

That was not gonna happen.

If there was the slightest chance he could gain Anne's love, he would not inflict his father on her. The corollary was that he should not take the chance of inflicting himself on her either.

"THE GOVERNMENT DOES not allow people to stay in the hospital unless they are unconscious or recently missing a body part," Vince said over his cell phone. "They're sending Thor home today."

"But they can't!" Anne said. "How will your stepmother manage a man with a broken leg, not to mention cracked ribs and head trauma?"

"The doctor says the brain-swelling has subsided. You don't wrap broken ribs any longer unless they're threatening to poke through your lungs. His are not displaced. He's supposed to refrain from coughing and…"

Anne broke out laughing. "I'll bet he doesn't want to cough. I've broken ribs falling off horses. They ache to this day when the weather's bad. Coughing with a fresh break makes you want a big fat shot of morphine. Which you don't get, by the way."

"Mary Alice and Thor added a master suite twenty years ago on the main floor of our house in case either of them became disabled. No stairs except from the front porch. Cody's crew have already built a ramp to take care of that. Thor's going to have to actually use his wheelchair full-time and not as a way to get attention. There's already one of those walk-in baths in their suite."

"Your step-mother cannot handle him alone. What if he falls?"

"The boys will help, and I'm staying until after the Fourth picnic. Daddy's doing amazingly well, all things considered. He's already starting to get his snarl back, but we're not letting him get away with it. This whole episode frightened him badly. I intend to keep him aware of his own mortality, until he starts being polite to us."

"Are you hiring a care-giver?"

"Probably part-time, until he can balance safely on a walker." Vince chortled. "He hates it like poison. He'd rather use a pair of canes, but he drops them. What he really needs is his own Tom Thumb to stabilize his balance."

Over dinner at the café with Edward and Victoria, Anne told them about Vince's update.

"Why not give him one?" Victoria asked.

"One what?"

"Tom Thumb. This would be the perfect graduation exam. He'd be doing the job we've trained him for with a person with an actual disability. Not like Becca, who can make allowances and correct herself."

Edward took his wife's hand, and said quietly, "Hon, if he can't correct himself, what happens if he falls and Tom can't keep him up? You'd have a real liability problem there, not to mention the possibility that you'd cause more harm."

Victoria waved him away. "This is still an exploratory program. We never provide guarantees of success. Besides, Anne will be right there the whole time…"

Anne choked on her iced tea. "Anne will do what? Vince says that old man was a not-so-holy terror before he was hurt. He's probably like a bear with a sore paw now that he's an invalid. I have duties here. Harriet and Big Mary are turning into a precious driving pair. You've seen how cute they look together. You promised we'd enter them in the driving classes at the Williamston horse show. Not much time."

"More than a month away," Victoria said. "Look, if Vince agrees, you can drive Tom down one day next week. Stay four or five days, and if things work out, you leave Tom and drive yourself home."

"Leave Tom for how long?"

"However long Thor's going to need him."

"No way!" Anne pushed her chair away from the table.

"Anne," Victoria said in a reasonable tone. "We are training companion animals. Sooner or later they're all going to people who need them."

Anne shook her head vigorously. "Not Tom. He's my practice horse. The one I learn on. Besides, Victoria, from the first time I saw him he's been my angel. He might not mind working for another owner, but I sure would. And definitely not for an old devil like Thor Peterson."

The other patrons and staff gaped at her.

"Anne, you're shouting," Victoria whispered.

"Honey," Edward said. "Listen to Anne."

"But…"

"Victoria," Anne said. "I love Tom and he

loves me. Don't expect me to let him go to a man who treats his own family like dirt. Who's to say how he'd treat Tom?" She shoved her chair away from the table and ran out, leaving Victoria openmouthed.

"You'd probably have caused Anne less pain if you'd cut her heart out," Edward said. "Let's go home. You need to fix this."

AFTER VICTORIA AND Edward came home from the café and she sent him off to watch television, Victoria walked down the hill to the cottage, which was never locked, came in and found Anne lying facedown across her bed, sobbing.

"I am so sorry," Victoria said. "I never meant to treat you and Tom as though you two don't matter."

Anne swung around and wiped her fingers over her cheeks. She'd obviously been crying since she came back to the cottage.

"When Becca sent Aeolus away," Anne said. "It liked to have killed her. She still can't mention his name without tearing up. She loved— no, make that loves—Aeolus. When you talked about sending Tom away so casually, it hurt. Tom is little, but in every way that matters, he's a giant and he's mine. Except tonight I realized he's not. He's yours and you can send him away whenever you want to."

"Where's your purse?" Victoria asked.

"On the desk. Why?"

Victoria went to the desk, opened Anne's purse, pulled out her wallet, took a bill out and sat back down on the bed. "Here," she said and handed Anne a dollar. "Give that to me."

Puzzled, Anne handed it over. "What's this for?"

"You just bought Tom Thumb for the exorbitant price of one dollar."

Anne threw her arms around Victoria. "Thank you thank you thank you."

"In order to pay his board bills and his feed bills…"

"I'll pay them if I have to go back to tending bar every night after I work the horses."

Victoria shook her head. "Not to worry. Tom is still an employee of Martin's Minis and has a free ride so long as we continue to use him as a consultant. Agreed? We don't have to think about actually breaking even on this program for another four and a half months. By that time Edward should have finished setting up the trust fund for the training expenses so that we can accept tax-free donations and insurance payments and grants. Right now the clients' horses are paying the bills for the minis. I should have gone through all this before."

"As just an employee, I didn't need to know. I figured you'd tell me when and if I did. I knew I was hired for six months, but not how you planned to pay me."

"Trust me. We are solvent and should continue to be. And you do need to know all this stuff. Obviously, I don't intend to let you go after six months."

Anne shoved off the bed.

"Where are you going?" Victoria asked. "It's pitch-black out there."

"I am going to find my newly acquired horse and give him a treat. Oh, and let's not tell anyone about this. They might treat him differently."

"So might you," Victoria said, then shook her head. "Nah."

"VINCE WANTS TO stay until after the Fourth of July," Barbara Carew said. "I gave him the time. His family needs him, but I wish he'd hurry back. I'm doing both our jobs. I'm afraid they'll convince him to stay there." She set the small hoof she'd been trimming back on the ground. "I took a little extra off Harriet's heels this time. Vince and I agreed it might give her a slightly longer stride like Molly's. If they're going to be in draft as a pair, their strides need to match. I want to handle it myself to see if that does the trick. If it works, the farrier can do it next time."

"Thanks," Anne said as she took Harriet back to the pasture. "That's your last job today. Come on up to the patio for a soda with me and Victoria."

"Don't need to ask twice."

As they walked over from the paddock, her voice studiedly casual, Barbara asked, "How are things going for Vince down home? He pretty much leaves me messages. I think he's avoiding me."

Anne gave her a situation report on Vince's father as she knew it. "Vince calls most evenings to give me an update."

"And with you two?"

"What 'you two'? He's there and busy. I'm here and busy. He might as well be on temporary duty with the military in Alaska."

"Why not visit him for the holiday? He did ask you."

"Vince and I have discussed it over and over again. At this point I've about decided I'm taking Tom to see if Vince's father can use a helper horse."

"Is that wise?" Victoria asked.

"For Tom or me?" She handed Barbara a diet soda from the cooler. Victoria already had one.

"Actually," Victoria said, "I was thinking about you, but it might be tough on Tom as well. He's not used to being on duty all the time. And with a difficult man."

"No way would I leave Tom there when I leave, but Vince and I agreed it would be a valuable short-term test of his ability to work with a stranger with different needs from Becca's. Have you ever met Mr. Peterson?"

Victoria gave a theatrical shudder. "Once. At a cattle show at the Williamston County Fair years ago. His cattle took home a passel of blue ribbons, but he wanted all of them in the breeds he raised. He is tall, gray-haired, very good-looking and in great shape for a man his age. Edward thought he was charming. I took one look at the way he glared at the officials and decided I didn't like him. Later on, I saw him tear a strip off another of the judges when he didn't win best overall bull. I decided then I *really* didn't like him."

"If you do go," Barbara asked, "When are you leaving?"

"The Petersons have a big party on the Fourth of July. They call it a family reunion, but Vince says everybody for miles around turns up for barbecue. I assumed they'd cancel it because of Mr. Peterson's accident, but Vince says not. I'll drive down the afternoon of the second and come home the fifth. I'll bring Tom back with me. I assume Vince will come then or shortly afterwards, but we haven't talked about it. I can help with preparations and cleanup afterwards. Vince says there's a pony paddock and stall Tom can use while Mr. Peterson's trying Tom to see if he can work with a VSE. Mr. Peterson's old mare is in the next stall with his own paddock, so Tom will have company."

"You've got it all worked out."

"We have the logistics worked out. The family dynamics, not so much."

"This is just an excuse to see Vince."

Anne drew herself up. "Not at all. Well, maybe. He said some things… I have to find out whether he meant them and what they mean to me. To us. If there is an *us* now or at some point in the future."

"How does this factor in to Vince's assertion that he's never getting married?"

"That's one of the reasons I'm driving to Mississippi."

Tom spent most of the drive down into Mississippi with his head over Anne's shoulder so he could look out the window of the big SUV. He did take a two-hour nap and snored softly. Since the drive was so long, Anne had brought his piddle pad, but she was hesitant to get Tom out to use it even at one of the roadside parks. Several owners let their dogs out to run free. A big dog might view the little horse as prey. Tom might bolt into the road.

When the dog area was finally empty, Anne laid down Tom's piddle pad under a shady pine, said, "Go now," waited while he did his business, then cleaned up after him and walked back toward the truck.

"Look, baby," a woman's voice called out. She was part of a group of four adults and one little girl who sat at one of the picnic tables eating fried chicken. "It's a little bitty horse!"

"That ain't no horse," said the man beside her. "It's some kind'a funny lookin' dog. Zerleen, don't you run over there and get bit and have to take them rabies shots. Zerleen!"

Anne held up a hand to stop the charging child. Her mother was hot-footing after her. The father had not moved except to open another can of soda.

"He's a minihorse," Anne said to the child.

"Can I pet him?"

Anne held on to the halter and line, while Tom did his eye blinking thing. The enraptured child petted him softly and screamed when her mother tried to pull her away.

Finally, Anne and Tom made it safely back into the car. She fed Tom a couple of baby carrots before she started her engine and pulled back onto the road.

"Happy now?" she asked. Tom hummed at her.

By the time she found her way along the back roads that led to the Peterson cattle farm, she felt grubby and decided she smelled like Tom. What would happen when she opened the door of the car and climbed out? Would she and Vince rush into one another's arms?

Probably not. Knowing Vince, he'd stand as far off as he could and ask why she was so late arriving. Definitely no public displays of affection.

She found the sign for the Petersons' farm beside a pair of outsize and elaborately carved wrought-iron gates that stood open either side of a long gravel road flanked by magnolias. She couldn't see a house through the thick trees.

Halfway up the drive, the magnolia alley

opened onto a manicured green lawn fronting a white house with columns and shiny black shutters.

"Whew," she said. "Tom, I do believe we have landed in Tara."

As she drove closer she realized that the house was much simpler than her initial impression. It was a two-story white farmhouse with a broad front porch lined with rocking chairs and tall ferns in pots. Probably no more than fifty or sixty years old. Not Tara.

Across the lawn and separated from the yard by dark red crepe myrtle trees sat several big metal barns. Past the barns stretched pasture that seemed to go on forever. She did not see the first sign of a cow. Or a dog, for that matter. They must have dogs to move the cattle. She'd have to keep a close hold on Tom. If a strange dog tried to herd him, he'd probably get one of Tom's sharp little hooves across his nose. Taking a chunk out of one of the owner's cattle dogs was not the best way to make friends with her host.

She parked at the foot of the front porch. She could move the car later if there was a designated space for guests. The second set of keys in her luggage guaranteed she would not be trapped if she mislaid the first set, which she frequently did.

"Okay, Tom, my man, here we go," she said and slid out from behind the wheel.

Vince came out of the front door, jumped off the porch steps, ran to her, caught her in his arms and kissed her.

What a kiss! It was as though he'd been saving up every atom of missing her to expend in this first mind-blowing kiss.

If this was what Mississippi did to him, she was all for it. For the short term, at any rate.

Finally, he released her, stepped back and said formally, "Welcome to Peterson Farms." He moved aside. "Mary Alice, this is Anne MacDonald, Victoria Martin's trainer. Anne, Mary Alice Peterson, my stepmother."

Mary Alice's small, soft hand was engulfed by Anne's large, rough one. Anne was glad she'd done her nails. Not a fancy salon manicure, but the polish wasn't chipped yet.

"Now, I must meet the mini," Mary Alice said.

Tom agreed. From his position halfway over the front seat, he was humming in anticipation of exploring new grass and loving on new people.

"He is adorable." Mary Alice scratched his withers.

Not new to horses, Anne observed.

"I assume you want to settle him before you settle yourself. Animal people always do."

"Yes, ma'am, if it's all right. He's had a long ride."

"So have you, and it's Mary Alice." She slipped her hand under Anne's elbow. "Vince, please look after Tom, then you can take Anne's things upstairs to her room."

Vince winked at Anne. "Yes, Mary Alice."

ANNE'S ROOM WAS large and airy with French doors onto a balcony that overlooked the barns at the side of the house rather than the lawn at the front. The canopied bed was tall enough to require a set of stairs to climb into it. The smell from the barns was of clean cattle, an odor Anne wasn't as familiar with as essence of horse. She kind of liked it.

Dinner was served at a round oak table that might have come down from Minnesota with the original Yankee carpetbagger ancestor. She was surprised that in a house this big she had seen no servants.

Nor had she seen or heard from Thor Peterson. There were only three places at the table, so apparently he wasn't joining them, but must still be taking a tray in his room.

"Do you have plenty of help?" Anne asked after they were seated at the table and relishing the pork tenderloin, hot biscuits and fresh vegetables. "Surely you don't try to handle your husband by yourself."

"Thor loathes having strangers in the house. I do have one of those quick cleaning teams once a week. I guess I'll have to hire somebody to look after Thor, even if he does put up an almighty fuss. You're right. I can't handle him alone. The boys help, but Cody and Joshua work all the time as it is. Either Cody's Nicki or Joshua's Nell comes over, so I can run to the grocery and do my errands. It's not that easy to find somebody out here in the country."

"I've already got some feelers out to find somebody for you, Mary Alice," Vince said. "I still know people who know people. While I'm down here, I'll help handle Daddy. You aren't cooking anything for the barbecue, are you?"

Mary Alice sighed. "The boys are doing the barbecue like always and we're having the rest catered. After Thor's accident I wanted to cancel, but the local politicians see it as the highlight of the campaign season. It's a chance to shake hands with all the cousins they haven't seen since last year's reunion. Everybody's a cousin when they're campaigning for reelection. I had to go ahead with it."

Mary Alice caught Anne's eye. "Thor is still sleeping a great deal of the time. I'm pouring protein shakes down him, but as Vince has no doubt told you, Thor can be difficult. I'm hoping that the minihorse will stimulate his interest in life. At the moment, he is afraid of falling, but he says the walker makes him feel old. I tell him he *is* old, so not to sweat it."

"Let's hope a horse like Tom will get him on his feet," Anne said.

"Speaking of Thor, I need to check on him." Mary Alice excused herself and disappeared toward the back of the house.

Vince stiffened and followed her with his eyes.

When they were finished eating, Vince bussed the table while Anne stacked the dishwasher. He seemed to be listening.

A baritone voice boomed from the back of the house. "I said get me up *now*. I am not meeting any lady guest in my own house in pajamas and no robe. Move, woman."

"Uh-oh," whispered Vince. "Don't *you* move. I'll see to him."

So that was Thor Peterson. He didn't sound sick.

Vince's rumble covered Thor's baritone, but

Anne couldn't understand most of the words because he was keeping his voice low and calm. Then she heard him say quietly, but with command, "You call yourself a gentleman. Act like one."

When he appeared back in the kitchen, he said, "Come on, let's get out of here. I'll drive you over the farm."

"But your stepmother's getting your father up…"

"Go," Mary Alice said from the hall. "He's already asleep again, and I will be soon. I need all the sleep I can get these days."

Vince led Anne out the back door and across the parking lot to a green four-door Mini-Cooper. "Mary Alice's car. Daddy's new truck is in the garage with my van. She says if she drives a small car, Daddy will stay out of it."

"Does he always speak to her that way?"

"Not generally while I'm here. I've told her not to put up with it. She's trying. She didn't hop to get the bathrobe he asked for. She used to."

The farm was large and lush, even in the summer. There were cattle guards across the farm roads, so they didn't have to climb out to open gates. The cows wandered up to check them out, then wandered off again. "I like those red ones," Anne said.

"Santa Gertrudis." He pointed across her. "The black ones are Angus. Don't worry. There's not going to be a pop quiz." At the back of the pasture stood a large metal storage shed. "This is where the accident happened. Those are his skid marks. He may never be safe to drive again, but if he had a pair of VSEs to pull a cart around the property, he might feel less imprisoned."

"Tom hasn't driven much, and never in a pair."

Vince stopped the car, leaned on the steering wheel and stared through the windshield at the avalanche of stars above them. "He also needs the same help Becca needs keeping his balance. He's a big man. A mini may not be strong enough to keep him on his feet. We'll have to see."

"Can he be trusted to keep his temper?"

"He generally saves his tantrums for his family."

VINCE TOOK HIS right hand off the steering wheel, leaned across and kissed her. "I've missed you."

"You haven't had time."

"Want to bet? I've got to go back to Williamston soon. Barbara's losing patience with me. It's not fair to leave her without help."

"You do plan to come back to Williamston, don't you?"

He leaned against the seat, closed his eyes and ran his hand down his face. "More than ever. Mary Alice understands."

"Have you told your father?"

"I'm dreading it. We haven't spoken about my staying, but from time to time I catch him looking at me and gloating as though he thinks he's won. Thing is, if I did move home, he'd discover he's lost. I would not put up with his crap. With me behind them, none of the others would, either. It's already happening. Cody made some major changes in the feed for the heifers without asking him first. When he yelled at Cody, Cody walked out on him and left him sputtering. Joshua and the wives are there for Mary Alice, but when they come to the house, they try to avoid him. Mary Alice has got her and daddy an appointment for marriage counseling. He'd get a whole lot more out of life, if he tried a little patience."

She chuckled and shook her head at him.

"What?"

"This from you, Vince, the most impatient veterinarian in the western hemisphere?"

"Am not."

"Are too."

He kissed her again, deep and sweet. And held it until his phone rang. "What now?" he said when he answered it. "Yeah. Be right there." He hung up. "Even the people I like drive me nuts when I'm down here."

"What's the problem?"

"Mary Alice needs help getting him into bed. He's being difficult. Tomorrow is Joshua's turn to get him up and dressed. Tomorrow while everybody else sets up for the barbecue, you can show Daddy how to work with Tom."

She nodded. "And keep him out of your hair."

"You got it."

ANNE TOOK CARE of Tom before breakfast without waking the rest of the household. She had brought his oats along, since changing feed could cause colic. He had made friends with the big walking horse mare in the stall beside him and leaned against her side of the stall when Anne went in to look after him.

Anne helped with breakfast and carried Thor's tray to him. At least Thor didn't need

to use a ladder to climb into his king-sized bed.
He could raise and lower his bed frame. She
was surprised that both sides of the bed had
been slept in. Mary Alice could not be comfortable sleeping beside a man wearing a cast.
She'd suggest to Vince that they bring in another bed for her. The room was huge.

Thor was not quite awake when she deliv-
ered his tray and did not ask who she was.
She didn't remember which son was in charge
of getting him up, but he hadn't arrived yet.
Thor's short gray hair stood up on his head and
his beard was solid white.

"Hey, Pop, sorry I'm late," came a voice be-
hind her. "Oops, sorry, ma'am. You must be
Anne. I'm Josh." He stuck out a broad hand.
She expected a squeeze, but he touched her
gently, and gave her a lovely smile. "I'll get
Daddy settled before I go back to work."

Vince had told her Joshua was the smallest
of the Peterson boys. He was nowhere near
small by Anne's standards. He was dressed in
starched chinos and a short-sleeved white dress
shirt with a red power tie that proclaimed, *I
am not a farmer. I am a CPA.*

After Mary Alice left to drive to Cody's
house to help with the barbecue, Anne got
Tom tacked up and walked him back to the

front porch. Thor sat in his wheelchair. Joshua rocked at his side.

Anne shook hands with Thor. His smile was wide and friendly. If she hadn't known better from Vince, she'd have found him attractive.

He took one look at Tom and roared with laughter. "You can't be serious, young lady. That thing can't hold up a big man like me. I'd be prone on the ground before we start."

"It's called a *face plant*, Daddy," Joshua said. "As in falling flat-out on your face." He snickered.

In an instant the charming old gentleman was replaced by an ill-tempered curmudgeon. "You'd like that, wouldn't you?" Thor snapped. "You all wish that truck had'a killed me, so you could do whatever you want with the place. Sell off the land to a developer, more than like."

Anne was appalled. She expected Joshua to come out fighting. Instead, he stood, turned on his heel, walked around the corner of the house and out of sight.

"Come back here. I'm talking to you."

Joshua did not reappear.

"Hate to have a pretty lady like you hear that." Back to charm. "They think 'cause I'm hurt they don't have to listen to me. Once Vince moves back in…"

"Mr. Peterson, can you stand on your own?"

"Of course I can. Walk, too. Couple of steps right now, more later. This is set up to be a walking cast. Not a bad break in the first place. Don't want to fall if I lose my balance. You think that bitty horse can keep me on my feet?"

Vince came out the front door. "I can, if Tom can't. Come on, Dad, up you go."

While Vince lifted his father to his feet, Anne set about getting Tom in position to *forward*.

Tom held back. At first, he didn't want to walk up the ramp.

Once he did walk to the head of the stairs, he refused to go near Mr. Peterson. He moved behind Anne and peered around her like a kid hiding behind its mother's skirts.

"He's never acted like this before," Anne said. He had to pick today to revert to behaving like an untrained donkey. She felt her impatience grow. "Tom, cut this out. Forward. Right this minute."

He gave a high-pitched neigh. It was answered from the barn. That mare must be distracting him.

"Shoot, you sure this thing's a gelding?"

Mr. Peterson snickered, then smacked the back of his wheelchair and guffawed. "He's fallen in love with my mare. Can't do anything about it unless we stood her in the basement and him in the attic. Vince, I told you when you wanted to bring this boy down, these little ponies are worthless." He raised his eyebrows and grinned an alarmingly triumphant grin at Anne.

Why did Tom have to pick this moment in front of Vince and his family to act up? He *never* acted up. She avoided Vince's gaze. If he looked at her as though he was sorry for her or disappointed with her, she'd probably burst into tears. She wanted to climb in a hole and disappear. Tom had been perfect at the nursing home, so it wasn't being in a strange place. She backed him down the ramp onto the lawn.

"Forward," she said between her teeth.

Tom looked up at her like his angelic self and walked forward by her side.

"How come he won't do that with me?" Thor called to her. "Maybe he don't like men."

"He likes men fine. Vince, come here a second. Take Tom for a walk over to the crepe myrtles and back, please."

"Sure."

Tom matched him step for step on a loose rein.

"Let's try it again," Anne suggested. Tom took two steps up the ramp, stopped dead and refused to budge despite repeated commands and pulling him forward with the reins.

"Sorry, Anne, I'd like to stay and help, but I promised the others I'd come help set up the barbecue. Daddy, let me get you back in your wheelchair. Anne, can you roll him inside? He can wait out here while you put Tom Thumb back into his paddock."

Anne fought tears and hoped her voice sounded normal. "Of course. Thank you, Vince."

"We'll try again this afternoon late, okay? Possibly he's just tired and in a new place."

She nodded.

While Vince settled his father, she settled Tom back in his stall. Was he getting ready to colic? What on earth was the matter with her angel? Was he getting sick? She had to admit that part of bringing Tom down here was to show off her prowess to Vince's father. In retrospect, that was silly, but normal to want his family to think she had talents of her own.

Poor Tom. She knew he hadn't had a great deal of training or been in many strange situations. His reaction was her fault. She'd been arrogant, a show-off. And she'd paid for it.

Vince drove away toward his brothers' houses as she climbed back onto the porch. She wanted to load Tom up and drive home in a state of total humiliation.

"Sorry, Mr. Peterson. He's never acted like this before."

"Too little for any good anyway. Told ya, he's a gelding. Some of 'em hate real men like me."

Finally, it hit her. "He likes most men fine, Mr. Peterson. He doesn't like *you*."

"Say what?"

"For some reason, he doesn't trust you. Maybe it's because you smell like medicine." *Or maybe he can read you like a book and doesn't want any part of you.*

"You listen, girlie. I been breaking horses since before you were born. You leave that thing down here with me for a month, I guarantee he'll obey me."

"Not in this lifetime."

"I'll tan his hide good. Tell you what. I'll buy him. Charge me anything you like."

"No."

"I'll bet Victoria Martin would take some cash money for him. She sells those minis as a business."

"No."

"Bring me the telephone. I'll call her right this minute."

"Victoria doesn't own him. I do. You do not have enough money or land or investments to buy one hair of his tail." She walked behind his wheelchair so that he had to twist it to look at her.

"Get *your* tail back here, girl. I want that horse. I'll pay you more money than you'll see in a year working for Victoria Martin."

"No, you won't, because I won't sell him."

"Then I'll get you fired. You try getting a job with horses after I'm through with you. I get what I want when I want it."

Her laugh started down around her toes. She collapsed into the nearest rocking chair and laughed so hard she was afraid she was having hysterics. She thought about slapping her own face to make herself quit and laughed even harder.

"What is the matter with you, girl?"

"You get what you want? What on earth happened to you to let you think you could treat people—family—the way you do with no consequences? You get what you want? A family? Don't you believe you have one of those. You don't. They don't like you a bit better than Tom Thumb does. You want Vince home? You haven't got him. You do have a wife who loves you, heaven only knows why, but even she is getting fed up with you. You want to die alone? You've got a swell chance of achieving that, but I doubt it'll happen when you choose."

Thor started to speak, but Anne held up a hand.

"When I first met Vince, I thought he was a pompous jerk with an ego as big as the moon. Actually, his ego is as fragile as a breath of wind, all thanks to you. I suspect they are all fragile men, your sons, big as they are, but Vince has beaten you every step of the way. Wonder of wonders, he still loves you, but he's sick of the way you treat the rest of the people he loves. To my consternation, I have managed to fall in love with *him*. I intend to fight for him, even if I'm fighting *him* most of all."

She was afraid Thor would have a stroke. Instead, he seemed relaxed and cheerful. Back to charming. He'd enjoyed her tirade.

"Well, girl, that's saying it flat-out. Maybe if I'd ever found a woman like you, I wouldn't have had to marry four of them. They were all disappointments, just like the current one. The heck with my son. How about you marry *me*. I'm the one with the money. I can still sire another son to leave this place to."

"You're kidding, right? Why would I marry a man who tries to eat his own children?" She walked inside.

"Come back here," he shouted. "I haven't finished…"

"Yes, you have. I'm headed on home now and taking Tom with me. You better start making your peace with your kinfolk. Do yourself a favor, Mr. Peterson. Go find a good psychologist and try to become a mentally healthy man before it's too late. Oh, and apologize to Mary Alice for all the grief you've caused her. She deserves diamonds and a cruise to the Bahamas."

"Soon as I'm well, I'm divorcing her," he grumbled.

"Then you are a bigger idiot than I thought you were."

She turned away and stuck her hands in her pockets. For a woman who loathed confrontation, she'd managed to hold her own and even score some points. Not that he'd pay attention.

She jumped when she saw Vince standing in the shadows by the fireplace.

"When did you come back? I thought you'd gone to help dig the barbecue pit?"

"All done before I got there. I came the back

way. Figured I'd save you from Daddy. Turns out he's the one needed rescuing."

"You heard all that?"

He nodded.

"I'm sorry if I offended you, but I'm not sorry about what I said to your father. Marry him? Not likely. He can't have been serious."

"He was serious right at that moment. Mary Alice would slice him into coleslaw if he so much as mentioned divorce to her. He's not really crazy. He knows she loves him. Somewhere in that dried up heart of his, I think he loves her back. He's be miserable without her."

"Then tell him to tell her so. Come on. We need to get him in. He shouldn't be outside in this heat."

CHAPTER TWENTY

"You can't leave before the barbecue tomorrow," Vince said as he drove down the farm road toward his brothers' houses. "Tom is happy with Daddy's mare to keep him company."

"Your father will want to try to use him again."

"I guarantee he won't. You haven't met the sane members of my family yet."

"They're getting ready for your party. They don't need a stranger underfoot. I'll make an excuse to leave early. Something Victoria needs me for in Williamston. Nobody needs to know things didn't work out with Tom and your father." She was glad now that she and Victoria had worked out an early exit strategy. All she had to do was text Victoria to send a message asking her to come home early. She didn't want to deal with Thor again.

But Thor came along with Vince. She loved Vince.

"You think I care what people think?" Vince said. "Here's Cody's and Nicki's place. Not as big as the main house, but not bad for a farmer."

Party or no, Cody's wife Nicki fed them lunch, then left Anne in their air-conditioned solarium while she met with the caterer in town. Vince walked over to the nearest pasture to check out the cows. He was obviously giving Anne a chance to get to know Cody.

Cody settled himself in a shabby leather recliner and offered Anne an equally shabby love seat. "Want me to make coffee?"

"I'm fine, thanks."

"Want some advice?" he asked.

"Should I?" She'd already decided she liked Cody.

"I'll give it to you anyway for free. Run, don't walk, away from my brother."

"Any special reason? Does he have six wives or a gambling habit?"

"Worse. He's one of the Peterson boys. We are a bad risk marriage-wise."

"Who said anything about marriage?" Anne asked.

Cody, who looked strong enough to practice cow-tipping without assistance, leaned back in his chair, kicked his boots off on the tile floor and yawned hugely. "Vince hasn't showed much interest in a female down here since he broke up with his prom date in high school. Then here you show up complete with a little bitty horse, and he can't keep his eyes off you. He's crazy about you. I'm just afraid you're crazy about him right back. Bad idea."

"Everybody including Vince keeps telling me that."

"We Petersons are genetically predisposed to divorce. It's in the Peterson DNA. We don't do marriage well as a general rule, not even long-term relationships. Every time we try one, we mess it up. Vince was smart enough to figure that out. The rest of us are trying to overcome our genetic disposition. Be grateful when he walks away."

"Grateful? And you're one of the sane ones?"

"Trust me, if he wasn't crazy about you, he wouldn't consider kicking you out of his life."

"But *you* have a solid marriage, Cody. Two beautiful sons…"

"Yeah, but I keep waiting for the whole thing to implode, and it would be my fault. The only word for Nicki is *dogged*. She holds me together with spit and construction glue.

"I spent my last two years at the University

of Alabama drunk, stoned out of my gourd and being a first-class tomcat," Cody said. "Then I met Nicki. She forced me to stay in school and make passing grades. Not good passing grades, but good enough to earn my degree. Would you believe, I have a bachelor's in botany. I *hate* plants, but I love cows, so I need to know about plants. I run the local agricultural extension agent so ragged he hates to see me coming. I know just enough to be dangerous."

"Nicki got you sober and off the drugs?"

He snorted. "First, she held my head a lot when I tossed my cookies after a weekend binge. I have no idea why she hung in there. She says she loves me. What other people do is love. What Nicki does for me is a whole other thing."

"Didn't she ever get fed up?"

"Oh, yeah. She's not Joan of Arc. No martyrdom for my Nicki. I finally pushed her too far. She was four months' pregnant when she walked out. She said she was not about to raise a child with a drunken, drugged-out daddy. Heck of a way to tell me she was pregnant. Bam! I'd pushed and pushed to try to get her to leave me. Then when she did, all I could say was, 'See, I said you'd leave me.'

"After Nicki left me I walked into my first

AA meeting with a swollen jaw and two loose teeth. Hit a couple of rough spots, but I've been clean and sober since that night.

"But I know I could go out right this minute, walk into a bar, drive home knee-walking drunk and maybe kill somebody. Me, maybe. My kids need both parents. One of the reasons I stay sober is that my daddy would love it if I fell off the wagon and Nicki left me."

"Why on earth would Thor want that?"

"He'd win. I'd failed at the same thing he's never been able to do—love and be loved. He's jealous of everyone he thinks is happier or richer than he thinks he should be. Now that his body's not as strong as it was—and believe me, even after the accident he's still strong—he's mad at everybody."

"Why do you stay here?"

"Daddy'd say I'm waiting for him to die so I can inherit my part of the farm. I'm not. I love this place. Nicki loves it, my boys love it. I like having family around, knowing my people have been on this land since right after the Civil War. I think my daddy loves it, too. More'n he loves any human people, anyway. Besides, I like cows."

"He's afraid he'll die alone."

"More'n likely will if he keeps on like this.

He's lost Vince, and Joshua avoids him as much as he can. Josh is an accountant, not a farmer. He would do better in a big city, but Daddy keeps making him offers he can't refuse."

"You plan to stay."

"I'd like this to be the place where the family comes for reunions like the one we're about to have. Where the cousins fish and hunt together. Where they get married and christen their children in the garden. I'm good at what I do. I intend to make money for all of us."

"You want to be the patriarch."

"Yeah, I guess I do. Heck, I pretty much am already. Daddy tries to spoil things, but Nicki and I are bound and determined not to let him do it. I'm sad for him, really. Somewhere along the way when he was growing up or when my mother left him, he decided it was safer to hate. Been practicing on us ever since."

Vince walked in from the pasture and nodded at Cody. "You on Daddy Duty the rest of the day?"

"For my sins."

"Then Anne and I are driving down to see if Nell and Joshua would like us to pick up the boys after soccer practice."

"Not necessary. They're all four spending the night in town. The coach is having a sleepover for the team. Keeps them out of our hair."

Vince shook his head. "That's no coincidence."

Cody came and slapped his brother on the back. "Nell and Nicki exerted a little pressure and furnished enough food for a whole soccer team. World would be a better place if we men turned it over to soccer moms."

JOSHUA AND NELL'S miniature Parthenon sat in a grove of loblolly pines half a mile down the road from Cody and Nicki.

After introductions, Nell set out iced tea on the kitchen table. "Vince, go get Josh. He's down by the pond attempting to fish. He never catches anything we can eat."

After Vince left, Nell patted her tummy and said, "I'm still trying to lose my baby weight. Since Josh Jr. is seven, I guess I'm fooling myself." She pulled a cookie sheet with chocolate chip cookies from the oven. "Only six more batches to make. Every year I bake more, and every year we run out." She moved the sheet to a warming rack and pulled another from the oven. "Have one while it's hot. I love hot cookies." She wiped her hands on her apron, looked down at her stomach, and said, "Guess you can tell, huh? Anyway, it's nice to finally meet you. Vince has been driving everybody nuts talking about you since he got here. Take my advice. Have an affair, but don't marry him."

"Cody said basically the same thing. I have seen no evidence that Vince is Bluebeard or Count Dracula. He has a temper he's working to control with people. He's fine with animals. He doesn't plan to get married ever, and I don't plan to get married for a while. We enjoy each other's company when we're not fighting over some sticky point of veterinary procedure."

"You're in love with him."

"Why does everyone keep telling me that? Shouldn't I be the first to know?"

"Honey, you do know. You're afraid to tell him for fear he'll run the other direction Probably will. Little boys don't ever get over having their mothers abandon them. Who's gonna trust a female again after that? If your mother can dump you, any woman can dump you. Obvious answer? Do not put yourself in the position where they can. I'm fond of Vince, but he is not good husband material. He's always going to be looking for your packed suitcase under the bed. Right beside the one he's planning to use to disappear on *you*."

"You mean walk out on me."

"Vince doesn't handle confrontation well. At least not with women. I am friends with some of his ex-girlfriends. They start to get serious and suddenly Vince stops calling. No break-up phone call. Not even an email. All I'm saying is enjoy the party but don't expect it to last."

By the time Vince came back to pick Anne up and snitch a few cookies, Anne had decided to stay until after the barbecue.

Maybe she wanted to prove Nell wrong. With the exception of Thor, she liked Vince's family and the way they accepted her not as a guest, but as another member of the barbecue helpers.

She could avoid Thor.

Cody's work crew began to move tables and chairs onto the front lawn of the big house at about four and were done and lounging in the grass, drinking beer, by six. They had the easy familiarity of country men who had grown up together and spoke in casual insults.

Thor did not appear. The door to his bedroom was shut.

Anne thought, *In his wheelchair he might have been the center of attention. Just the way he likes it.*

The Fourth of July, the day of the Peterson reunion barbecue, was Mississippi hot and humid with a sun that demanded hats and sun-screen. The three brothers had been barbecu-ing several small hogs since midnight. The odor of ribs and pulled pork lay over the lawns and garden. Anne had been to a number of barbecues, but never one this size in a private home. Cars began to drive in around five in the afternoon, filled the parking lot and lined the long driveway.

Anne wished that Sonny Prather were here to see this. He'd be in his element. She finally gave up explaining that no, she wasn't kin, and no, she couldn't vote in Mississippi because she was registered in Tennessee.

She finally met all four of the new genera-tion of Peterson males. She could see the Pe-terson gene pool in them even as young as they were. If Vince had sons they would most likely grow to look like them—tall for their ages, rangy and big-boned.

What would it be like to raise sons like these? Vince's sons. To belong among these people? She watched Vince work the crowd. She considered herself more comfortable in small groups than large and had believed that Vince was as well. Now she wasn't so certain.

Pleading his injuries, Thor sat inside the air-conditioned living room in his wheelchair and held court. It was like a Southern version of a mafia movie, until Mary Alice whisked him away for a nap. The minute he was gone, the whole atmosphere of the party lightened.

At eleven in the evening the fireworks began. In Tennessee private fireworks were illegal, so municipalities mounted their own display. In Mississippi fireworks were sold by the roadside.

The Petersons must have spent a fortune on theirs.

Remembering the thunderstorm at Martin's, Anne slipped away just before the first rocket exploded. She carried a bag of horse treats for Tom and shared them with Thor's mare. The mare never raised her head from her hay. She was used to fireworks.

Anne thought Tom would pitch a mini-size fit at the first boom. He was a long way from home and his herd. As soon as he saw Anne, however, he settled with his head over the stall gate where she could stroke him.

As Anne slipped back out of the barn, an absolutely stunning blonde woman came toward her, hand outstretched. "Hey. I'm Cheryl from across the road. I grew up with the boys—well,

Vince, actually. I was just dyin' to meet the girl who finally caught him.''

So this was the woman that Thor had chosen to marry his son. He might have done worse. She was tall, lanky and dressed in immaculate white linen slacks under a coral silk shirt.

"I certainly haven't caught him.''

Cheryl gave out a tinkly laugh. "Everybody thought Vince and I'd get married sooner or later. Finally, I got good sense and moved on.'' She held out her left hand and wriggled the fingers. Her diamond engagement ring must have weighed over four carats and was surrounded by smaller diamonds. "Time Vince found somebody and kept ahold of her. You treat him good, now.'' She toddled off on high-heeled espadrilles.

Anne scurried out to watch the rest of the fireworks.

She had expected to meet Vince at the fireworks display, but she couldn't spot him in the crowd.

Nell's words came back to her. When Vince was facing an uncomfortable confrontation with one of his girlfriends. He disappeared.

Nonsense. She wasn't just a girlfriend. He had told her he loved her. He had invited her and only her to be with him at this barbecue.

Had he lost his nerve when people linked them together?

No, he must be inside with his father. The old man must need him for something. She stepped up onto the porch, expecting to find him in the living room. Thor was there in his wheelchair surrounded by acquaintances, but no Vince.

She was becoming anxious. Vince should be looking for her, too. Unless he was distancing himself, sending the guests a message that she wasn't important. Just another guest.

Exactly what were they to one another? He had said he loved her, but he had never said he was changing his mind about marrying. As a matter of fact, he hadn't mentioned love since she arrived in Mississippi. He certainly never introduced her to anyone as especially important to him.

She loved him. That meant admitting that you were committed to the other person. In her book it meant acknowledging you were a couple.

It meant marriage.

People who loved one another got married, had babies, took out mortgages. Were seen as a couple. Laughed together, cried together, worked toward the same goals. Out in public. If Vince was offering her anything, it wasn't that.

Had he decided to walk away? Just like that?

She found a seat under an oak that must have been a hundred years old when the Petersons left Minnesota. Why had they never christened the farm with a fancy name? It was simply *Peterson's*. It gave the whole place a feeling of impermanence, even after a hundred and fifty years.

She hadn't expected Vince to hover around her tonight, but she hadn't expected him to disappear, either. He was one of the hosts. But he'd said he loved her. She was here. Shouldn't he want to spend as much time as he could with her?

Some women spent lifetimes trying to change men. It never worked. He'd warned her on the front end that he didn't believe in marriage, that he ran from women who wanted permanence. Cody had warned her. Nell had warned her.

Now that she had given in to loving him, served her right if he broke her heart. Vince had told her from the start he wasn't suited to be married. She should have listened.

She walked her back up the tree until she

stood erect. She'd set herself up for heartbreak. It always seemed to happen.

But even with Robert she had never felt what she felt for Vince. Love. She wanted to be with him. She felt complete when they were together, even when they disagreed.

But he'd abandoned her among strangers at a party he'd invited her to. Not the way she'd been brought up. You "danced with the feller what brung ya."

If she could just find him, talk to him...find out whether this was the finale or a simple misunderstanding.

But he was nowhere to be found. She asked several people if they'd seen him. No one had.

She felt embarrassed asking perfect strangers if they had seen Vince.

The fireworks were over. She'd barely registered them.

At his size, Vince should be easy to spot. Nope, no Vince.

Telling her he loved her was not good enough. She doggone well deserved a man who wanted her as much as she wanted him.

She wouldn't hang around waiting for him to give her more than words and the occasional kiss. She'd survived before she met him. She'd survive now. The very thought caught at her heart so that she could barely breathe.

The caterers had broken down the buffet. Now they were setting up chairs around a portable dance floor. Musicians were plugging in equipment. Fairy lights flickered in the oak trees.

This party showed signs of going all night, but she was exhausted. Her head was cranking up to a tension headache. There was not a Peterson in sight.

"I want to go home," she whispered. When she was sick she always wanted to crawl home to her nest to recover. At the moment she was sick at heart. She needed to crawl home to deal with it alone.

What home?

The only home she had was her little cottage at Martin's Minis. She wanted to be there. As nice as the Petersons had been, they were strangers. She wanted her friends.

And the horses.

Her luggage was still in her bedroom. Tom's harness was still in the barn. Nice people did not break off a visit early without saying goodbye to their hosts and definitely not to the family of the man she loved. She did not feel nice.

She did not want to be miserable in someone else's house, either.

Across the lawn she spotted Mary Alice talking to Joshua. No Vince. She ran over to them and asked, "Have you seen Vince?"

"He's around somewhere," Joshua said and waved his hand at the remaining guests.

"Are you all right, dear?" Mary Alice asked.

"Not exactly." She took a deep breath and prepared to lie her lungs out. "Victoria, my boss, sent me a text saying there's some kind of emergency. She needs me back as quickly as I can get there."

"Just call her," Mary Alice said. "It could be your father."

That's why she gave up lying, Anne thought. It always made things worse. "Barbara would have notified me if it were my father. When I called Victoria back it went to voice mail. I should just go."

"But it's midnight. You won't get there until dawn. At least let Vince ride with you."

"I really don't want to wait until he surfaces. I've driven ten-horse trailers all over the country at night. I'll be fine. I'll call you when I get there." She turned toward the porch and ran, head down. "I'm so sorry," she said. "Everyone's been so kind."

"Happens all the time with people who have animals," Joshua called after her. "I'll find Vince for you while you pack up."

But he didn't. With Joshua and Mary Alice's help, Anne was on the road to Memphis in twenty minutes.

Tom sensed she was upset. He leaned over the back seat and whuffled to her until she yelled at him to be quiet. Then she had to apologize.

When Vince came back to Barbara's, they would meet as colleagues. He would probably not understand why she had left because she couldn't find him.

In reality she'd never been able to find him. He'd always kept a wall between them as though she might disappear on him the way his mother did. As he had. He didn't dare to get too close. Not loving Anne was safer than loving her and facing the possibility of losing her.

Love was risky. You held hands and jumped off the cliff into life. She was willing to take that risk. Vince avoided it. Going through life alone was safe for Vince, but she was tired of safe. She hit the steering wheel with both hands. "All he had to do was be there, Tom. He chose not to be. I want a man who chooses me."

At Martin's, Victoria helped Anne unload

and fed her breakfast. Anne was aware that Victoria was tingling to know why she was home early, but she didn't ask.

Anne didn't tell. She did talk about Tom's rejection of Thor. She made the episode sound hilarious instead of embarrassing. She talked about the rest of the family, and how much she liked Mary Alice.

She did not mention Vince's name.

"Victoria, how would it be if I went to that place in North Carolina that trains the minis earlier than we'd planned for me to go?" She avoided Victoria's gaze. "It's obvious I need the training if I'm going to get the minis ready to work on their own by the end of six months."

"How much earlier do you want to leave?"

"Like now." Anne held up a hand. "Just listen. Becca can train some of the basics with Big Mary and Harriett. Darrell and Calvin are looking after the barns and pastures. North Carolina should be cooler than here…"

"Hades is cooler than here," Victoria said.

"I might take Trusty, so I can do some trail-riding in the Blue Ridge on a full-size horse."

Victoria nodded. "Let me make some phone calls. Maybe we can work it out. What's this really about? What happened down there?"

"Nothing worth discussing. Thanks, Victoria, you are a peach. Now, I need a swim while it's cool. Then, if you don't mind, I am going to sleep."

She didn't swim laps often. Too much like work. This morning, however, she pushed herself until her arms and legs felt paralyzed, then crawled out, stretched out on the chaise longue, pulled her hat down over her face and cried. Who was she fooling? She'd never get over Vince. She loved him. Wanted marriage, a home, tall sons and beautiful daughters. She might even ask Elaine to teach her to cook.

Without warning her chaise jerked to the side and upended. She rolled into the pool and swallowed a mouthful of water.

"What were you *thinking*?"

Vince.

Sputtering from her sudden dunking, she brushed the water out of her eyes and looked up—way up—into Vince's angry face. He was still dressed in the same clothes he'd worn to the party. Beard stubble stuck out along his jaw, and he hadn't combed his hair.

"What are *you* thinking? Vince Peterson. You might have drowned me."

"I considered it seriously. They used to dunk witches. Dunk you enough, maybe you'll stop driving me insane."

"You? I was doing you a favor, letting you off the hook. Obviously, you went too far when you said you loved me. May not mean anything to you, but it does to me. In my family, *love* means you plan to stick around, make a life. You've said all along that's not what it means to you. Last night I figured out I want my kind of love. Your kind isn't good enough. So I left."

He walked down the pool steps until the water reached above his knee, grabbed her around the waist, slung her up and sat her down on the lip of the pool. "What are you talking about?"

"What else do you call it when a man invites a woman home to meet his family, then avoids her as if she'd developed Ebola? Even your stepmother had no idea where you'd got to. Then your sister-in-law says I should have an affair with you and not expect marriage, because you don't do marriage?"

"I do now." He turned so that he could lean one hand on either side of her. "What if I screw it up? I don't want to hurt you."

"There are two of us. I could screw it up, too."

"Then what?"

She took his face in her hands. "Then, dummy, we unscrew it. Together."

He wrapped his arms around her waist and pulled her to her feet and into his arms. He kissed her not at all gently. Eventually, they broke the kiss. She said from the hollow of her shoulder, "Where were you? I looked everywhere. I didn't want to wander around in the dark crying 'Heathcliff, Heathcliff.'"

"Good thing. I wouldn't have answered." He kissed her again. "I'm sorry I scared you. I'm not used to having somebody bother to know where I am. I was across the street at Cheryl's, sliding a prolapsed uterus back into one of their cows. Her dad caught me and dragged me back across the road with him. Took longer than I thought. When I came back to the party, Joshua found me and said you'd taken your toy horse and left. Then Mary Alice said that you were upset and thought I'd abandoned you. So I came after you. Now, about this marriage proposal thing…"

"What marriage proposal thing?"

"The thing where I kneel at your feet…"

"Vince, if you kneel where you are, you'll be under water. Can you please get out of the pool?"

He lifted himself out of the water and stood her up beside him. "Okay now?" His slacks were dripping. He still wore his boots.

He sank onto one knee, which meant his eyes were nearly on a level with hers. "On the drive up here I finally figured out that I'd better do marriage *with* you, because I can't possibly do *life* without you. I'll try to protect you from my family to the best of my ability. Marry me. I promise I will cherish you all the days of my life."

She stared down at him with her eyes wide and her mouth open.

"Say something!"

"Uh-huh." She paused. "Yes, yes, of course I'll marry you. I have to marry you. I love you."

"And divorce will never be an option. Deal?"

She nodded. "Deal."

EPILOGUE

"I'VE SEEN COUPLES hang their wedding rings on their dog in place of a ring bearer, but this is my first ring-bearing horse. Are you certain you want to do this?" said Stephen MacDonald's friend, Walt, the Episcopal priest who had confirmed Stephen and Barbara's marriage in his small church in Holly Springs.

Anne and Vince had chosen to be married at the equally small church in Williamston. Walt was still going to perform the service. He'd known Anne since he'd married Stephen MacDonald and Barbara Carew. He wanted to see Anne married.

"What if he—uh—Tom Thumb—has incontinence issues during the service?"

"He won't, will you, Tom?"

Tom rumbled deep in his throat and laid his head on Anne's lap. She gave him a peppermint. He sighed.

"The flowers draped all over him won't scare him?"

"Nope. We've been practicing. He might eat a couple if he can reach them, but we're not decorating with anything poisonous. He's only one small horse, Father Walt, not a herd of wild mustangs. We were considering using a couple of the others as ushers but decided that would be tempting fate. We didn't think they could follow the seating chart."

"You *are* kidding, right? I suppose I should be grateful for that."

"We're only taking four on our honeymoon."

"On your honeymoon? Horses?"

"We're driving them to North Carolina to spend two weeks polishing up our training skills and learning some new ones. Victoria already has a waiting list of people who want them."

"Are they expensive?" Walt asked. "Can those who need them afford them?"

"They're free to the people who need them, but the farm can now accept donations. Most people give as much as they can afford. There are grants out there that can work, too. The same groups who provide Seeing Eye dogs and helper dogs for the disabled support helper horses as well. You have to have room for them, of course. An apartment won't do. Then there are compatibility and training tests. Some people are simply not suitable. They have requirements that a mini can't meet or don't have the temperament or space to look after them properly. The group that we'll be working with in North Carolina has developed tests to match training with skills and personalities."

"Surely Martin's Minis can't afford to subsidize the program. Victoria is a businesswoman with a boarding barn, not a charity."

"Vince's brother Joshua is now working with Victoria's husband, Edward, setting up a trust so we can manage the revenue. Then the Peterson wives are planning a charity benefit for later in the fall after it cools off. Victoria won't get rich, but she won't starve either, and neither will the horses."

"Speaking of rich, is Vince's father coming to the wedding?"

"He said he wouldn't, but his wife, Mary Alice, is bringing him whether he likes it or not. He still limps, but he's using only one cane, not a walker. He hated the walker. He decided against divorcing Mary Alice, by the way, when she made him quit bullying her. They're going to marriage counseling."

"Good for them."

"He's had to give up driving automobiles

since his accident, and is not happy about it because it tips the balance of power to Mary Alice. He has promised to behave today, but Vince doesn't trust him. His bad temper is too ingrained. He likes to be the center of attention too much. His motto is, 'If you can't be a shining light, be a horrible example.' Mary Alice says he's going soft, because he's scared of losing everyone in his family and winding up alone, but when you have that much practice being a curmudgeon, it's tough to be Mr. Nice Guy. He knows he can't touch me and Vince, and the wives are teaching their husbands to ignore him."

"I'm surprised Barbara and Victoria are going to let you two go off on your own for two whole weeks. How is Barbara going to manage?"

"One of Vince's friends is coming to fill in. The horses are our passport. When we get back to Martin's I'll be taking over the mini end of the business from Victoria, so she can go back to running her boarding barn full-time. Vince will move into the cottage I've been living in until we need more room." She blushed and dropped her eyes.

"Babies?"

"At least one, if we're lucky. But not right away. I'm sneaky. This way Vince has to move his stuff from The Hovel, while I don't have to move a thing. Now, Father, if you don't mind, I have to put Tom's sneakers on and get dressed myself. Tom, slippers."

The little horse stood beside Anne's chair and waited for her to tie his sneakers on his hooves.

"See, Father, I'm using blue shoelaces as my something blue."

Outside the room Anne had used to dress Tom and herself, the little church was decorated with autumn flowers and foliage. Masses of rust-colored chrysanthemums banked the altar and hung in pots at the ends of each pew. The October temperature had dropped to eighty-five, and the leaves had begun to change color at last.

Anne had chosen a sleek cream silk wedding dress with a short train that detached for dancing. All the white dresses she had tried on made her look washed-out, but the cream set off the rose in her skin tones perfectly.

She and Vince had planned to have a simple service followed by champagne and nibbles in the parish hall for a few family and friends. Once Emma, Barbara, Anne's sister Elaine, Barbara's daughter Caitlyn, and the Peterson wives found out about the engagement, however, the number of invitations sent out increased exponentially. Now the little church was filled to capacity.

Joshua's nose was a bit out of joint when Vince chose Cody to be his best man, but he lowered it when Vince decided to have both brothers stand up with him.

"Unusual, but not unheard of," Walt said. "I hope there's enough room to fit all three of them in. They're the size of a professional football team."

Becca had been elected to chaperone Tom as he walked down the aisle, while Seth's mother, Laila, organized babysitting in the church's Sunday school for Seth and Emma's daughter, Diana, and any other prepubescent children that arrived with their parents. "Small children do not belong at weddings," she said. "No doubt they would chase that horse down the aisle and cause a riot. Victoria agrees with me."

"Happy the bride the sun shines on," Stephen MacDonald said when he met his daughter in the narthex at the rear of the church.

"Does it mention how eighty-five-degree temperature affects the omens?" Anne said. "I told the verger to crank the air-conditioning down low enough to hang meat. With all these people in this little church, we're going to need it."

"Don't worry. It will be fine." Stephen kissed her cheek and whispered, "I hope you know what you're doing," but he smiled when he said it.

"This is not nearly as crazy as your wedding to Barbara."

At the head of the aisle, Elaine, Anne's matron of honor, her baby bump just starting to show, handed Anne her bridal bouquet of meadow flowers with ribbon streamers in autumn colors.

Anne had chosen not to wear a veil. She'd told Victoria, "I have nightmares of Tom wrapping himself in yards of tulle, galloping down the aisle and jumping the chancel rail. No veil."

At the front of the church, the organ burst forth with *Trumpet Voluntary*.

Tom lifted his head and leaned against Anne nervously, but held his position. She shifted her bouquet to her right hand so that she could use her left to pat his head. "Good boy."

She took her father's arm, leaned down and said to Tom, "Forward." Forward to Vince, to life, to forever.

And they were off.

* * * * *

MUST ♥ DOGS COLLECTION

SAVE 30% AND GET A FREE GIFT!

Finding true love can be "ruff"— but not when adorable dogs help to play matchmaker in these inspiring romantic "tails."

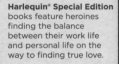

Get 4 FREE REWARDS!

We'll send you 2 FREE Books
<u>plus</u> 2 FREE Mystery Gifts.

Harlequin® Romance Larger-Print books feature uplifting escapes that will warm your heart with the ultimate feel-good tales.

FREE
Value Over
$20

YES! Please send me 2 FREE Harlequin® Romance Larger-Print novels and my 2 FREE gifts (gifts are worth about $10 retail). After receiving them, if I don't wish to receive any more books, I can return the shipping statement and cancel. If I don't cancel, I will receive 4 brand-new novels every month and be billed just $5.34 per book in the U.S. or $5.74 per book in Canada. That's a savings of at least 15% off the cover price! It's quite a bargain! Shipping and handling is just 50¢ per book in the U.S. and 75¢ per book in Canada.* I understand that accepting the 2 free books and gifts places me under no obligation to buy anything. I can always return a shipment and cancel at any time. The free books and gifts are mine to keep no matter what I decide.

119/319 HDN GMYY

Name (please print)

Address   Apt. #

City   State/Province   Zip/Postal Code

Mail to the **Reader Service:**
IN U.S.A.: P.O. Box 1341, Buffalo, NY 14240-8531
IN CANADA: P.O. Box 603, Fort Erie, Ontario L2A 5X3

Want to try 2 free books from another series? Call 1-800-873-8635 or visit www.ReaderService.com.

HRLP19

READERSERVICE.COM

Manage your account online!
- Review your order history
- Manage your payments
- Update your address

*We've designed the
Reader Service website
just for you.*

Enjoy all the features!
- Discover new series available to you, and read excerpts from any series.
- Respond to mailings and special monthly offers.
- Browse the Bonus Bucks catalog and online-only exculsives.
- Share your feedback.

Visit us at:
ReaderService.com

RS16R